THE INDIA-RUBBER MEN

THE INDIA-RUBBER MEN

EDGAR WALLACE

WILDSIDE PRESS

Originally published in 1929.
Published by Wildside Press LLC.
wildsidpress.com

CHAPTER I

In the murk of a foggy morning a row-boat moved steadily down stream. Two pairs of oars moved as one, for the rowers were skilled watermen. They kept to the Surrey shore, following the slightly irregular course imposed by the vital necessity of keeping to the unrevealing background formed by moored barges.

Somewhere in the east the sun was rising, but the skies were dark and thick; lamps burnt on river and shore. Billingsgate Market was radiant with light, and over the wharves where cargo boats were at anchor white arc lights stared like stars.

The river was waking; the "chuff-chuff" of donkey engines, the rattle and squeak of swaying derricks, the faint roar of chains running through came to the men in the skiff.

They were clear of a long barge line, and the nose of the boat was turned to the northern shore, when on the dark background grew a darker object. The stroke rower jerked round his head and saw the lines of the launch which lay across his course, and dropped his oars.

"Wade!" he grunted.

Out of the blackness came a cheerful hail.

"Hallo, sweetheart! Whither away?"

The police launch, skilfully manœuvred, edged alongside the skiff. Somebody caught the gunwale with a boat-hook.

"It's only me, Mr. Wade. We was takin' the skiff down to Dorlin's to lay it up," said the bow oarsman. He had a high falsetto voice and punctuated his speech with involuntary sniffs.

"Not Mr. Offer?" The voice in the police boat was charged with extravagant surprise. "Not Sniffy Offer? Why, sweetheart, what are you doing at this hour? A raw morning, when the young and the ailing should be tucked up in their little beds. Let me have a look at you."

A powerful light was switched on and flooded the interior of the skiff with devastating thoroughness. The two men sitting, oars in hand, blinked painfully.

"Little case of something here," said the hateful voice of Inspector John Wade. "Looks like a case of whisky—and, bless my life, if there isn't another one!"

"We found 'em floating in the river," pleaded the man called Sniffy. "Me an' Harry fished 'em out."

"Been fishing? I'll bet you have! Make fast your boat and step into the launch—and step lively, sweetheart!"

The two river thieves said nothing until they were on the launch and headed for the riverside police station.

"You don't have to be clever to catch us, Wade, do you? Here's London full of undiscovered murders an' robberies, an' all you can do is to pull a coupla river hooks! Look at that woman found in Cranston Gardens with her throat cut—look at the Inja-Rubber Men——"

"Shut up!" growled his companion.

"Proceed, Sniffy," said Mr. Wade gently. "I am not at all sensitive. You were talking of the India-Rubber Men? You were reproaching me—you were trying to make me and the Metropolitan Police Force feel exceedingly small. Go right ahead, Sniffy. Whip me with scorpions."

"Shut up, Sniffy!" warned the second prisoner again, and Sniffy was silent through all the gibes and taunts and provocative irony which assailed him.

"Now, where was this whisky going—tell me that? The destination of whisky, cases of whisky—stolen cases of whisky—interests me, Sniffy. I am in training for a bootlegger. Spill the truth, Sniffy, and I'll keep it locked in my bosom."

There was no other answer than a succession of indignant sniffs.

"Come, sweetheart, tell papa." They could not see the grin on the dark, lean face of John Wade, but they could hear the chuckle in his voice. "Was it to gladden the hearts of poor sailormen at the 'Mecca'? That would be almost an admirable act. Poor fellows who sail the seas are entitled to their comforts. Now was it for dear old Golly——"

The worm turned.

"You ain't entitled to ask these questions under the Ac', Wade, *you* know that! I could have your coat off your back for questionin' me. An' castin' asper——" He boggled at the word.

"Asparagus!" suggested Wade helpfully.

"Committin' libel, that's what you're doin'."

The launch pulled up beside a heaving float and was hauled tight. Somebody in the darkness asked a question.

"Only two young fishermen, Sergeant," said Wade.

"Put 'em on ice!"

That day Wade made a call at the Mecca Club, and on its manager, Mrs. Annabel Oaks.

Mrs. Oaks had been compelled by an interfering constabulary to register her "club" as a common lodging-house, a disadvantage of which was that it was subject to police supervision. At any hour of the day or night it was competent for an inspector of police to walk in and look round, which could be, and on many occasions was, extremely inconvenient.

She complained savagely to her guests.

"Nice thing, eh? A club for officers, and any flat footed copper can walk in and look you over!"

It might be conceived that Mrs. Oaks was indiscreet in publishing a truth that might scare away a percentage of her boarders. But the "Mecca" was conveniently placed for under-officers of the Mercantile Marine. Here men were near to the dock offices of various steamship lines, and the living, if plain, was cheap, while many of the clients who patronised her establishment found the "club" convenient in another respect. Suppose one got a ship out of London, it was possible to owe the money due for keep until the debtor returned from his voyage.

"Mum" Oaks was very obliging, especially if the men were likeable. He was likeable if he did not give himself airs and sound his "h's" too punctiliously, or if he took his drop of drink like a man and didn't raise hell and want to fight Golly or anybody else who happened to be around.

The Marine Officers' Club and Recreation Rooms had not always been a club. Because of its initials it had come to be known as the "Moccer," and from "Moccer" to "Mecca" was an easy transition. Not, as Mum said virtuously, that they'd ever take in a seagoing gentleman who was not white, and if, as by all accounts was the case, Mecca was a foreign country inhabited by niggers, well, any so-called Mecca people who came to the club for lodgings would get a pretty saucy answer—either from herself or Golly!

Golly seemed wholly incapable of giving anybody a saucy answer. He was a mild little man, rather spare of frame and short. A reddish moustache drooped over an unmasterful chin. He had once been a ship's steward; in moments of inebriation his claims rose as high as a purser, and once, on a terrific occasion, he stated that he had been the captain of an Atlantic liner; but he was very ill after that.

He sang sentimental ballads in a high falsetto voice, and it was his weakness that he found a resemblance in himself to the popular idols of the screen; and, in moments when he was free from observation, he did a little quiet and dignified acting, following the instructions of "Ten Steps to Stardom," by a Well Known Screen Favourite of Hollywood—so well known that it was not necessary to put his name to this interesting work.

Mr. Oaks had aspirations to opera as well as to the screen. The tenants of Mecca often threw up their windows and commented upon Golly's voice—for he sang best when he was chopping wood, and he seemed always to be chopping wood.

Mum was hardly as motherly as her name. She was spare, not to say thin. Her greying hair was bobbed, which did not add to her attractiveness, for the face which the lank hair framed was hard, almost repulsive. A section of her guests called her (behind her back) Old Mother Iron Face, but mostly she was Mum to a hundred junior officers of cargo ships which moved up and down the seas of the world.

The premises of "Mecca" were half wooden and half brick. The brick portion had been the malt-house of a forgotten brewery, and was by far the more comfortable. Before the club was a strip of wharfage, covered with rank grass and embellished with two garden seats. Every year Golly sowed flower seeds in a foot-wide border under the house, and every year nothing happened. It was almost as ineffectual as his fishing.

The wharf edge was warped and rotten; the ancient baulks of timber that supported what Mum called "the front" split and crumbled. There was some talk of building a stone wall for patrons to lean against, but nothing came of it.

The view was always fine, for here the Pool was broad and the river crowded with shipping. There was generally a cable boat tied at Fenny's on the Surrey side, and the German ships had their moorings near by. You could see scores of seagoing barges moored abreast, with their house pennants fluttering at the tops of tall masts, and at the wharves up and down the river there were generally one or two cargo boats.

Lila Smith used to stand, fascinated, at the big window of the dining-room and watch the slow moving steamers come cautiously up river. She had seen the lights of the eel boats and the G.T.C. fish-carriers and the orange ships from Spain, and got to know them by their peculiar lines. She knew the tugs, too, the big *Johnny O* and *Tommy O*, and the *John and Mary* and *Sarah Lane* and the *Fairway*—those lords of the river—and she could tell them even at nights.

Club lodgers who had returned from long voyages remarked that Lila was no longer a child. She had never lacked dignity; now there was a charm which none had observed before, and which it was difficult to label. She had always been pretty in a round-faced, big-eyed way. But the prettiness had grown definite; nature had given the face of the child new values.

She often stood at the window, a shabby figure in a rusty black dress and down-at-heel shoes, gazing thoughtfully at the river pageant: the sound of a deep siren brought her there, the impatient toot-toot of a tugboat, the rattle and roar of anchor chains.

"That new feller in seven wants some tea, Lila—don't stand mooning there like a stuck pig; get your wits about you, will you?"

Thus Mum, who came into the room and caught the girl at her favourite occupation.

"Yes, Auntie."

Lila Smith flew to the kitchen. That rasping, complaining voice terrified her—had always terrified her. She wished sometimes for another kind of life; had a vague idea that she knew just what that life was like. It had trees in it, and great spaces like Greenwich Park, and people who were most deferential. More often than not she was dreaming of this when she was watching the ships go up and down the river.

She was dreaming now, as she poured out the tea and sent the slatternly maid into No. 7 with the thick cup and the thicker slabs of bread and butter.

The small square window which brought air into the stuffy kitchen was wide open. Outside the morning was cold, but the primrose sun laced the river with waggling streaks of pale gold. Suddenly she looked up.

A man was looking at her from the wharf: a tall man, with a brown, attractive face. He was bare-headed, and his close-cropped brown hair had a curl in it.

"Good morning, princess!"

She smiled in her frightened way—a smile that dawned and faded, leaving her face a little more serious.

"Good morning, Mr. Wade!"

She was a little breathless. He was the one being in the world who had this effect upon her. It was not because she was frightened, though she was well aware of his disgraceful profession—Mum always said that policemen were crooks who hadn't the pluck to thieve—nor yet because of the furtive character of these rare meetings.

He had a tremendous significance for her, but the reason for his importance was confusingly obscure. For a long time she had regarded him as an old man, as old as Golly; and then one day she grew old herself and found him a contemporary.

He never asked her awkward questions, nor sought information

9

on domestic affairs, and Mum's fierce cross-examinations which followed every interview produced no cause for disquiet in the Oaks household.

"Why do they call you 'busy,' Mr. Wade?"

She asked the question on the impulse of the moment and was frightened before the words were out.

"Because I *am* busy, princess," he said gravely—she never quite knew when he was being serious and when he was laughing at her when he used that tone and inflection of voice. "I am so busy that I am an offence in the eyes of all loafers. Industry is my weakness."

He paused and looked at her oddly.

"Now as to that experience?" he suggested.

She was instantly agitated.

"I wish you'd forget I ever said it," she said, with a quick fearful look at the door. "It was silly of me. . . I—I wasn't telling the truth, Mr. Wade. I was just trying to make a sensation——"

"You couldn't tell a lie," he interrupted calmly. "You're trying to tell one now, but you can't. When you said: 'Don't think I have a bad time—sometimes I have a wonderful experience,' you meant it." He raised his hand with a lordly gesture. "We'll not discuss it. How are you keeping in these days?"

She, too, had heard Mum's heavy footfall and drew back a pace. She was gazing past him and was conscious of her deceitfulness when Mum came scowling into the room.

"Hallo, Mr. Wade—got nothing better to do than keep my gel gossiping?"

Her voice was high and venomously vibrant. Of all hateful faces, John Wade's was the most loathsome in her eyes.

With a gesture she sent Lila from the room and slammed the door behind the girl.

"Don't come here cross-questioning children. Be a man and knock at the front door."

"You haven't got a front door," said Mr. Wade reproachfully. "And why so angry, child? I came in the friendliest spirit to interview Golly——"

"He's on the wharf—an' don't call me 'child'!" snapped the woman savagely.

Mr. Wade, whose weakness was the employment of endearing epithets, shrugged his shoulders.

"I go," he said simply.

Golly he had seen, and was well aware that Golly had seen him. The little man was chopping wood, and, as the detective approached, he put down his hatchet and rose with a painful expression, which deepened when he heard the detective's drawling inquiry.

"Whisky? What do I know about whisky? . . . Yes, I know Sniffy. A common longshore loafer that I wouldn't have in this here club. A low man with low companions." He spoke very rapidly. "The Good Book says: 'As a bird is known by his note, so is a man by the company he keeps'——"

"I don't believe it," said Mr. Wade. "Heard anything about the India-Rubber Men lately."

Mr. Oaks spread out his arms in a gesture of patient weariness.

"I don't know no more about the Inja-Rubber Men than what the organs of public opinion, to wit, the newspapers, talk about. We got the police; we pay 'em rates 'n' taxes, we feed 'em——"

"And well fed they are," agreed John Wade, his eyes twinkling. "I never see a fat policeman without thinking of you, Golly."

But Golly was not to be turned aside.

"Inja-Rubber Men! Burglars 'n' bank robbers! Would I know 'um? Am I a bank? Am I a safe deposit? Am I rollin' in millions?"

"Unanswerable," murmured Mr. Wade, and went back to the question of stolen whisky, and, when Mr. Golly Oaks closed his eyes and delivered an oration on the probity of all associated with the Mecca Club, this brown-faced, young-looking man listened in silence, staring at the orator as an owl might stare if owls had big, blue eyes.

"Encore!" he said when Golly reached the end of his apologia. "You ought to be in Parliament, angel-face. Gosh! I'd like to hear you on the subject of Prohibition."

With a nod, he turned and went back to the police launch, hidden under the crazy face of the wharf.

CHAPTER II

Three nights later. . . .

The engineer, who was also the steersman of the police launch, remarked mechanically that it was cold, even for that time of the year; and John Wade, to whom the remark was not altogether unfamiliar, answered sardonically.

He often referred to himself as an old man; he was, in point of fact, thirty-five, which is not a great age, and indeed is rather young in an inspector of Thames police.

"I've often thought, sir——" began the engineer sentimentally, as the launch shot under Blackfriars Bridge and edged towards the Embankment.

"I doubt it," said Mr. Wade. "I very much doubt it, sergeant. Maybe when you're off duty——"

"I've often thought," continued the unperturbed sergeant, "that life is very much like a river——"

"If you feel mawkish, sergeant, restrain yourself until we tie up. I am not in a sentimental mood to-night."

"It will come," said the sergeant unabashed, "when you've met the girl of your heart. Bachelors don't know what sentiment is. Take babies——"

Wade did not listen. The launch was running close to the Embankment side of the river. It was a night of stars, and there was no sign of the thin fog which was to descend on London the following night. He had spent the most annoying evening, searching evil-smelling barges. That afternoon he had removed a dead body from the river. The morning had been occupied at the Thames Police Court, prosecuting a drunken tug skipper, who, in a moment of delirium, had laid out his little crew and would have laid out the tug too—for it was headed straight for a granite-faced wharf—if a police boat had not ranged alongside, and Wade, with his own hands and a rubber truncheon, put the drunken skipper to sleep, and spun the wheel only just in time to avert disaster.

Now, on top of these minor disasters, he had been stopped on his way to a comfortable bed with instructions to report at Scotland

Yard; and he was perfectly sure what was the reason for that call—the India-Rubber Men. As a reader of crime reports in which he had no particular part, he was interested in the India-Rubber Men; as a police officer he carried out certain inquiries concerning them; and for the past week they had become something of a nuisance. It was perhaps a fatal error to advance a theory—he had done this and was now to suffer for meddling.

They called these marauders the India-Rubber Men because there was no other name that fitted them. They were certainly elastic in their plans and in their movements; but the nickname developed after the one and only glimpse which brief authority had had of the ruthless bank smashers. They wore rubber gas-masks and rubber gloves and crêpe rubber shoes. Each man, when seen, carried a long automatic in his belt, and three dangling cylinders which the experts described as gas bombs. This latter was probably their principal armament.

They had been seen the night they cleared out Colley & Moore, the Bond Street jewellers; and that week-end when they opened the vault of the Northern and Southern Bank and left behind them a night watchman, who was dead before the police arrived. The reason for his death was apparent; in his clasped hand was a portion of a rubber gas-mask, which he had torn from one of the robbers. He had seen the face of the rubber man and had been killed for his enterprise.

"I shouldn't be surprised," said the sergeant steersman, bringing the launch a little nearer the Embankment's edge, "if the Wapping lot weren't in this india-rubber business. That gang wouldn't think twice——"

Wade, looking ahead, had seen indistinctly something which might be human leaning over the parapet of the Embankment. The launch was not twenty yards away when he saw the bulk of the figure increase, and realised that whoever it was was standing on the parapet. In another second it had disappeared, and he saw a splash of white where it had fallen into the water.

The steersman had seen it too. The little boat shuddered as the engines went astern.

"On your right, sir. You'll reach him with your hands."

Wade was on his knees now, leaning over the edge of the boat, the steersman throwing his weight on the opposite side of the boat and bracing himself to keep it balanced.

For a second the tiny black thing on the water vanished. It reappeared right under the gunwale of the launch, and, reaching down, John Wade gripped an upflung arm and dragged the whimpering thing into the boat. It was a woman.

"Must you commit suicide, my good wench, when I'm on my way to an important conference?" he demanded savagely. "Give a light here, sergeant!"

A lantern flashed. He looked down into a pair of wild eyes. A grey-haired woman, whose face was terribly thin and lined, and in whose wide-open eyes glared an unearthly fire.

"You mustn't have it. . . . I must take it with me!" she gasped.

She was clutching something tight to her bosom. It looked like a piece of sodden paper.

"I'm not going to take anything from you," he said soothingly.

The sergeant passed him a brandy flask, and he forced the neck between the woman's teeth. She struggled and choked.

"Don't . . . give me that. . . . I want to go to my baby. . . . The colonel said——"

"Never mind what the soldier said," snarled the inspector. "Get this hooch into you—it killed auntie, but why shouldn't it make you dance?"

He pulled a blanket from a locker and threw it over her, and in doing so he caught a glimpse of the thing that she held. It was the photograph of a child's face. He only saw it for a second in the light of his lantern, but never after did he forget that picture. Until that moment he had thought all children were alike; but there was something very distinctive, something very unusual, in that portrait of round-eyed childhood. And then he recognised the photograph and gasped.

"Lord help us! Who is that?"

He saw the likeness now—distinct, beyond question. It was Lila Smith! A baby's face, but Lila Smith.

"Who is this?" he repeated.

"You shan't have it! You shan't have it!" She struggled feebly. "You wicked man . . ."

Her voice sank to a murmur, and then the tired fingers relaxed.

"Rush for the pier, Toller. I think she's gone."

When he tried to take the photograph from the clenched hand, it squeezed up into an indistinguishable mass.

As to the identity of this unknown woman he did not even speculate. Such cases as these were common. Sometimes the police launch was not in time, and there were nights spent manipulating long drag ropes. Strange things come up from the bed of old Thames: once they had hooked the wheel of a Roman chariot; once they brought to light what remained of a man chained from head to foot, and bearing unmistakable evidence of murder. The live ones appeared at the police court and were conventionally penitent; the dead ones filled unknown graves, and occupied half an hour of a busy coroner's time.

14

Lila Smith? He tried to restore the photograph to a recognisable form, but it was too far gone.

The launch ran under the pier, and a Thames policeman caught the painter scientifically and tied it up. Another policeman vanished in the gloom and brought back a wheeled hand ambulance, and into this the woman was lifted, and whisked away to Westminster Hospital.

Wade was still frowning when he came into the superintendent's room and found the Big Four in conference.

"I'm sorry I'm late, sir," he said. "A lady decided to end her life right under my nose, and that held me up."

The Chief Constable sat back in his chair and yawned. He had been working since six o'clock that morning.

"What is this yarn of yours of the Rubber Men?" he asked briefly. He took a paper from a dossier and opened it. "Here's your report. You say there's a racing boat been seen working up and down the river—about the time of these robberies. Who has seen it distinctly?"

John Wade shook his head.

"Nobody, sir—it has not been seen, except at a distance. I have an idea it is painted black; it certainly carries no lights, and there's no question at all that it goes at a devil of a speed. The first clue we had that it was working was when bargemen complained of the wash it made. It's been heard, of course; but even here, whoever is running it has used mufflers, which is very unusual in a motor-boat."

"She carries no lights?"

"No, sir. The only two men who have ever had a close view of her is a river thief named Donovan, whom I took for breaking cargo two months ago, and another. He said that he and another man were in a small boat one night, and they were crossing the river—innocently, he claims, but I should imagine to get aboard a lighter—when this launch came out of the blue and they had a very narrow escape from being run down. If the boat hadn't been moving at a terrific speed and hadn't turned off in its own length, Mr. Donovan would have been stoking sulphur! As far as I could find out, he could give no description of the boat, except that he said it was very short and hadn't the lines of a motor-boat at all. I have checked up the appearance of this craft as well as I can, and it has generally coincided with one of the robberies."

"Where has it been seen?" asked the Chief Constable.

He was a long-faced man who had the appearance of being half asleep and never was.

"As far west as Chelsea Bridge," said Wade. "It was seen there by the second man, who is also a river thief in a mild way, but is

15

more likely to be a receiver. He has a sort of warehouse in Hammersmith, which we raided a little time ago—his name is Gridlesohn. I'm fairly sure he's a receiver because he's so ready to squeak—apparently he resents these land thieves taking to the river, because it means extra vigilance and extra danger to his own 'rats.' In that respect he has my sympathy. I've caught three of them in the last month."

Jennings, one of the big chiefs, blew a cloud of smoke up to the ceiling and shook his head.

"Why should the Rubber Men take to the river? That's what I want to know. There are twenty ways out of London, and the river's the slowest. You can go from Scotland Yard to any part of the town in a taxi, and not one policeman in a thousand would dream of taking the slightest notice of it. My own opinion is that after their last big job the Rubber Men are not going to operate again for years."

A third member of the party, a studious-looking man of fifty who was in control of the Foreign Branch, interrupted here.

"This is certainly the work of an international crowd. The New York police have had rubber men working there; and in France the Bank of Marseilles was smashed and the cashier killed, in exactly similar circumstances to the busting of the Northern and Southern Bank. As to their being finished in London——"

The telephone buzzer sounded. The Chief Constable took up the phone and listened.

"When?" he asked. A long pause, and then: "I'll come right away."

He hung up the phone and rose from his chair.

"The constable on point duty reports that the lights have gone out in the manager's office of Frisby's Bank. He put his lamp on to the side of the window and thought he saw a man in the room. He has had the intelligence to phone through to his divisional inspector—mark that constable's name for promotion, will you, Lane?"

Two of the four were already out of the room. By the time Wade got to the courtyard, three police tenders were drawn up by the kerb and detectives were still climbing aboard when the cars moved off.

Frisby's Bank was in the lower end of St. Giles's Street: it was one of the few private banks that had branches in the West End. It was a small, modern building, connected by a bridge across a courtyard with an older house, and stood on the corner of a block, practically under the eye of a constable on point duty—it was he who phoned.

By the time they reached the place the street was alive with police officers and a cordon had already been established round the bank. The manager's office faced a side street, and here was the general safe of the office. Two lights burnt day and night, and the safe was visible from the point where the policeman controlled the traffic.

The constable's story was quickly told. He was standing on the corner of the street, waiting for his relief, and Big Ben was striking the last note of twelve, when he saw the two lights go out. He ran across the road, tried the door and hammered with his fist on the panel. He then went back to the cashier's office, and, climbing on to the railings which surrounded that side of the bank and protected a small area, he turned the light of his electric lamp on to the window. It was then that he saw, or thought he saw, a man move quickly into the shadow of the safe.

A big crowd had assembled, attracted by the cordon even at the late hour; traffic had been diverted, and the streets within fifty yards of the bank had been cleared. While the constable had been telling what had happened, the bank manager, who had been telephoned for, arrived with the keys. There was, he said, a night watchman on duty, and the fact that he had not answered the repeated knockings was ominous. Detectives had already entered buildings to the left and right of the bank, and were stationed on the roof.

The premises were in a sense unique; there was a courtyard guarded by two big gates at the side of the building, and this separated the modern premises from an old Georgian house, also the property of the bank, in which was housed the staff. The top floor was in the occupation of the night watchman, a widower of fifty, and his daughter, who controlled the office cleaners. The only value of the courtyard, explained the manager, was that it gave a certain privacy to the bank's collecting van, and it also served to park his own and his assistants' cars during the daytime.

All these explanations were given very hurriedly, the while he was fitting, with a trembling hand, the key in the door—for he was pardonably nervous, though, as the Chief Constable explained, there was no need, for he would not be asked to enter the bank after it was opened.

At last the door swung back.

"You had better take charge of the search, Wade—give Mr. Wade a gun."

Somebody thrust an automatic into his hand, and he entered the dark outer office. The door leading to the manager's room was fastened; the key had been turned on the other side; but the Flying Squad had brought the necessary tools, and in a few minutes the lock was smashed and the manager's office was open to them.

Wade stepped quickly in, a gun in one hand and an electric torch in the other. The room was empty, but a second door, leading, he gathered, in the direction of the courtyard, was ajar. He pushed this open, stopped . . .

Bang!

A bullet went past him, smashed into the surface of the wall and covered his face with powdered plaster. He kicked the door open farther. The second shot came nearer. He thrust his hand round the jamb of the door and sprayed the interior with ten shots. He did not hear the answering fire, and would not have known that the burglars had replied if he had not found his sleeve ripped to rags.

In a whisper he demanded a pistol from the detective who had crept to his side, passing his own back. As he did so he heard the sound of quickly moving footsteps, and a door slam. Again he put his pistol inside and fired two shots; this time there was no answer, and when he pushed in the lamp to draw the fire, the provocation was unrewarded.

It might be a trap, but he must take the risk. In a moment he was in the room, his lamp flashing quickly from left to right. It was a small office below the level of the manager's: a plain room, lined with steel shelves on which were a number of boxes. In one corner was a steel door; behind that he could hear the soft purr of a motor-car. He tried the door; it yielded a little. He had the sensation that it was being held by somebody on the other side, and tugged. It opened suddenly—he had a glimpse of a car moving swiftly towards the gates, and then:

Rat-tat-tat-tat!

It was the quick stammer of a machine gun. A big black car swept into the street, and from its interior came the staccato rattle of automatic rifles. The police, taken by surprise, fell back; the crowd behind the cordon scattered, and the long car flew forward, venomously spitting fire from the back seat. The bullets whistled and smacked against the building; glass crashed; there was a wild scurry of people to cover. Before they could realise what had happened, the car had disappeared into St. James's Park.

CHAPTER III

It was not until the next morning that Wade remembered the would-be suicide and her photograph. Business took him to Scotland Yard, and he went on to the nearby hospital to make inquiries. To his amazement he found that the woman had left. By a mistake, which might have been the sergeant's, no charge had been preferred against her, and when she had demanded that she should be allowed to leave, no obstacle was offered.

"A creature of the most amazing vitality," said the house surgeon. "I thought she was dead when she came in, but in twenty-four hours she had walked out on her own two feet. . . . attempted suicide, was it? Well, we had no intimation. The policeman who brought her here thought she had fallen into the water by accident. By the way, she was frantic about a photograph she had lost. In fact, she got so hysterical that I nearly detained her."

"Did she give any name?"

The young surgeon shook his head.

"Anna. She didn't tell us her surname. My own opinion is that she's slightly demented—not so bad, of course, that one would certify her, even if one could."

John Wade was mildly puzzled. He was not very interested in this unknown drab, and, but for the photograph, she would have slipped from his mind instantly.

Conference followed conference at Scotland Yard. The India-Rubber Men had become a leading feature in quite a number of newspapers. There were the inevitable questions in Parliament and the as inevitable suggestion for a commission to inquire into the operations of the Criminal Investigation Department.

The bank's loss was not so heavy as it might have been, for the men had been disturbed in their work, but the robbery which followed was serious enough. A small factory, the property of a group of jewellers, was burgled; a safe, set in a concrete wall, was forced, and manufactured jewellery to the value of between eighty and a hundred thousand pounds vanished.

The first intimation the police had was a telephone message, evidently from one of the members of the gang, saying that the night watchman might need attention. A police tender was rushed to the factory, and the man was discovered unconscious on the ground. He could give no account of what had happened; he had seen nobody, he remembered nothing, and the police were left without a clue, for on this occasion the India-Rubber Men left not so much as a chisel behind them.

John Wade could read the account of this new crime without discomfort. He belonged to the river, and only by accident had been in the earlier hold-up. The usual inquiry had been put through, but the river police could contribute no information. Nevertheless, he was called in to the interminable conferences, and had little time to satisfy his own curiosity.

If the mysterious Anna passed quickly from his mind, the incident of the photograph recurred again and again. It was not until a week after the jewel theft that he was able to spare time to call at "Mecca."

Mum was out when he climbed up to the crazy wharf and made his way to the open window. From the woodshed came the howl of Golly's melancholy voice and the clump-clump of his hatchet. John Wade found the serving-room empty, and waited patiently, quite prepared to see Mum's disapproving face at any moment.

"Hallo, Lady Jane!"

Lila came into the room so quickly, noiselessly and unexpectedly, that he had the illusion that she had materialised out of nothing.

"Mrs. Oaks is out." She volunteered the information. "And please don't stay long, Mr. Wade. Auntie doesn't like you coming here, and really you were very unkind about Golly. He wouldn't dream of buying stolen goods——"

John Wade smiled.

"'If you see that man Wade, you tell him that your uncle is a good, honest citizen,'" he mocked, and by her quick flush knew that he had hit truly.

Then, while she was still embarrassed, he asked:

"Who is Anna?"

She turned her head and stared at him.

"Anna?" she said slowly. "I don't know—I told you I didn't know a long time ago, didn't I?"

"No, you didn't."

John Wade had a very excellent memory, and he was fairly certain that the name of Anna had never occurred between them.

The wonder he had glimpsed in her face was more apparent now; she was looking past him at a small tugboat thrusting its way against

20

the falling stream.

"I'm often puzzled who Anna was. . . . I don't know anybody by that name. Yet I know it so well. Isn't it curious?" Her sensitive lips twitched in the faintest smile. "She's a dream, I suppose."

"Like the experience?" he bantered her, and saw her mouth open in consternation.

"No, that isn't a dream," she said hastily. "It was silly of me to tell you about it. . . . I really mustn't."

It seemed to her that she had spoken of "the experience" many times to him; in reality, she had only made two references to the occasional adventure in which she was the central figure. She did not know that the first time she had mentioned it he had been amused, and not very greatly interested. He had thought she was exaggerating some little jaunt, setting a commonplace happening in a shrine of romance. The second time he was arrested by a note in her voice and had made a blunt inquiry. The more unwilling she was to tell him, the keener he was to know.

He was too experienced a cross-examiner to pursue his questions, and when she asked him gravely whether he was very busy, he accepted the turn of the subject.

"I don't think you *are* busy," she said. "It seems a terribly lazy life. You do nothing but ride up and down the river—I often see you. What do the Thames police do?"

"Ride up and down the river and lead a lazy life."

"But truly?" she insisted. "People say there are thieves on the river, but I've never seen one. Nobody's ever stolen anything from 'Mecca.' I suppose there's nothing of value here——"

He laughed at this, and that laugh was an extravagant compliment.

Such occasional visits as he paid to "Mecca" were invariably spoilt for her by a sense of apprehension that Mum would make an unwelcome and embarrassing appearance, and usually she was secretly praying that he would leave almost as soon as he had come. On this occasion, when it seemed there was no reason why he should go, he made an early departure, leaving her with a feeling of disappointment, which changed very quickly to relief, for he had not been gone for ten minutes when she heard Mum's voice.

Mum had been to the City and had returned with a visitor—the one man whom Lila Smith actively disliked. Mr. Raggit Lane very rarely came to "Mecca." A tall, spare man, with a thin, ascetic face, he would have been good-looking but for the lift of one corner of his lip that produced the illusion of a permanent sneer. He was always well dressed, finickingly so. He wore none of the ostentation of ephemeral wealth which was expressed by other habitués of the home in scarf-pins and rings and heavy gold watch-guards. Lila's dislike of him was based upon his use of perfume. Nobody had ever told her that it was bad form in a man to scent himself: Mum rather approved the practice.

Mr. Lane's hands were always well manicured, his black hair brilliantly polished. He wore a small signet ring upon one finger, but no other form of jewellery whatever.

Mum was very vague about his profession, but Lila gathered that he followed the sea; she gathered this because Mr. Lane, with re-markable condescension, had once given her a small embroidered shawl which he had picked up in China.

Almost as soon as Mrs. Oaks arrived, Lila was summoned to the sitting-room. Mum's sitting-room was the holy of holies, into which only very privileged people entered. It was a large room with two long, opaque windows. The walls were painted, the floor covered with parquet.

Lila came in, drying her hands on her apron, and met the long scrutiny of Raggit Lane's glass eye.

"Hallo!" He looked at her with unfeigned admiration. He had not seen the girl for a year, and in that year a remarkable change had oc-curred in her. "She's got pretty, Oaks."

He always called Mum "Oaks," and she never showed the least resentment.

"Let's have a look at you."

He caught her by the shoulder to swing her round to the light. A sudden anger shook the girl, and she disengaged herself violently.

"Don't touch me. How dare you touch me!"

Her voice had a new note. Mum gaped at her, amazed.

"Why, Lila——" she began.

"The girl's right. I'm sorry, Lila. Forgot you were grown up."

But Lila seemed not to hear. She turned and walked quickly from the room. It was her first demonstration of independence that Mum had witnessed, and she was speechless with astonishment.

"What's the matter with the girl?" she demanded shrilly. "I've never seen her like that before! If she starts giving herself airs with me she'll know all about it!"

Raggit Lane chuckled, took a cigarette from a thin gold case and lit it.

"She isn't a kid any more, that's all—there's nothing to make a fuss about. I didn't believe you when you said she'd got pretty, but she's all that."

"The last time you were here, I said: 'Come and have a look at her,' but you wouldn't believe me," said Mum, with the satisfaction of one whose predictions had been justified.

Mr. Lane blew a cloud of smoke to the ceiling.

"The last time I was in London there were many reasons why I shouldn't come," he said slowly.

There was an awkward pause.

"Where have you come from now?" she asked.

"The Black Sea—Constantia."

He was evidently thinking of something else, and answered her questions mechanically.

"How is the old man?" she asked after a long silence.

"Eh? The old man? Oh, he's all right." And then, bringing all his attention to her: "I don't want him to know I've been to-day."

Mum smiled.

"You don't want him to know you've been at all, do you? You can trust me, Mr. Lane—I never discuss anything with him except Lila; and I don't see him more than an hour every year."

The smooth brows of Mr. Lane met in a deep frown.

"He's getting touchy, very difficult. Of course I could always say that I came here by accident. It's an officers' club. But I don't want to use that excuse until it's necessary. Where's Golly?"

She listened.

"Chopping wood," she said.

Another long silence. Then:

"Who is this Lila girl?"

Mrs. Oaks would do much for her good-looking visitor, but he had asked her a question which she could not with safety answer.

"The thing that worries me about Lila is this fellow Wade. He's always hanging around the house. I don't know whether it's because he's after the girl or what. You never know what a copper's doing."

"Inspector Wade?" Mr. Lane fingered his chin thoughtfully. "He's a pretty clever man, isn't he?"

Mum smiled derisively.

"Ain't they all clever by their own account? From what I hear, they nearly got him the other day, these India-Rubber people. I wish they had!"

Lane laughed softly.

"The India-Rubber Men seem to be rather busy," he said. "Who are they?"

She shook her head.

"I don't know anything about 'em," she said decisively. "I keep myself to myself and mind my own business. It's hard enough to get your own living without troubling about how other people get theirs.

Half of it's newspaper lies—they'll say anything for a sensation."

"Now what about a trade, Oaks?"

She got up from the chair in which she was sitting.

"I'll see what the girl's doing," she said, and left the room.

She was back in a few minutes, closed and locked the door behind her and, going to the fire-place, rolled back the hearth-rug. With a bodkin she pried up an irregular section of the parquet floor. Beneath was a patch of felt, which she lifted, disclosing a steel trapdoor set in the floor. It was less than a foot square and was fastened with a patent lock. Inserting a key, she turned it, and with some difficulty raised the heavy steel door. The receptacle beneath was evidently much larger than the opening and, groping, she brought to light half a dozen little canvas bags, which she handed to the man one by one. He placed these on a table beneath the opaque glass window, and opened them carefully.

"That's a cheap lot," she said, as he unrolled the strip of cloth and disclosed a variety of articles that ranged between cheap ear-rings and big, flamboyant brooches of low-grade gold. "The one with the red ribbon's the best."

He looked at the stuff disparagingly until he came to the package tied with red ribbon. There were several good pieces here: a ten-carat emerald, a cushion-shaped diamond ring, a necklace, a pendant, and five fairly large-sized pearls. He looked at these curiously.

"I suppose the string broke when they snatched?"

She shook her head, her thin lips set in a straight line.

"I don't ask any questions. I don't know where they come from. If I'm offered a bargain I buy it. I always say, if you ask no questions you hear no lies."

He was examining one of the pearls through a small magnifying-glass.

"That one you'd better throw in the fire," he said, handing the gem to her. "It is marked and would be recognised anywhere."

Obediently she threw the pearl, which must have been worth six or seven hundred pounds, into the fire. She never argued with Mr. Raggit Lane, having learned by experience the futility of questioning his judgment.

He made his choice, dropped the selected articles into his pocket, and returned the remainder to the woman.

"The gold isn't worth much—it is hardly worth boiling," he said. "I should drop these things into the river."

Mrs. Oaks sighed.

"It's a waste," she said plaintively, "but you know best——"

There was a sharp rap of knuckles on the panel. Mrs. Oaks

looked up.

"Who's that?" she asked shrilly.

"I should like to have two words with you, Mrs. Oaks."

It was the voice of John Wade!

Not a muscle of the woman's face moved.

"Who are you when you're at home?" she demanded.

"Inspector Wade."

"One minute."

Quickly she gathered the packages together, dropped them into the safe, closed and locked it, replaced felt and parquet and rolled back the hearth-rug. While she was doing this, Lane had opened the big wardrobe at the end of the room, had entered and closed it.

Mrs. Oaks gave one glance at the fire, poked a round, glowing globule that had once been a pearl, and unlocked the door.

"Come in, Wade," she said coolly.

John Wade walked into the room and shot a swift glance around.

"Sorry to interrupt your prayer meeting," he said.

"I was changing my stockings if you want to know," snapped Mum tartly.

"I don't want to know anything so indelicate, Lady Godiva."

He sniffed.

"Having a quiet little smoke? Naughty, naughty! You're getting quite fast in your old age."

Mrs. Oaks bottled her wrath.

"What do you want?" she asked.

But John Wade was looking round the apartment with every evidence of admiration.

"Charming room," he said. "Your ladyship's boudoir? And you smoke Egyptian cigarettes, too—that's bad for the heart, child."

"What do you want?" she demanded.

To her alarm, his eyes were glued on the big wardrobe.

"I came to ask you a question, but I seem to have arrived at a very awkward moment. Quite an unimportant question—nothing whatever to do with my professional duties—but I won't wait."

He walked to the door, beaming back at her with that delightful smile of his.

"I'm afraid your boy friend will be suffocated unless you let him out very soon," he said, and closed the door with extravagant care.

She flung it open after him and followed him to the front door of "Mecca." His crowning insult was left to the last. Bending towards her, he murmured sympathetically:

"I shan't tell Golly!"

Before she could tap her coherent stream of invective he had

25

gone. She came back to her room and locked the door behind her.

"Come out, Mr. Lane," she said, her voice tremulous with anger. "It was only that fly policeman."

Mr. Lane came into the room a little dishevelled. He smoothed his hair, and it was patent that he was less angry than concerned.

"He knew I was here. Does he know who I am?"

"God knows what he knew!" snapped the woman. "One of these fine mornings that fellow's going to be picked out of the river with his head bashed in. And the day that happens I'm going to church for the first time in twenty-five years."

"Wade—h'm!" Lane was fondling his chin.

Then he began to empty his pockets.

"Put those back, I'll take 'em another time."

"There's no danger——" began Mrs. Oaks.

Raggit Lane smiled.

"I don't take risks. Send a boy with 'em . . . you know where. . . . I'll have them picked up."

He adjusted his tie, collected his hat and cane from the wardrobe and, Mrs. Oaks having reported all clear, went out into the street and made his unhurried way to the main thoroughfare where his taxi was waiting. Once or twice he looked round, but there was no sign of a watcher. Yet, even when his cab was entering the City, he found no relief from the uncomfortable feeling that he was being followed.

That afternoon Wade went personally to Scotland Yard for information.

"Do you know a dark-looking gentleman who smells like a flower-shop and dresses like a duke?" he asked Inspector Elk, who was an authority on all strange people.

"Sounds like everybody to me," said Elk wearily. "Can't understand this craze for scent. A brother-in-law of mine——"

Wade cut short his reminiscences. He drew from his pocket a sheet of paper. He had a taste for drawing and could sketch a very respectable likeness of Mr. Raggit Lane.

Elk studied the sketch, scratched his ear and shook his head.

"It might be anybody. I don't know him. What's his name?"

"That I'll find out. At present I'm without information," said Wade. "None of the servants at 'Mecca' knows him—one of my men has been making inquiries. I have never seen him before. I only saw him by accident. I remembered an inquiry I wanted to make about some stolen whisky—one of those fellows who'll come up at the Sessions this week put up a half-squeak. I landed at the main stairs and went round to the front of the house, and then I saw him with the old lady. They drove up in a cab just as I got there. She was so darned friendly with him that I thought he couldn't be much good."

Mr. Elk sighed and closed his eyes.

"You can't charge him with being a friend of Mum Oaks," he said. "That's no offence—you haven't got a cigar in your pocket, I suppose? I didn't think you had. You young officers smoke too many cigarettes—now that brother-in-law of mine——"

"It wasn't he," said Wade, and made his escape.

The rest of the day was his own, and he employed it in a characteristic fashion. In reality John Wade had no spare time. He was a man who loved his profession, lived for it, and thought of nothing which did not touch at some angle upon police work. His ideal occupation was to loaf through the busy streets of the West End, watching people. The study of human beings was an absorbing hobby; their gestures, their facial expressions, the conventions of movement. He collected them as other men collect stamps. He would sit for hours in a teashop, watching two men talk, and jotting down on any odd scrap of paper their peculiarities of expression. He knew the gesture which accompanied a lie, the droop of eyelids inseparable from vanity. He could tell at a dozen yards whether a man was talking of himself or of somebody else.

Towards evening it came on to rain, not heavily but a chill, uncomfortable drizzle. He made his way to a small restaurant in Soho at an earlier hour than he intended. Usually he liked to sit over his dinner, ruminating upon such events of the day as needed examination; but to-night dinner proved to be an uninteresting meal; because of the early hour the restaurant was almost deserted, and it was eight o'clock when he came into the street.

The rain had ceased, but it was quite dark. He wandered aimlessly towards Shaftesbury Avenue, intending to make his way back to his little house in Wapping on foot. He crossed Shaftesbury Avenue, and, passing through Leicester Square, came to one of the streets that lead into the Strand.

There was a newly fashionable restaurant here—a discreet place which had been lately discovered by the epicure. In London the reputations of restaurants rise and fade inexplicably.

He was sauntering along the rain-soaked pavement when a big limousine came noiselessly from the other end of the street and stopped before the restaurant. John Wade halted. He was not curious as to the people who were being assisted from the car by the stout commissionaire; his chief desire was not to barge into them as they crossed the pavement.

The man who got out was tall and broadly built; his head was bald, his hard, old face was covered with a hundred wrinkles.

"Come on, my dear," he said impatiently.

He had a deep, booming voice which interested the detective.

The old man put out his hand and assisted his companion to the pavement. She was dressed in white, over which was a coat of silver tissue with a deep ermine collar. A slim, radiant figure of youth; from her *coiffeured* golden hair to the tips of her silver shoes she was a vision of loveliness. For a moment John Wade did not see her face, and then, as she came under the overhead light, she turned her head. She did not see John Wade, but he saw her and his jaw dropped. It was Lila Smith!

They had passed into the restaurant before he could stir himself into movement. All thought of his little home in Wapping had vanished from his mind. He waited till the obsequious commissionaire had returned to his station at the door, and then strolled up to him.

"Was that Colonel Martin I saw go in there?" he asked.

The commissionaire looked at him suspiciously. It was not the first time that some stranger had endeavoured to establish the identity of ladies and gentlemen who dined at that restaurant.

"No, it wasn't," he said.

"Queer. I could have sworn it was he," said Wade, and would have passed the man, but the commissionaire blocked his way.

"This isn't the way to the restaurant, sir. These are the private rooms and banquet halls. The restaurant opens on to the next street."

John Wade saw that the man and Lila were disappearing through a glass door and had turned left, evidently to a staircase.

"Now perhaps you'll tell me something I want to know." His voice was authoritative. "My name is Wade; I am an inspector of police. If you will call the constable who's standing at the corner of the street he can probably identify me."

"That's all right, Mr. Wade." The commissionaire was almost apologetic. "I recognise you now—I've seen your face in the papers. You quite understand I couldn't answer questions——"

"I quite understand that," said Wade amiably. "Who was that man who went in just now?"

The man shook his head.

"I haven't the slightest idea, sir. He and the young lady dine here about once a year—certainly not more often. The last time she came she was only a kid. I think he must be her father. One of the head waiters said he's an officer in the Indian Army and only comes home every year."

"He always brings her here, does he?"

"He may take her somewhere else, but I've seen them here together."

"And she's always well dressed?"

"Why, yes, sir," said the commissionaire in surprise. "She's quite a young lady. She's at school somewhere."

John Wade considered the situation quickly.

"What room have they got?"

"Number Eighteen." Then the commissionaire remembered. "I can tell you his name, sir—it'll be in the book."

He disappeared down the passage and returned very soon.

"Brown—Mr. Brown. He's a rich man, according to the head waiter. Is there anything wrong about them?" he asked anxiously.

There had been something wrong about quite a number of people who dined at the Lydbrake.

"I don't know," said the detective shortly. "I suppose there's no way of getting a glimpse of them? I don't want you to see the head waiter or make a fuss about it that'll start people talking."

The commissionaire thought.

"Number Nineteen isn't occupied. You might walk up into that, Mr. Wade. I can easily tell the head waiter that you want to write a letter. But you understand, sir, I don't know who you are—I'd probably lose my job."

John Wade was assuring him on this point when there came on to the scene one whom John Wade was to meet again in less pleasant circumstances. The meeting was coincidental. Neither had sought the other. In such a way men meet their future wives and other men meet ruin.

Wade was aware of the swaying figure in evening dress. He stood beyond the patch of light thrown from an overhead glass canopy. As the detective moved to the entrance—

"I say—tha's a pretty girl! Tha's a beauty!"

He lurched into the light, a thick-set young man, red of face and with a small red moustache. His pale blue eyes stared owlishly down the corridor.

"Whosh that, Bennett?"

"I don't know their names, m'lord."

He was rather drunk, this coarse-handed, coarse-featured young man. John Wade gave him one glance before he turned into the restaurant, and a few seconds later was walking up the softly carpeted stairs. A waiter was entering Number Eighteen as he came into the corridor but took no notice of him. Wade opened the door of Nineteen and stepped in, closing it behind him. He felt for the light switch and found it.

He was in a small, rather ornately furnished dining-room; the walls were panelled in rosewood. At the farther end, near the window, was a door which evidently led into Eighteen. He went softly to this. There was no sound of voices, and, turning the handle with great caution, he pulled the door slightly ajar, and found, to his annoyance, that there was a second door beyond.

Voices were faintly audible; the deep, gruff note of the man, the softer voice of Lila. So this was "the experience"! Every year, like a modern Cinderella, she doffed her old clothes and her worn-out shoes and, dressed in the best and most expensive of fashions, dined with this old man.

The whole of the evening must have been spent in preparation for this little jaunt. There must have been hairdressers called in secretly. . . . months of preparation, of dress-fitting, all carried out secretly, under Mum's supervision. She had not known she was going out that night, he could swear; she would have been more excited, less her placid self. He listened at the panel, could hear nothing; tried the keyhole, with no better result. Greatly daring, he turned the handle softly, but the door was locked.

He went to the light switch and turned it off, and, tiptoeing back, lay prone, his ear to the floor. There was a slight space between the bottom of the door and the carpet, and he could hear scraps of the conversation.

". . . no, Mr. Brown, she's very good to me . . ."

He heard the man say something about education and France; but there was curiously little conversation. From time to time the door of the room opened and closed when the waiter came in and set new dishes. Once he heard the man say something about Constantinople. He was describing the place to the girl.

If anything was said which had the slightest bearing upon their strange relationship, John Wade did not hear it. Always she addressed him as "Mr. Brown." There was nothing to suggest they were father and daughter.

At last Wade heard the man demand his bill, and, rising, he dusted his knees, slipped out of the room, and was sitting in a taxi when the big limousine drew up to the door, and the girl and her strange companion came out. "Mr. Brown" stopped only to slip a Treasury note into the commissionaire's hand, and then the car moved off.

Both Wade's taxicab and the driver had been well chosen; the cab was just behind the bigger car as it sped through the deserted streets of the City. They passed Aldgate, along the Mile End Road, and were near to Wapping when the car turned into a side street and stopped. Fortunately, Wade's cab had been a little out-distanced; he overshot the road, stopped the cab, and, springing out, reached the end of the street in time to see Lila pass into a house. Almost immediately the car moved on, disappearing round a second corner, and Wade made his way to the house.

It was a one-story villa. The windows were dark. He waited a little while, and then a second taxicab came into the street and stopped at the door. The detective strolled on, crossed the road and came back to where, from a doorway, he was able to watch what followed.

Five minutes later the door of the villa opened and Lila and a woman came out. She was wearing a black raincoat, and he guessed rather than knew that she had resumed her shabby attire. The woman he had no difficulty in recognising as Mum, even if he had not heard her sharp voice directing the cabman.

Waiting until they were gone, he again crossed the road and, opening the little iron wicket-gate, passed up the flagged path to the door of the house. By the light of his small electric torch he found the bell and pressed it. He heard it ring, but no answer came, and he rang again.

The door was fastened by a Yale lock. He went into the little forecourt and tried the front window, but the catch was fastened.

Running down by the side of the house was a narrow pathway which led to the back of the premises. There was a little door here, the lock of which was easily forced with a penknife. Presently he found the kitchen door; it was locked and bolted; but he had better luck with the kitchen window, which had not been fastened.

It took him a few minutes to open this. The sash squeaked noisily, and if there had been anybody in the house they must have heard. But when he flung his leg over the sill and dropped into the darkness of the kitchen, there was no sound.

Nobody knew better than John Wade that he was satisfying his curiosity at the expense of the law, which he was most outrageously breaking; but this knowledge caused him not the slightest uneasiness, even though at that moment the police force was passing through a period of unpopularity.

The kitchen was unfurnished; the permanent dresser fixed to the wall was covered with dust. There was not so much as a strip of linoleum on the bare boards.

He opened the door and stepped into the passage. Here he had evidence that the house was used, for he found a thick carpet under his feet, though apparently nobody had ever troubled to clean it, for his feet stirred up little clouds of dust. There were pictures hanging on the wall; cheap engravings which were hardly visible under the coating of grime which covered the glass.

He opened the door of the back room. There was a bed here, covered with a dusty quilt, and the cheap furnishings of the place were in an equal state of neglect. In the front room the blinds were drawn. It had once been a very commonplace parlour, but here also the tawdry furniture had not been used for years.

Going up the carpeted stairs, he reached a landing from which three doors opened. One led to a bath-room; this had been recently used, for, as he opened the door, there came to him a waft of delicate perfume. The bath-room floor was clean; the bath itself had been used that evening, and there were towels, still damp, hanging over the back of a chair. The big mirror, too, was polished, and on the little table before it somebody had left a washleather pad and an orange stick. He found a paper bag half filled with bath salts; the soap in the dish was of a most expensive brand and was hardly used. It was here, then, that Cinderella had prepared her toilet.

He passed into the front room. It was scrupulously clean, and laid out on the bed was the dress he had seen Lila wearing, even to the silver shoes. There were no stockings; she must have been wearing those when she went away.

He made a more careful search of the room. The windows were covered with thick felt, so that it was impossible that light should escape. There was no electric current in the house; light was evidently supplied by a big paraffin table-lamp, which, after closing the door, he lit, the better to conduct his investigations.

Near the bed, let into an alcove of the wall, was a long, sunken cupboard. He tried to open this, but it fastened with a patent lock and the door was obviously of very solid construction. A table, two chairs—one of them very comfortable—a long mirror leaning against the wall and performing the function of a cheval glass—these were the only articles the room contained.

He turned out the light and made an examination of the back room. Evidently this was not used, for it bore the same appearance of neglect that he had seen in the other rooms. It contained an untidy bed which was covered by a dust-soiled linen sheet.

Wade went down the stairs slowly and thoughtfully. This house puzzled him. Did Brown, or Mum, or whoever was concerned, keep this villa vacant all the year as a changing place for Lila? And if they did . . .

He had reached the foot of the stairs when he heard the sound of a key being inserted in the lock of the front door. Swiftly he went back to the cover of the kitchen, and waited. The front door opened; he heard a man whispering, then the door closed. They were coming towards him. For some reason which he could not explain, a shiver went down John Wade's spine. He was not a nervous man, and this was an uncanny experience—more uncanny than Lila's furtive outings.

One of them stopped at the back room, opened the door and went in. Neither showed a light, but presently Wade saw a gleam of yellow under the bottom of the closed door. There was a queer, musty smell in the house; his nostrils were very sensitive, and, even before he listened and heard the fierce chatter of a voice, he knew that the men who had passed into the back room were Chinamen.

Even as he listened, he heard a quick step on the flagstones outside, and had only time to get back to the kitchen when a third man came through the front door. He asked something in Chinese; the door opened and one of the men came out. Wade did not see the face of the new-comer, but he was European and wore a black raincoat turned up over his ears. Then he too disappeared into the room; the door was closed and locked.

The new-comer was at any rate European—that was evident from his height. Wade crept forward and listened at the door. Two voices were talking urgently; the third did not speak. There was a menace in the deeper note of the new arrival, almost a plea in the whine of the one Chinaman who spoke. Somebody came to the door and turned the handle, forgetting it was locked, and again John Wade retreated to the kitchen. Presently the lock snapped back, the handle turned and the three went out. They passed through the front door together, the last man closing it gently.

They were hardly in the street before Wade was after them. They walked together across the main arterial road, turned down a narrow street, with the detective on their trail. Presently they reached one of the waterside streets, a place of warehouses, narrow entries that gave to worn, slippery stairs leading to the dark waters of the river. They stood for a while, talking together, then one of them sat down with his back to the wall. In the uncertain light it was difficult to see which of the three it was, but he was hardly seated before the other two men moved on and became indistinct blurs in the light of the street lamps as they passed.

John Wade was in a dilemma. Did they suspect he was following them? Had this man been left to check the shadow? John walked on, came nearer and nearer to the man sitting against the wall. It was one of the Chinamen, he saw. The pavement glistened from a recent shower, but it glistened more brightly in the place where the Chinaman sat, for three little rivulets of blood were trickling down to the gutter.

John Wade's police whistle shrilled through the empty streets. He blew as he ran swiftly in the direction the two men had taken, and presently he came upon a policeman running towards him. The policeman had met nobody. In a few minutes a dozen policemen were searching the neighbourhood, but the tall European and the China-man were not found.

CHAPTER IV

Late that night John Wade reported to his immediate chief.

"We found in his blouse about six ounces of platinum setting; I think, from their style, they are part of the effects of the jewel robbery," he said.

"The curious thing about the man is that he was dumb. At least, the doctor says so. No identity marks that one can find. I've had his finger-prints taken, and I had a big man in the Chinese colony down to see him, but he hasn't been recognised."

It was past midnight when John Wade arrived at "Mecca," and this time he did not come alone. Golly, in his shirt-sleeves, was sitting in the serving-room, smoking a short and foul clay pipe.

"Mum's in bed, I suppose?" Wade asked.

"She's been out to-night."

"I know very well she's been out," said Wade shortly. "That's what I want to see her about."

Golly got down from the table on which he had been sitting, shot a baleful glare at the two detectives in the background, and disappeared. When he returned it was to summon him to Mum's presence. She was in her sitting-room, a tight-lipped, resentful figure of a woman.

"What's the idea?" she asked sharply.

"For the moment," said John, "the idea is murder, and it's a pretty bad idea."

He saw her face fall.

"Murder?" she said incredulously.

"A Chinaman was murdered to-night by one of two men, who, previous to the murder, admitted themselves into a small house in Langras Road, where you had been earlier in the evening with Lila."

She was not acting—her surprise was genuine. But she was not so startled that she would betray herself. Almost instantly she came back with her excuse.

"That's right, I was in the house in Langras Road to-night. It belongs to my sister-in-law; we've been trying to let it for years."

"You took Lila there?" challenged John.

"Did I say I didn't?" she asked sourly. "I took her there to change her things. She was meeting"—there was a pause—"her father. Do you want to know who he is, Mr. Busy, because, if you do, you're going to be disappointed."

John Wade's eyes narrowed.

"Be very civil, Mrs. Oaks, and this will be a more or less pleasant visit. If you want to be associated with this murder you can get fresh with me. I'm not threatening you, I'm telling you the truth. If I can't get all the information I want here, I shall take you to the station. Is that clear?"

He saw fury in the woman's eyes, but her voice was meekness itself.

"I'm sorry, Mr. Wade, but naturally I'm a little upset. Where was he killed—in the house?"

"Did you know Chinamen used that place?" asked John.

She shook her head emphatically.

"I never knew anybody used it except me. I go there every few months to tidy it up—me and Lila go."

"Who is Lila's father?"

But here she was adamant.

"I'm not going to create any scandal—you understand what I mean. The gentleman's got another family."

"Does Lila know that?"

Mrs. Oaks hesitated.

"No, she doesn't. She thinks that he's a friend interested in her. He pays for Lila's keep, and when he's in England, he sends me the money to dress her up and take her out to dinner with him."

"Is he English?"

"American."

The answer came a little too quickly.

"He lives on Long Island or New York or somewhere. An American gentleman. I've never seen Chinamen in the house, Mr. Wade, I'll swear it. If there was any there to-night, I didn't know about them—Chinamen frighten me anyway. You're not going to upset the poor child by cross-examining her? She's only just gone to bed."

"How many sets of keys are there—I mean to the house in Langras Road?"

She considered.

"I've only seen one set."

"Do you keep it all the time?"

She nodded.

"Do you know anybody who had another set?"

She was equally emphatic on this point.

Wade was convinced that she spoke the truth. At any rate, she had made no attempt to conceal the happenings of the evening. It was unprofessional in him that he felt terribly sorry for Lila at that moment: this explanation of "the experience" was so obviously plausible.

Nothing could be gained by speaking to the girl—Mum Oaks seemed only too anxious to supply him with information.

"Has 'Mr. Brown' got a key of the house?"

She was rather startled when he used the name by which the old man was known to her.

"So far as I know he hasn't a key, and I don't see why he should have. I've never told him about the house in Langras Road."

John Wade thought a moment.

"Give me those you have," he said.

She searched a bag that was on the table, producing a ring on which one key dangled.

John Wade eyed her steadily.

"And the key of the cupboard."

For a fraction of a second he saw alarm in her eyes.

"Cupboard? Which cupboard?"

"There's a cupboard in the bedroom where Lila changed."

She shook her head.

"I don't know anything about that. That's the only key I have."

The detective smiled.

"Then I'm afraid we shall have to break open that cupboard," he said pleasantly.

She had recovered herself immediately.

"I'm afraid you will," she said coolly. And then, suddenly, she snapped: "What do you want?"

John turned his head. Lila was standing in the doorway, wrapped in a dingy old kimono; the elegance of her hair and the whiteness of the manicured hands that held the shabby gown in place seemed oddly incongruous. She looked in surprise from Mum to John Wade.

"I—I thought—you told me to come down for some milk——"

"You can go up again," said the woman harshly.

"Do you think she murdered the Chinaman?" asked Mum, heavily humorous. "She looks like a murderer, doesn't she?"

He ignored her sarcasm.

"I want the name and address of Lila's father—the man she dined with to-night."

"I can't give it to you," said the woman defiantly. "I don't know it, I tell you. You know as much as I do—he's a Mr. Brown. Where he lives I don't know. I usually get a telegram from him."

"And he doesn't know the house in Langras Road, you say?" said Wade quietly. "How does he pick her up?"

For a moment the woman was nonplussed.

"A hired car comes for her, and I take her as far as St. Paul's Churchyard, if you want to know; then I get out and he gets in."

"Yet he brought the girl back to Langras Road," persisted Wade. "You're tying yourself in knots, Mrs. Oaks."

But she was dogged on one point: the mysterious Mr. Brown had never been inside the villa.

John Wade drove back to the house of mystery, admitted himself with the key, and, there being no further need for secrecy, he carried out a very complete search of the house.

He had one shock; he found the cupboard open and empty. Somebody had been there since he left. Lila's clothes had been thrown on to the floor, evidently to make space for the contents of the wardrobe.

The room in which the conference between the two Chinamen and the European had taken place yielded another curious clue. There was a certain dampness about this room; he found patches of wet on the floor, and one of the chairs was still moist. It had been raining steadily in the region of Wapping, and a heavy downpour came on immediately after the discovery of the murder, so that, when the dead man was taken away, his clothes were saturated. There was a reason why the European should be dry: he wore a long raincoat. But the second Chinaman . . . he wore only his blouse, yet he had not left any evidence of his presence.

How had they come to the house? Had they walked? Nobody had seen them, not even the taxi-driver he had left at the end of the street, and who was still waiting for him, as John Wade remembered, after the discovery of the murder, his taximeter ticking expensively.

In the man's blouse had been found a scrap of Chinese writing on a thin, narrow slip of paper. By the time Wade returned to the police station this had been interpreted. This might have been done earlier, but the paper was not found until the head of the Chinese colony had viewed the body and failed to identify it.

The sergeant at the desk handed the translation with a smile.

"No clue here, Mr. Wade. It's just directions for finding this police station."

John read and frowned.

"He was coming here and they intercepted him. I wondered if that was the idea."

"Was he putting up a squeak?" asked the sergeant.

"It almost looks like it."

He went into his room. On his desk there had been laid out

the twisted trinkets which had been taken from the Chinaman's blouse. Most of them were settings from which the stones had been wrenched, and, except for one article, they were of platinum. The exception was a man's gold signet ring, heavily worn. There was a half obliterated crest on the flat seal—a temple before which was a figure in classic robes. This was so faint that it was difficult to recover the outlines. On the inside, almost worn from visibility, were the words: "Lil to Larry."

The room which John Wade used as an office was a small apartment leading from the charge-room, and approached from behind the sergeant's desk. There was a window, heavily barred, and a second door leading to the courtyard. The desk was under the barred window, and the two men were leaning across this, turning over the settings, when John felt a cold draught playing about his legs. It was ordinarily a draughty room, but this discomfort was unusual, and he looked round idly to discover the cause. And then he saw something which made him turn with a jerk . . .

"Don't move, either of you!" said a muffled voice behind the rubber mask. "If you shout, you'll finish it in hell!"

Two men were in the room—one half in and half out of the doorway, the other between the door and the desk. They wore coarse black overalls; their faces were hidden behind light gas-masks, their hands were covered in tight red rubber gloves. Two heavy-calibred automatics covered the police officers.

"Step back to that wall," said the man in the doorway, coming farther into the room, and John Wade and the sergeant obeyed. "Keep up your hands, please. It will be easier to shoot and clear then, you know."

The man nearest the desk took two noiseless strides forward, peered down at the trinkets, selected something and backed towards the door.

John Wade was no fool. He was unarmed; the nearest pistol was in the drawer of the desk, and he had no doubt at all that, in sacrificing his own life, he would sign the death-warrant of the sergeant.

The two figures moved with uncanny quietness. John, glancing down, saw that their feet were covered with thick felt overshoes, attached to which, he guessed, were rubber soles.

They were out of the room, and the door slammed and locked, in three seconds. John made a dive for the table, pulled open the drawer, and, gun in hand, rushed into the charge-room, almost knocking down the policeman on duty at the door. He saw two figures flying along the street, but did not see the slowly moving car until he was within a dozen yards of it. The two men leaped aboard, the car accelerated noisily, and sped at a tremendous pace along the deserted thoroughfare. There was no chance of catching them. He flew back to the station, to find that the sergeant had already mustered every possible reserve.

"You'll not catch them. Phone all stations," said John shortly, and went back to the charge-room.

He saw at a glance what the intruders had taken—the gold signet ring had disappeared. He could now reconstruct the story of the murdered Chinaman. This man had come to betray his masters, and had brought this setting as evidence. He was dumb and unable to make himself understood, and had either brought the ring to prove the identity of some member of the gang, or had stolen it as an act of revenge. This latter seemed most likely. The India-Rubber Men would not have taken the risk to recover the ring if some especial importance was not attached to it. A sentimental one, perhaps.

The case was clearer now. It was a crime definitely nailed to this remarkable gang.

The next morning the police threw a wide net. Every Chinese suspect was pulled in for examination. Haunts that regarded themselves as sacrosanct, so long was it since they had been raided, were subjected to police visitation. The long riverside area, the Chinese lodging-houses, the queer little dens where Orientals congregate—they were all combed. It added to the difficulties that there were in the Pool of London at that period a dozen ships which contained a fair sprinkling of Chinese hands: they were employed as cooks and stewards, and in some cases as deck-hands; but no information of any value reached police head-quarters from there.

Mum Oaks had paid two visits to Scotland Yard, and had been interrogated, but she could not lighten the mystery. It was unfortunate that this period followed a new order, issued by the Secretary of State, limiting the power of police interrogation; but Wade had an idea that even the terrors of the Spanish Inquisition would not have made Mum Oaks tell all she knew.

On her second and last visit he accompanied her down the stone stairs into New Scotland Yard.

"Angel," he said extravagantly, "you are doing a very silly thing. Why the dickens don't you tell pap all you know?"

She was in a white heat of fury. As the days had passed without the realisation of her fears, and as she had discovered the limitations of police action, her assurance and insolence had grown.

"Is that all you want of me?" she demanded.

Golly, who had been waiting for her outside, came timidly towards her, a pathetic figure.

"My poor, persecuted wife——" he began.

"You shut up!" she snapped. "Have you anything more to say to me?"

"Nothing, child," said Wade unpleasantly, "except that when I do get the India-Rubber Men——"

"The India-Rubber Men!" she sneered. "A fat lot you'd do with the India-Rubber Men! Didn't they come into the police station and pinch a ring——" She had said too much. Her lips closed like a rat-trap; but it was too late.

"How did you know that, Mrs. Oaks?" His voice was silky. "Now, who's been telling you all about that ring?"

She did not answer.

"Nobody knew but four people; I was one of them, Sergeant Crewe was one; the other two were the gentlemen who made the call."

He waited.

"It's all over London," she said at last. "You don't suppose fellows would do a thing like that without telling the world, do you?"

She expected to be held for further cross-examination. To her surprise and relief, he waved his hand at the archway standing at the entrance of the Yard.

"Pass along," he said good-humouredly.

And then, as a parting shot:

"Remember me to your boy friend in the wardrobe."

When he winked at her, Mum Oaks could have killed him.

By a peculiar combination of circumstances Inspector Wade was within twenty-four hours of meeting the boy friend face to face.

What the police called the Haymarket incident occurred about ten o'clock that night. This is the hour when the West End is more or less of a wilderness. The theatres are full; the waiting cars stand in rows along dark back streets in their vicinity; and the traffic in Piccadilly Circus is so light that there is practically no need for control. Later, when the theatres empty, there will be chaos, but at ten o'clock the streets are a paradise for the timid motorist.

Two men walked down the Haymarket at a leisurely pace and turned towards St. James's Square. They were talking together as they sauntered, and apparently did not notice the woman who stood on the corner of the square. A policeman who was walking in the same direction, and following them, saw the woman suddenly dart forward to one of the men and grip him by the coat. The policeman saw the scuffle, heard the shrill, screaming voice of the man's assailant, and, running forward, pulled the woman away.

"I know you!" she screamed.

41

By this time two other officers were running towards the four people, and one of those crowds which come from nowhere in London had gathered.

"No, I don't know the woman," said the taller man. "She just flew at me. Let her go—I think she's drunk."

"I'm sober—you know I'm sober, Starcy. That's your name—Starcy!"

She struggled violently in the grip of the two policemen.

"I'm afraid you'll have to charge her, sir," said the officer who had been first on the spot.

The man who had been assaulted would have made his escape, but now it was impossible.

"I shan't prosecute. Here's my card. . . . no, my name is not Starcy. I've never seen the woman before."

He said something under his breath to the policeman, but the constable shook his head.

"Can't be done, sir," he said.

And then there appeared another in the queer little drama. A stout, red-faced man pushed his way through the crowd. He was slightly inebriated, and evidently the policeman knew him, for he touched his helmet.

"Good evening, m'lord."

"What's the trouble, eh? Bit of a scrap?"

"It's all right, Lord Siniford, there's just a little disturbance. I don't think I'd wait here if I were you."

The gaunt-faced woman, held by the two policemen, suddenly strained forward and peered at the lordly intruder.

"Tommy!" she breathed. "You remember Anna, Tommy? . . . I used to give you cakes, Tommy. You remember Anna?"

The new-comer gaped at her.

"Good God!" he croaked. "Why, Anna . . . ."

And then, with a sudden jerk, she released herself from the policeman's grasp, and, gripping the man by the shoulder, began to speak in a rapid undertone.

"Eh? What's that?" Lord Siniford's voice was shrill. "What's that?"

The policeman pulled her back, and began to edge her through the crowd. Lord Siniford stood, staring after her, oblivious of the curious glances which were turned upon him. Then, with an oath, he followed the policemen and their prisoner. His face had lost some of its colour; he was breathing heavily, and was considerably more sober than he had been when he had intruded upon the scene.

CHAPTER V

Inspector Wade had a small cottage in Wapping. It stood at the end of a drab street and was surprisingly rural in its surroundings, for it boasted a small garden and at least three lime trees. That section of Wapping society which takes an uncharitable view of the probity of police officers pointed to the fact that the property was Mr. Wade's own freehold, and hinted at secret malpractices which had made him wealthy. The fact that the house and the little bit of land had been left to him by his father, who had lived in it all his life, did not lessen the suspicions of his neighbours, who never lived anywhere longer than their defrauded landlords permitted. By their code, all police officers grow rich from illicit practices—from the acceptance of bribes, to a little private thieving on their own.

Wade had an ex-police officer as servant and caretaker, a very wise choice, for there were times when his unpopularity might have produced unpleasant results. As it was, two attempts had been made by the Wapping Lot to enter the house. Once a fire had been started at the back of the premises, and once, when he brought Liddy Coles to the scaffold, his windows had been smashed, and he had found a revolver bullet embedded in the wall of his sitting-room.

He had fallen into his first sleep when the telephone bell rang, and he heard the melancholy voice of Inspector Elk.

"Remember that suicide you pulled out of the river—the woman you were talking about?"

"Anna?" asked John Wade sleepily. At the moment he was not interested in would-be suicides.

"That's the lady. She was pinched to-night for assaulting Captain Aikness." He spelt the word. "Of the good ship *Seal of Troy*."

"This is very sensational, Inspector," said John sarcastically. "But have you called me out of my warm bed——"

"Hold hard," said Elk. "She was bailed out by Lord Sini-ford"—he spelt the name laboriously—"a soak who's got a flat in St. James's Street. Does that interest you?"

"I'm thrilled," snarled Wade.

"Wait a bit," urged Elk's plaintive voice. "That gold signet ring was found in the woman's hand when she was brought in. She couldn't account for it . . . she had a fit of hysterics, and we had to bring in the divisional surgeon. When they opened her hand they found the ring."

John Wade was wide awake now. He thought quickly.

"She was bailed by Lord Siniford? Yes, I've heard of the man. Did he know her?"

"Apparently he did. She knew him—called him Tommy, or something. I wouldn't have called you up if it hadn't been for the ring."

"I'll be up in a quarter of an hour," said Wade.

He dressed quickly, got out his motor-cycle and drove through the drizzle to Scotland Yard. That Elk should be at Scotland Yard at two in the morning was not remarkable. He seldom left before. What he did nobody knew. His detractors advanced the theory that he had no home, but this was hardly true.

The ring had been sent to the Yard and was lying on a sheet of white paper on Elk's table when the detective arrived.

"Why did they let her out on bail?"

"The ring wasn't identified until she'd gone. The sergeant happened to look inside and remembered the report. Naturally, the divisional inspector sent down to Lord Siniford's flat to pull her in, but Siniford wasn't there, nor was the woman."

Wade knew Lord Siniford by reputation. He was loosely described as a man-about-town. He lived in an expensive flat in St. James's Street, and was a member of one or two clubs which were not particular as to the status or private character of their membership.

Siniford was the holder of an impoverished peerage. He had neither land nor money; the American marriage he had made had not proved successful, either from his or his wife's point of view, and had been dissolved. He had appeared on the boards of a few shaky companies; was so constantly in the County Court that he became an institution; had even been reduced to sleeping on the Thames Embankment. Then, unexpectedly, money had come to him, nobody knew whence. His debts were paid off, and it was generally believed that, whilst he had no great command of wealth, he must be in receipt of a respectable income.

His late wife was given the credit of being his benefactor, but this proved to be untrue when her father sued him for some money he had borrowed during his brief married life.

He was a frequenter of bars, an occasional visitor to race-courses; had owned a couple of horses, but had retired from the Turf with some precipitation after an inquiry into the running of one of them.

The police knew him as a good-natured creature, but their respect for him was somewhat tempered by information which came to their hands, but which need not be particularised in a narrative which may be read by young people.

He had not returned when John Wade arrived at the flat, and his slovenly servant could volunteer no precise information.

"His lordship comes in when he likes," he said vaguely. "Police, are you? Ah, yes, they've been here before. His lordship bailed a woman out, but they didn't come here."

"Has he got a car?" asked John Wade.

"Yes; he keeps it at a garage—I don't know the name of it."

"Then remember, will you?" snapped the detective.

The servant's memory returned conveniently, and John went on to a garage off Dean Street and learned that the car had been taken out just before midnight.

He had finished his inquiries and had come out into the street, when he saw a little car turn the corner and approach him, slowing at the garage entrance. A man got out, and John Wade recognised in Lord Siniford the man he had seen at the entrance of the restaurant on the night Lila Smith and her mysterious guardian had dined *tête-à-tête*.

He lost no time in preamble.

"I'm a police officer, Lord Siniford; my name is Wade."

The man stared at him near-sightedly.

"Oh, I know you. You were the bird I saw the other night. The commissionaire told me who you were. What do you want?"

"I want to see the woman for whom you stood bail."

"Oh, you do, do you?" Lord Siniford was a little amused. "Well, my dear fellow, you'd better go and find her."

He was perfectly sober: either the drive or some shock had produced this effect.

"I believe she called you Tommy. You knew her?"

"Don't ask me silly questions, my good fellow."

"Do you know her?"

"Not from a crow," said his lordship cheerfully.

"Then will you explain why you bailed her, and stated to the police sergeant that you had known her for some years?"

The request took his lordship aback.

"Well, I do know her. She's an old servant of our family—Anna Smith."

"Make it Robinson," suggested Wade unpleasantly.

He expected an outburst, but it did not come.

"Where have you taken her?" Wade broke the awkward silence which followed.

"She asked me to put her down near her house in Camberwell," was the glib reply.

"It doesn't take you two hours to get from here to Camberwell and back, does it?"

He heard the man breathing heavily.

"I refuse to make any statement to the police. I've simply taken her to her house in Camberwell——"

Wade interrupted him.

"She stated at the police station that she lived in Holloway, which seems a long way from Camberwell. Lord Siniford, I think you would be wise if you told me all you know about this woman. I have a very special reason for asking. A ring was found in her possession which was stolen a few days ago from a police station. It is very necessary that I should see her at once and question her on that subject."

"A ring?" Siniford was obviously puzzled. "I don't know anything about a ring. She didn't tell me . . ." And then, rousing himself: "I can't tell you any more about this woman than I have told you. She lives in Camberwell somewhere—at least, that's where I dropped her. She'll appear to-morrow at the police station, I suppose, or it'll cost me a tenner."

John Wade smiled in the darkness.

"Suppose you've taken her to some place where we can't see her and can't question her?"

Lord Siniford was aroused.

"You're damned impertinent!" he said loudly. "I've simply done a good, kind—er—Christian act for an old servant of the family—dash it! could a gentleman do any less? And here you're telling me that I'm helping a common—er—thief who steals rings! It's disgraceful! I shall see the Chief Commissioner in the morning."

"See him to-night," said Wade. "I'll give you his telephone number."

There was nothing to be got out of this man. The only thing to do was to wait for the woman to be charged at Marlborough Street, and he was in attendance at the court when her name was called. There was no response; but a solicitor, evidently instructed at the eleventh hour by Siniford, rose and said that his clerk had not been able to get in touch with the woman.

"He's taken her to the country somewhere," said Wade to the local inspector. "Do you know anything about him?"

The officer shook his head.

"No, except that he's the usual kind of waster one meets up

46

West."

"Has he a country house?"

The inspector smiled.

"No, he hasn't. I'll tell you something, though," he said, remembering. "In the old days he got into quite a lot of trouble by taking country cottages and leaving without paying his rent. He's probably rented a place on the river—that was his pet hunting ground. I've known him to take as many as three houses in a year and bilk each landlord in turn. Since he's had money he's probably given up that game, but he may still have a weakness for the river. I'll put through an inquiry."

The inquiry, however, proved to be unproductive, when it was minuted on to Wade.

If the accused did not attend, neither had the prosecutor. John had been anxious to see the assaulted man and discover from him some cause for the demented Anna's action. And here the case came within his province, for the *Seal of Troy* was lying in the Pool. He had seen her several times as he had passed up and down the river, a 5,000-ton tramp, differing from no other tramp save that she had two funnels. She was lying in midstream, taking in a cargo of machinery. He had seen the heavily laden lighters at her side, had watched the huge packing-cases being swung into her hold.

At three o'clock that afternoon his launch came up by the companion-way and he went up the side of the ship. He was met by a dark-faced officer, who, he thought, was a South American.

"Captain Aikness is ashore," he said. "I am the second officer."

John Wade showed his card and was conducted down the companion-way to a small and surprisingly well furnished saloon. The walls were panelled with mahogany; there were two or three deep leather arm-chairs, and at the end of the saloon a small fire-place.

"This is the officers' dining-room," explained his guide. "It is our good fortune that we have an owner who treats officers like human beings—it is appreciated. Will you sit down, Mr. Wade?"

John Wade sat down on one of the leather-covered chairs flanking the long mahogany table that ran down the centre of the saloon.

"Captain Aikness had some little trouble, I believe, late last night. A woman attacked him in London, and there has been a police court prosecution," said the second officer, his dark eyes fixed upon John. "I hope she was not sent to prison? Captain Aikness was very distressed."

"She was not sent to prison because she didn't appear," said John. "She jumped her bail."

The officer's eyebrows rose.

"Indeed? That is very satisfactory. I will tell the captain when he returns."

There was nothing to be gained by waiting. John Wade followed his conductor to the upper deck, took a polite farewell and descended to his waiting launch.

"Take her round the bow of this boat," he ordered, and the little launch circled out into the stream, turned under the sharp bows of the *Seal of Troy* and came back along the shore side.

Wade had no other intention than to bring the launch into slack water and to avoid two lighters which were being manœuvred to the side of the ship. Looking up incuriously at the hull, he saw, towards the stern, three big, square portholes, and wondered if the owner provided sleeping accommodation as luxurious as the saloon. The portholes were open. From one of these a pair of short blue curtains were blowing. It was these that attracted his attention to the "window."

The launch was opposite the middle of the three when he saw through the porthole the face of a man. Only for a second—a brown, wrinkled face and a glistening, bald head. Almost as he saw it, the man withdrew quickly from view, but not quickly enough.

John Wade had recognised the mysterious Mr. Brown, who once a year took Lila Smith to dine at a fashionable restaurant.

CHAPTER VI

There was no shadow of doubt that it was the man; less doubt that that man was Captain Aikness. John's lips opened to order the return of the launch to the companion-way, but he checked himself. If he went back he would hear merely a repetition of the lie that Captain Aikness was not on board. He had no authority to search the ship; there was no excuse for a warrant for a search. Did the man know he was recognised? Why should he? So far as he knew, Wade had never seen him, unless——

What communication was there between Captain Aikness and "Mecca"? Was the common interest of Mum Oaks and the skipper of the *Seal of Troy* entirely confined to the well-being and care of Lila? She had said she did not know who "Mr. Brown" was. But Mum was a liar of liars.

"Go downstream for half a mile, then turn up again," he instructed his sergeant. "When you come up, keep close inshore, so that we pass the *Seal of Troy* as near as possible."

The lighters had been fastened alongside by the time the launch came back abreast of the big tramp. There was an officer on the aft bridge, directing the stowage. Two or three men, obviously labourers, stood around the hatchway. There was no sign either of the Italian officer or of the man he had glimpsed.

The launch passed the ship slowly; it was moving against a heavy tide. Once clear, it turned to cross the river. Wade took up a pair of glasses and carefully scrutinised the portholes. He thought once he saw a face appear and disappear at a square, window-like opening, but it might have been imagination. He put down the glasses and stood up.

"Make for Favy Stairs," he ordered.

The launch heeled over as the tide swung the stern of the launch downstream.

Smack!

Something hit the cover of the little cabin amidships, smashing the glass and ripping a strut of the wooden frame to splinters.

"For Gawd's sake," cried the startled engineer.

"Go right ahead and take no notice," interrupted John.

"What was it, Mr. Wade? Are you hurt?"

Wade had stumbled forward on his knees.

"A crazy sea-gull, dear lad. Don't ask such damned silly questions!" he growled. "As for me—I'm dead. Wait till the inquest before you speak again!"

The nerve of it, in broad daylight! The shot had come from the ship; there was no doubt about that. The roar and rattle of the derricks would drown the sound of a shot, even if they had not used a silencer. But the nerve of it! His emotion at the moment was one of unfeigned admiration.

The launch came to a floating station and tied up.

"Help me ashore—I'll rest a bit heavily—that's propaganda," he ordered.

It was a picturesquely wounded man who was hauled and carried across the float. He calculated that the bullet had missed him by less than an inch—it had only been the swerve of the stern as she caught the tide that had saved his life.

Half an hour later three chiefs from Scotland Yard arrived by car and inspected the damage before they returned to the cabin where John was concealed.

"It may have been some rat laying for you, Wade. There are a dozen places they can shoot from the shore, and God knows you're not popular."

"Rats do not carry rifles—they're rather difficult to conceal," said Wade.

The chief nodded.

"If you searched the ship you'd find nothing, and you'd probably lose a lot. You can bet your life they expect a search, and they've got forty-five alibis all sitting up and making noises! What do you suggest?"

"Send a police boat with a couple of officers inquiring down the river as to whether they've seen or heard a rifle fired," said Wade. "Send them on to the *Seal of Troy* to make their inquiries there. Let 'em drag every ship, barge, riverside wharf. I don't think it would be a bad idea if a hint was dropped that I was badly hurt. A few bandages, a sling, and a motor-ambulance is indicated."

"That kid's right," said Inspector Elk. "I'll take you home myself and stay with you. I'm one of the finest nurses that ever took a job as a policeman."

A little later, that section of Wapping society which had criminal sympathies was gratified to see a motor-ambulance drawn up at the door of John Wade's house, a stretcher tenderly withdrawn and borne into the house.

"He's got what was coming to him!" said an exultant spectator. "And he's been askin' for it!"

They worked very late on the *Seal of Troy*. Great branch lamps overhung her sides and the big packing-cases which filled the lighters went up one by one at the end of a long steel hawser. From one of these a grimy-looking labourer climbed up the monkey ladder and reached the deck, without his arrival attracting any attention. Even the dark-faced Brazilian officer, watching the operations from the after-bridge, did not notice his appearance. The man kept to the shadows, and was an interested audience, for riverside labourers will talk.

". . . Couple of river coppers came here, wanted to know who'd been shooting. Did you hear any shooting, Harry?"

"Lies," retorted some unknown and unseen cynic. "The police are always pretendin' something's happenin' on the river. They just make it up."

"They've been to every ship in the Pool. There was three blokes makin' inquiries . . . and they say Wade has croaked!"

The listener smiled to himself and threw another glance at the entrance to the alleyway. An ugly little quartermaster was on duty there. The port alleyway was locked and bolted. It was impossible to mount the companion-way without coming immediately under the observation of the dark-faced officer on the bridge.

The quartermaster-guard was interested in the loading of the ship. Once or twice he had strolled forward a few paces to see a load dropped in the hold, and now came a diversion: one of the big packing-cases swung against the side of the hold, the sling slipped; there was a wild hubbub of warning voices, and the quartermaster walked away from the door. Immediately the shabby stranger darted through.

He had to pass the galley, but the cook's back was turned to him, and presently he reached a narrow transverse alleyway from which descended a companion ladder.

Ordinarily, the quarters of ship's officers on a tramp are on the boat-deck, but either the *Seal of Troy* carried passengers, or else the officers were quartered in the cabins which gave from this alleyway. They were all locked save one, in which a light was burning. It was a large cabin with a bunk, under which was a number of drawers. There were two arm-chairs and a couch, and on the steel walls a number of framed etchings. On a small desk he saw the portrait of a middle-aged woman in a frame. It was better than most captains' cabins that he had seen on tramp steamers, and apparently all the accommodation on this deck was equally comfortable.

He came to the end of the companion-way and found himself in a dim unlighted place which he recognised as the lobby of the officers' dining saloon. The port and starboard doors of the saloon were closed, and obviously he could not reach the cabin where he had caught that momentary view of Mr. Brown's face without passing through the saloon.

He tried one door: it was locked. He passed to the other: this also was locked. As he released his hold of the handle he had a sense of danger, and sank down behind the cover afforded by a turn of the companion-way. He had hardly done so before the door was jerked open and a man came out.

The lobby was in semi-darkness. The officers' saloon was brightly illuminated, and the man was plainly visible. He wore the uniform of a ship's officer; the detective recognised him instantly. It was Mr. Raggit Lane, that visitor of Mum Oaks's whom he had surprised on one memorable occasion.

Lane peered into the dark lobby.

"Nobody," he said to somebody inside.

And then there came a deep, booming voice.

"I saw the handle turn. Don't be a fool—go and look. It may have been one of the quartermasters wanting something."

John Wade grinned to himself. It was the voice of Lila's guardian: there was no mistaking that bellow of sound. He heard Lane grumble something, then the door closed. Through the panel he heard the sound of that tremendous voice.

"Go and look, damn you!"

Wade came out of his place of concealment and was up the companion before the door opened again. He was now on the top deck, partially illuminated by the reflection of the branch lamps. From somewhere forward came the clang of the ship's bell, and then the detective saw a man standing at the head of the companion ladder, looking over into the water. Amidships there was a small space between two tanks, and into this he squeezed. As he did so, he heard the watcher by the ladder call a name, and out of the shadows came another man. There was a brief colloquy, and the second sailor went down the companion to the officers' saloon. He was gone a few minutes, and when he returned it was with Raggit Lane.

Somebody was at the ship's side. The watch on the companion ladder had gone down to interrogate the visitor, and Lane followed. He was out of sight for some time; when he came back he was alone. He crossed the deck and disappeared. Evidently he was consulting with Captain Aikness, for after a while he returned, and, leaning over the rail, hailed the man in the boat.

"Come up, sir," he said. "The captain will receive you."

There was light enough to see his saturnine face, ample light to recognise the visitor who came puffing up the ladder, cursing at its steepness, for Lord Siniford was no athlete.

"I'm sorry to bother you, my dear fellow," he said tremulously, "so very late at night, but it's most important and urgent business. . . I must see the captain. I left my man in the boat to take me off, and there's a couple of fellows with him. I told 'em if I didn't come off, to go ashore and tell somebody all about it——"

"You needn't worry, Lord Siniford. We would put you ashore ourselves, but if you prefer to go in your own launch, by all means do," said the suave Mr. Lane.

Wade heard scraps of the conversation, but he was too astounded to take in any more than that Lord Siniford had come in some apprehension, and had made careful preparations against the danger which he anticipated.

The man on guard at the companion ladder stood with his back to the bulwarks, whistling softly. If it had been possible for John Wade he would have squeezed his way through to the opposite deck, for he was growing very uncomfortable; one of the tanks contained hot water. But when he tried he found his way blocked by a stanchion.

To his relief, the look-out man turned his attention to the boat lying against the ship's side.

"Cast off that cutter," he said in a tone of authority. "Tie up to the lighter."

The reply which came from the dark water was unprintable, and the look-out man was amused. During the little interlude which followed, Wade squeezed his way back to the deck, and, slipping through the companion, gained the shoreward deck. What business could have brought Lord Siniford to this ship, except the urgent business of Anna and that assault which had taken place the night before? His garage had been watched all the morning, but his car had not been taken out, and he had slipped his shadowers. Little doubt that he had been with Anna all that day, and it was the result of what he had heard from that half-demented creature that had brought him to the *Seal of Troy* that night.

Wade wanted badly to see the men's quarters. There was no sign of deck-hands; the men on duty were of the quartermaster type. He tried to find an entrance to the engine-room amidships, but realised that it must be forward or in the well deck aft, both of which were too brilliantly illuminated for him to cross.

The lobby to the officers' dining-room was faintly illuminated. He made his way down, hoping that the door was not too thick. He could hear a rumble of voices. . . . Aikness was there, and once he heard the strident note of Lord Siniford, but could not distinguish his words.

There was nothing to do now but to go back the way he came. He turned and stopped. Standing in the alleyway was Raggit Lane, his hand thrust deep into the pocket of his pea-jacket, an amused smile on his sneering face.

"Do you want anything, my man?"

"No, sir," said John Wade. "I was looking for a glass of water."

"You've come on board from one of the lighters, I suppose?"

John knew instantly that he had been recognised and that the man was playing with him. There was a gun in his pocket—Wade could see the muzzle covering him. He made no sign that he recognised he was in danger. From his waistband he took a small tobacco box, opened it, and, carefully selecting a round, black plug, made to bite at it, and then, as if changing his mind, threw it through the open porthole.

"Suppose you and I have a little talk——" began Lane.

He stopped at that moment and turned his head to the porthole. Something was burning greenly on the river below. The sickly reflection of it showed on the white ceiling of the lobby.

"Just to tell them I'm here," smiled John pleasantly. "There are three police boats alongside, and before I left them I said: 'If things look troublesome I shall throw out a signal.' It ignites when it touches water—you know the chemical, Mr. Lane?"

Lane's face went dark.

"There's no kick coming, is there?"

"Not now that your hand is out of your pocket," said Wade. "In a few minutes I shall be asking you to show me that gun of yours, and if you give me any trouble about it, I don't think you'll sail with the *Seal of Troy.*"

Raggit Lane forced a smile.

"You river police are scared sick. We had a man here——"

"Spare me your recital. I know you had a man here, or two men here, looking for the gentleman who was such a rotten shot that he missed me at a hundred and fifty yards."

He saw the man's face twitch.

"Does that touch your *amour propre*?"

He turned his head as the sound of heavy feet came from the deck.

"It's all right, sergeant. Send a man down. Now I'll see that gun of yours, Mr. Raggit Lane."

Reluctantly the man took the pistol from his pocket. At that moment the door of the saloon opened and the big bulk of Captain Aikness appeared. This time he made no attempt to conceal himself.

"What's all this racket?" he asked harshly.

"Captain Aikness, I believe?"

The old man towered half a head above him.

"I'm just asking your officer to explain why he's carrying a pistol. He can probably produce the necessary licence."

The old man glowered at him.

"A ship's officer is allowed to carry a gun—you know that, Mr. What's-your-name."

"Wade is my name, captain." There was a twinkle in John Wade's eyes. "Wholly unfamiliar to you, I'm sure."

"I've never heard of you before," said the other shortly, and again John smiled.

"Then Mum Oaks is as dumb as that unfortunate Chink whose throat was cut, either by another Chinaman or by"—he looked at Raggit Lane—"a rather thin gentleman who wore a raincoat, which," he said carefully, "was not unlike yours, Lane. Have you a licence for this gun?"

"It's not necessary," stormed the captain.

"It is necessary in the Port of London if it is carried on the person," said Wade. "I'll keep this." He slipped the pistol into his pocket. "You know where to apply for it."

He paused, with one foot on the lowest step of the companionway.

"Siniford would like to go ashore with me, perhaps?"

"Lord Siniford has decided to stay the night on board," was the surprising reply. "If you don't believe that, you'd better ask him—but why you should butt into my business I'd like to know!"

He stood aside for Wade to pass. Lord Siniford sat in one of the deep arm-chairs, a cigar between his teeth, apparently at ease. He gaped quickly at the untidy-looking man who came into the saloon, and did not for a moment recognise him. When he did he jumped up.

"What do you want?" he asked rapidly. "It's no use coming here; I can't give you any information."

"Are you going ashore to-night?"

"I'm staying aboard to-night, my dear fellow," said the other testily. "My friend Captain Aikness has very kindly put a cabin at my disposal."

He avoided the detective's eyes; obviously he was uneasy about something. John thought it was the embarrassment of being discovered on the ship at all.

The detective came back to the lobby.

"Satisfied?" said Aikness contemptuously.

"Quite satisfied."

He looked down at the rubber-tiled deck, and then:

"We found your signet ring. You can come along and get it when you like."

The big man blinked at him.

"A signet ring? I don't know what you mean. I've lost no signet ring," he said.

Wade nodded.

"I've an idea it might have been pulled off your hand when the woman was struggling with you. A ring with the crest of a temple and a figure of Aphrodite. Has that any significance for you?"

"None," said the captain instantly.

"It has for me," said John Wade. "Those figures represent the ancient seal of Troy. Rather a coincidence, captain. I don't know what the new seal of Troy is"—he kept his eyes fixed upon the blue eyes of the captain—"maybe an India-Rubber Man, with a gun in one hand and a rope round his neck!"

The face of Captain Aikness was a mask.

For a moment he tried to outstare John Wade, then, turning on his heel, he strode back into the saloon and slammed the door behind him.

CHAPTER VII

John Wade came back to the police float, to find the three Scotland Yard men awaiting him.

"I don't know what we can do," said the chief after he had finished his narrative. "A search warrant would probably discover nothing. We haven't any evidence to connect this ship with the India-Rubber Men. She's registered at Rio and sails under the Brazilian flag. If you searched the ship from stem to stern you would find nothing that would justify an arrest, and you couldn't possibly connect these people with the India-Rubber Men. I'm getting the boat checked up; probably it will be ready by the time we get back to the Yard. You had better come along, inspector."

It was a very elaborate and thorough piece of data which the clerical department had prepared. The *Seal of Troy* was once a unit in the Seal Line; had been purchased by a Brazilian named Dumarez ten years before, when a comparatively new boat. A careful scrutiny of Lloyd's List had enabled the police to check her movements. From the police point of view these were curiously unsatisfactory. She had certainly been in London, and once in New York, when the India-Rubber Men had been active, but there were many crimes attributed to this gang which were committed when she was thousands of miles from the scene of the robberies.

But Wade examined the typewritten record and made a discovery. Though she might be on the other side of the Atlantic when a crime was committed within reach of Marseilles, the *Seal of Troy* had invariably called at Marseilles within two months of the robbery.

"But the cost of running a ship is prohibitive," protested somebody. "You could not use a five thousand tonner as a blind——"

The chief pushed a piece of paper towards him.

"That argument doesn't hold water," he said. "The ship pays a dividend on its trading. And look at this total: it represents the amount of property stolen by the India-Rubber Men. Without reckoning bonds which are not negotiable, it runs to a million and a half in ten years, and that is only part of the loot. There's a heap we can't check up." He surveyed the total gloomily.

"Now I'll tell you something"—it was Elk who spoke—"if you get a warrant to search that ship you'll find nothing. At the first suggestion of a raid everything that's incriminating will be dumped in the river or destroyed some other way."

In the middle of the night the highest authority was consulted. The advice was tendered to leave the *Seal of Troy* untouched.

All that night, watchers on land and river kept the ship under observation, and when Lord Siniford landed at seven o'clock in the morning he was shadowed back to his flat in St. James's Street, whereupon he went to bed, and was not seen for the rest of the day.

At three o'clock in the afternoon the *Seal of Troy* cast off its last lighter and went slowly down river. In the evening it came to Gravesend, where it was boarded by a medical officer and his assistants. Information had come from London, explained the officer politely, that there was a suspected case of infectious disease on board, and he was not satisfied until he and his men had made a very thorough scrutiny of all reachable parts of the ship. Captain Aikness accompanied him to the companion-way and nodded a grim farewell.

"I'm afraid you won't have very much to tell Scotland Yard," he said, and the "medical officer" smiled cryptically.

The *Seal of Troy* was spoken off Dungeness, and later sighted and reported in the Atlantic. On the fourth day after her departure, John Wade received a radio message from the ship:

When I come back to London I would like to have a little talk with you.

It was signed "Aikness."

"That tells me a lot," said John Wade. "What an artist!"

But he did not explain his meaning.

"Anyway," said Elk, to whom he showed the message, "we're going to have a little peace from the Inja-Rubber Men."

His prophecy was premature. At ten o'clock that night a policeman saw smoke curling from the upper window of an empty store in Oxford Street. They were premises recently occupied by a furrier who had gone bankrupt. The policeman gave the alarm, and in a few minutes fire engines were on the spot. The flames spread with great rapidity; a district call was issued, and Oxford Street was filled with fire tenders and half the local police reserves were rushed to control the crowd. Fires are very interesting things.

The two plain-clothes officers who had been specially told off to patrol round the island site on which Northland's Bank was situated were attracted to the front of the premises, the more so since their position gave them a clear view. The Northland Bank carried a very large reserve of currency. There was an armed night policeman, but even he was interested in the fire and was peering through the window of the main office, when a cord was slipped over his neck and he was pulled down.

There was a light burning in this office all the night, and had the two private detectives turned their heads, they must have seen the assault—if they had looked at the psychological moment.

By the time the fire was subdued, and it had ceased to be a fascinating spectacle, the outside guard discovered that a back door had been forced, and, rushing into the premises, came across a half-dead caretaker, a steel door that stood wide open, and a practically empty bullion vault.

Only one man had seen the robbery: an old street tramp who slept at night in such doorways as afforded him shelter. He had seen too many exciting incidents to be attracted to the fire, and knew, moreover, that on such occasions the police have little sympathy with sight-seeing tramps. He had been awakened by the appearance of a motor-car, and had seen three men alight and melt, as it seemed, through the door at the back of the bank premises. The witness did not even know it was the bank premises, and would hardly have noticed the intruders again but for the fact that the roof of the burning building fell in, a brilliant light showed for a moment in the sky, and not only awakened him but enabled him to see the strange creatures in black, pear-shaped objects dangling from their belts and their faces covered with rubber and mica masks. Even then the slow-witted man thought they were firemen, wearing some special appliance, and not till after the bank robbery did he volunteer his information to a policeman, and was surprised and flattered to discover that his story was believed.

As to which direction the car had taken, there was no information. The police knew from long experience that the India-Rubber Men always followed the most crowded route. Literally, for them, there was safety in numbers.

John Wade, stepping into his launch for the morning patrol, had a private and confidential dispatch which told him no more than he had read in the late editions of the morning newspapers. A commentary on the happening was supplied later by a jubilant river thief who, his legs dangling over the edge of a wharf at which John, in the course of his duty, tied up, offered a few oblique criticisms of police methods. Sniffy had reason for jubilation, for, by a gross error of justice and a lot of hard swearing, he had succeeded in establishing his innocence at a recent sessions.

"I wonder all you officers don't fix your 'earts an' minds on gettin' these 'ere Inja-Rubber Men, Mr. Wade. You're wastin' your time lookin' for poor little hooks—everybody knows you can swear *their* lives away. But these Inja-Rubber Men have got you stone cold."

John Wade, sitting in the stern of the boat whilst his sergeant climbed ashore to make an inquiry, grinned at his late victim.

"I'm not looking for thieves, sweetheart; I'm studying perjury. One of these days I'm going to get you ten years, Sniffy, and the night you go in, I'm sending a big donation to the Home for Lost Dogs."

Sniffy sniffed hard.

"That's maliciousness pure an' simple," he said helplessly. "I wouldn't have your disposition for a million pounds, Mr. Wade."

"You'd cut your own mother's throat for a ten-pound note," retorted John Wade.

Sniffy did not sniff at this—he snorted.

The sergeant came back at this moment, and as the boat turned into midstream Sniffy shouted a parting gibe:

"Mind them Inja-Rubbers don't rub you out!"

John waved his hand cheerfully.

Between the river thieves and the police there was a deeper hostility than between the shore police and their shore confrères. And yet there was a deeper understanding; a certain camaraderie of the river, difficult to define. Your river rat showed fight, where the landsman would have taken his arrest quietly. He was more difficult to reform, less susceptible to the influence of missions and improvement societies. But in a queer way he was very proud of the efficiency of the force which worked to his undoing.

John Wade completed his round, leaving his most important call till the last. The "Mecca" was not an easy place to reach. There was one set of rotting wooden stairs, which were occasionally used for landing, but he preferred the accessibility of Fraser's Wharf which connected the frontage.

Fraser's Wharf, with its gaunt sheds, had been deserted until two months ago. There was no secret about Fraser's Wharf; indeed, there was no secret about any of the businesses which front upon the river. Their inner histories were known; the solvency of the great ironworks, the reason why this or that foundry failed, the difficulties and troubles of warehousing companies, were common property. The river watermen knew that Grigley's Shipbuilding Yard was tottering to financial destruction, at a time when its shareholders were blissfully expecting a dividend. Likewise they knew that Fraser's Wharf had remained empty for so long because of a Chancery action, and they regarded the place as being degraded when it suffered a rough-and-ready conversion into a garage.

There was no reason why Fraser's Wharf should not have enjoyed a certain amount of prosperity, for it was the one front where barges could lie alongside at low tide. Either the bottom had been dredged or there was a natural channel here, and whilst other barges lay at crazy angles on the mud, those that tied up at Fraser's sat on a level keel.

Unfortunately for the dead and gone Fraser, the frontage was too short; only one barge could lie up and unload at a time; and since other wharfage was available near by, the source of revenue from this service was a scanty one.

Wade tied up at the stairs, mounted to the wharf, and, stepping over the wire fence, walked along the front of the "Mecca." The familiar window was open, but the serving-room was empty. There was no sign of Golly, no sound of Mum's strident voice. He waited a little while, and then a new servant came into the room. She jumped and almost dropped a plate at the unexpected sight of him.

"Lila about?" asked John.

The girl looked at him suspiciously.

"Miss Lila's upstairs," she said.

Miss Lila? Nobody had ever given that prefix to Lila Smith.

"Will you ask her to come down and see me? Where is Mrs. Oaks?"

The girl shook her head.

"I don't know. I'm not supposed to talk to anybody. Mrs. Oaks said I wasn't——" Then, as a thought struck her: "Are you Mr. Wade?"

John nodded. The girl hesitated a moment.

"Wait a minute," she said, and went out.

John waited more than a minute before Lila came in to him. He opened his mouth in astonishment at the sight of her. No longer was she the down-at-heel menial; Cinderella was remarkably well dressed and shod.

"Hallo, Lila——" he began, and then he saw her face.

She had been weeping. Before he could ask a question, she came hurriedly to the window ledge and most unexpectedly laid a cool palm on the back of his hand.

"Don't stay, please!" she said in a low voice. "Mrs. Oaks is out. I'm having a nice time, and I'm going to school to learn French and German."

She said this quickly, almost mechanically. He had the impression that she was repeating a lesson.

"Where?" he asked at once.

She shook her head.

"I don't know—I think in France. Mum made me promise I wouldn't speak to you, but I had to. I told the girl to let me know when you came. You saw me the other night?"

He nodded.

"That was 'the experience.' It was silly of me, wasn't it, to make such a fuss about it—but I don't like it very much. It frightens me. I don't know why."

Every now and again she turned her head, listening.

"Lila, what is it all about? Who is Captain Brown?"

She shook her head.

"I don't know. He's always very sweet to me, but I'm terribly frightened of him. Do you believe that? It used to be wonderful, wearing those beautiful clothes; but this last time I got"—she shook her head again—"I don't know—frightened, I think."

"Who is he?"

She drew a long breath.

"Mum says he's a relation, and I suppose he is."

John Wade thought quickly.

"Is it possible to see you alone anywhere? If I came up one night on to the wharf——"

"No, no, no!" She was almost frantic in her refusal. "You mustn't come here by night."

She knew something, more terrifying than the experience she had described; something that really frightened her.

"You mustn't come—promise me!"

"Can you come to me? Do you ever go out alone?"

He saw her hesitate.

"You could send me a note. I'll meet you anywhere," he continued.

She looked at him steadily.

"Why?"

Here he floundered; he had no excuse but the most obvious one for such a clandestine meeting, and that was not an excuse which ever occurred to him.

"I'd like to help you, Lila. I want to do something for you; I think you need some kind of help."

She shook her head.

"I don't think it's possible . . . and I don't want to see you."

She spoke with difficulty, was breathless; the flush that was in her face when she came to him had gone, and she looked pale and rather tired.

"I trust you . . . you're so true."

He smiled at this.

"That's an odd word, but it describes the situation. Do you know where I live?" he asked again.

"Yes, I know." She looked at him straight in the eyes. "In the little house that stands by itself. You can get into the house over the flat roof of the kitchen, and there's an old well at the end of the garden."

He stared at her, and then suddenly she turned and ran from the room.

John Wade went slowly along the wharf, whistling softly to himself. There was a flat roof to the kitchen of his house, and the upper window was the one vulnerable point in his defence. He had thought nobody knew about the well at the bottom of the garden; it had been covered in with stout oak planks and turfed over in the lifetime of his father. He knew why she had given him this description—she had heard it from somebody who had a very excellent reason for making a reconnaissance of the place.

John Wade ordered the launch to go half a mile up stream, and here he went ashore again and strolled back to the entrance of the club. There was a tiny forecourt before the "Mecca," and two wooden forms on which, at most hours of the day, could be found two or three shipless officers of the Mercantile Marine and their friends. They regarded Wade with idle interest as he passed into the house and made an inquiry of the aged doorkeeper.

"Yes, Mr. Wade, she's just come in. If you'll hang on for half a tick I'll tell her."

John waited in the frowsy little lobby, its walls hung with cheap prints of sailing vessels, and after a while the man came back and conducted him to Mum's sanctum. She had evidently just come in from the street, for she still wore her gloves and her bonnet.

He had expected a brusque and chilly welcome, but Mum for once was on her best behaviour, and even smiled graciously at him.

One of the two things that instantly impressed him was the untidiness of the room. Though the morning was far advanced, neither broom nor duster had been applied. Mum's absence from the house was probably responsible, for he knew that this room was kept locked when she was out.

"Sit down, Mr. Wade. Excuse the room; it hasn't been tidied up this morning."

There are certain tell-tale signs that humanity bears on its face which are not to be mistaken. Mum's eyes were very tired; she had not had a great deal of sleep.

"You went to bed late last night, Mrs. Oaks?" said John amiably, and the smile left her face for a second.

"You're a regular detective, Mr. Wade. No, I didn't; I had neuralgia."

"And a party," said John gaily. "Cigars are not your vice."

There was a little pile of cigar-ash in the fire-place. There was something else in the room which had given him a thrill of exhilaration as he had entered. An unmistakable something which made him purr inside and set him all a-tingle.

"One or two of the gentlemen did come in and smoke," she said. "Fancy your noticing that!"

"How's Lila?"

"She's going to school, somewhere in the north of England—her father wishes it. He's a nice man, don't you think, Mr. Wade? It's a pity he's seafaring at his time of life."

"When do you expect Captain Aikness to be back?"

She did not express any surprise at hearing the name.

"Not before three months, perhaps not for a year. And, Mr. Wade, we've let that house in Langras Road."

"Where is Lila?" he asked, ignoring the attempt to drag him to a side issue.

"She's upstairs—got a bit of a headache, and I told her to stay in bed this morning."

She was looking at him steadily, and her eyes said as plainly as words: "Has he seen her?"

"Going to a school in the north of England, is she? She's rather old for school. By the way, I suppose Mr. Raggit Lane has also gone with the captain?"

The woman nodded.

"He's seafaring too. Golly went—he's been a steward before, and they were short of one. He isn't much use round the place, so I let him go." And then: "I hope, Mr. Wade, that you've taken no offence at what I said the other day to you up at Scotland Yard? I was very naturally upset, and what with being badgered by the police and knowing that you didn't like me——"

"Tell me one thing, Mrs. Oaks: does Captain Aikness know that Lane is a visitor to this place?"

It was a bow drawn at a venture, but he scored a bull's-eye. She was staggered by the question, opened her mouth to speak, but found articulation difficult, and was for the space of a few seconds a picture of acute embarrassment.

"Why, I don't know, Mr. Wade," she said haltingly. "I never talk about people's business. Mr. Lane doesn't often come here, and I always treat him as a friend."

"Not cause and effect, I hope?"

He stared thoughtfully at the fire-place, but out of the corner of his eye he saw that she was growing more and more uncomfortable.

"You sat up until quite an early hour this morning; that's very bad for your health, Mrs. Oaks," he said.

"It's funny how time passes when you're listening to people. His—he—one of the gentlemen who was here told us a lot of stories."

"I hope you won't repeat his bad example," said Wade. "What you were going to say was 'his lordship.' Do you know Lord Siniford rather well?"

She did not answer.

"He's becoming quite a friend of the family, isn't he?"

"I've told you all I know," she answered sullenly. She was not to be surprised into any further indiscretion, John saw, and he made his leisurely way back to the launch.

He had enough to reflect upon. Being human, his first consideration was the cryptic warning which Lila Smith had given him. She could not have been speaking idly when she described the position of the well and the accessibility of his cottage. But how had Lord Siniford come into that galley? What was his connection with "Mecca," and why had he come and spent half the night there, talking—with whom? There was no question who one of the other men was. Raggit Lane was something of a fop, and used a peculiar Eastern scent, whether in the shape of pomade or on his wearing apparel did not matter, and he had been at "Mecca" on the previous night. John Wade had a very delicate sense of smell, and the perfume peculiar to Mr. Lane came out to him as he had entered the Oaks' s sitting-room.

Lane was supposed to be at sea on the *Seal of Troy*; he, at any rate, was in town when the Oxford Street bank had been burgled.

The detective came off duty after lunch, and the first thing he did when he reached home was to make a very careful survey of the little cottage. The flat roof of the kitchen could be reached easily enough by the aid of a pair of steps. There were no bars on the window; the catch was one of the simplest; and the room into which an intruder would break was usually unoccupied day and night. It was, in fact, the room which John Wade used as a study.

He easily located the well, the existence of which he had almost forgotten, because his father had planted on top a small circular flower bed. On his way to town he stopped in the City and bought a small electric alarm.

He had been summoned, as he believed, to a conference, but found himself interviewing the Chief Constable.

"We're borrowing you for special duty, Wade," he said. "Inspector Elk is doing the routine work—he's making inquiries now. We'd like you to follow any line of inquiry you think may be profitable."

John Wade nodded, a gleam of satisfaction in his eyes.

"Then I'm going straight away to find Anna," he said, and the chief looked up at him.

"Anna? Oh, you mean the woman who jumped her bail? Does she come into it?"

"I don't know. That's just what I want to find out."

"Siniford's bail has been estreated," said the Chief Constable. "By the way, we've traced his country cottage. It's between Bourne End and Maidenhead; a very small affair on the banks of the river. He took a lease of it two years ago, but of course the rent has been paid and there has been no trouble with the tradesmen, as there used to be in the old days."

"Has he a housekeeper?" asked John, and then, quickly: "I'm sorry; if you'll put me on to the officer who made the inquiry——"

"There's no need," smiled the Chief Constable. "I've got it all in my head! No, he hasn't got a housekeeper. He had a man and woman who live somewhere near by, and these people looked after him—the man keeps the garden in some sort of order. From what I can gather they were fired a week ago. One of our men saw them both, but they could give no account of Anna. It was a sketchy inquiry, and if you like to follow that trail you might take it up where he left off."

It seemed to be a great waste of time for a very problematical result, but John Wade drove down to Maidenhead. His first call was at Freckly Heath, where he found the couple engaged by his lordship to look after the cottage. A slovenly-looking man, who was probably called "gardener" by courtesy, answered his knock.

"No, we're not working for him now, mister," he said. "The cottage has been let, or it's to be let—I don't know which. I haven't been there for more than a week. He paid me off; he told me he wouldn't want me again nor the missus. His lordship's a queer one: you never know what he's going to do next, and anyway the pay isn't very good and you don't always get it."

Wade called at a local house agents and had no difficulty in getting the keys of Reach Cottage. It was a sprawling bungalow, standing about fifty yards from the river's edge. The lawn was unkept, the garden showed evidence of neglect. He made an inspection of the house from the outside, but he was less concerned with the structure than with the evidence he could collect from the gravel drive and the little patch of lawn before the front of the cottage.

A heavy car had been driven up the drive; it had had a long chassis, and the driver had found some difficulty in turning. Wade could

66

read the wheel tracks very clearly. And there were drippings of a heavy lubricating oil. Following the short drive to its entrance, he made another discovery. There had been a gate here at some time, but it had been removed, and on one gate-post he found a new scar, as if something had driven against it. He measured the height and found that it corresponded to the height of the mud guard.

The entrance to the cottage lay along a narrow lane leading from a secondary road. The wheel tracks were very clear and very informative; at one place they led to the edge of a shallow ditch, for no reason. There was plenty of room even for a large car.

He knew Lord Siniford's machine—a small two-seater; but these tracks were not those of a light car. He read the signs thus: a car had been driven out of that drive at night; it had had no headlights. It would be very easy to foul the gate-post on a dark night, and as easy to drive along the edge, or beyond the edge, of the ditch.

When he entered the bungalow he found that none of the rooms was in disorder; the beds were neatly made and covered. In the scullery John made a discovery; two cardboard boxes bearing the name of a firm of ladies' outfitters in Maidenhead. He noted the name and address, and after a further inspection of the room drove to the town and interviewed the outfitter whose name appeared on the box.

A woman's dress, hat, shoes and stockings had been sent to the cottage less than a week before. The order had come from Lord Siniford himself and had been accompanied by cash—a necessary precaution, since his lordship's old reputation as a tardy payer had not been wholly forgotten.

By a piece of luck he was able to fix the time when the heavy car had left the cottage. It was the night of the Oxford Street burglary, and it was easy to establish this fact. The Bucks and Berkshire police had received a message telling them to hold up any suspicious-looking cars proceeding from London. The cordon which had been established between Slough and Maidenhead reported that a heavy limousine with dim lights had been seen turning on to the main road in the direction of Burnham, but had not been held up because the police had no instructions to question drivers proceeding to London. The near-side mudguard of the car was bent, this corresponding to the damage to the cottage gate. The further progress of the machine could not be traced, and, except that it went in the direction of London, no further information was forthcoming.

John Wade "tried back." He returned to the neighbourhood and conducted almost a house-to-house investigation. This dull, monotonous, uninteresting and seemingly fruitless task was a constituent of police work.

His very last inquiry provided him with a clue. This was at a cottage very near to a level crossing. Here the road passed across the railway, and the cottage to which he directed his inquiry was the only one, save the signalman's cabin, in sight. The cottager had been suffering from toothache and had spent the early part of the night walking up and down his garden. He had seen the car, which had slowed, as cars usually do, before crossing the uneven surface of a railroad, and had noticed that, sitting by the side of the driver, was a man muffled up in a heavy coat, who was singing softly to himself.

"Not exactly singing, but like a man with a sort of feminine voice, if you understand me," said the cottager. "There's a word for it, but I can't remember it——"

"Falsetto?" suggested John.

"That's it, sir. I mightn't have noticed it, but somebody put their head out of the window and told him to shut up."

John pursed his lips thoughtfully.

"Was it a big man or a little man who was singing?" he asked.

The cottager was not sure; he was rather inclined to the side of smallness . . . he seemed to remember the chauffeur who sat on the other side of the singer "towering above him."

"H'm!" said John, and went back to town with his mind intermittently on an individual who at that moment should have been singing falsetto on the bosom of the broad Atlantic.

Why had Lord Siniford been brought into this business? What was the business he had discussed with the captain of the *Seal of Troy*? Why had he subsequently spent the night at the "Mecca"? Were his lordship still in the impecunious situation which for years was normal with him, the explanation might have been simplified. He was any man's money in those days; a five-pound note was almost a fortune. But now he was in receipt of a good income.

Here John Wade paused to make a mental note that he would inquire into the source of that income. It might well be that this was not the first time Siniford had met Captain Aikness. There promised to be an interesting discovery at that angle of his investigations. But, however much he allowed his thoughts to stray, they came back to the singer who sat by the driver of the car which had taken Anna to London. And it was as though the very concentration of his thoughts materialised their subject, for that night he saw the man who was on his mind.

John had reported to Scotland Yard, made a brief minute of his day's work, and drove back to the unsavoury district in which he lived. His way took him through one of those busy little markets which distinguish certain thoroughfares in London. Stalls lined each side of the roadway; naphtha and acetylene lamps shone blindingly, and the sidewalks were crowded with poor shoppers, who here could obtain anything from a Sunday joint to a nearly new dress.

There was one portion of this market which was devoted to the garden. For the Londoner, however small may be his back yard, finds space to grow a flower or two, and the street vendors who cater to the arboreal tastes of the East End enjoyed a prosperous trade. Here you might find bulbs and shoots, weedy rose trees, pansies growing and blowing, late narcissus, early stocks.

There was a man at one of the stalls buying pansies, which, as he chose them, were fitted into a shallow, earthy box by the stallkeeper. He was picking the flowers with the greatest care, unaware that behind him an interested officer of the law was giving him his undivided attention.

He was an undersized man, dressed in the rough clothes of a navvy. Straps were belted artistically round his corduroy trousers; over his head was pulled a large new cap. A clean-shaven man with a weak chin and large, gold-rimmed spectacles, he pointed to the pansies, and John noticed that he chose only yellow ones. Presently his purchase was complete, the box was covered over with a cardboard lid, he paid his money, and, turning abruptly away, crossed the road and disappeared down a dark side street.

He may or may not have noticed John Wade; he certainly nearly dropped his box in a fright when the inspector tapped him on the shoulder. If he did not know him before, he knew him now, and the two eyelids behind the glasses blinked rapidly.

"Hallo!" he said. "What's the game?"

He intended to speak gruffly, but nature had not given him the necessary apparatus for deep-toned speech, and his voice was a hollow squeak.

"Hallo, sweetheart!" said John cheerfully. "The sea has done you a lot of good—it's blown away that horrible moustache of yours, and how brown you're looking!"

"Don't understand what you're talking about," said the little man shrilly, and added with simulated indignation: "It's a nice thing if a gentleman can't take home a few flowers——"

"You're not a gentleman, Golly, you're a navvy," said John gently. "You're a common labouring man with a beautiful soul! You like to see the little flowers lift their fairylike faces to the golden sun—and I don't blame you. It's much less messy than keeping chickens."

The other was silent but obviously embarrassed. He shifted his box of pansies from one arm to the other.

"I fear there's been some mistake," he said. "It's curious you should think I was somebody else, mister. But then, the police are always making mistakes."

"You've made a little mistake too, haven't you?" interrupted John. "How did you know I was a policeman? Now tell me all about your sea voyage. I gather you walked back? The *Seal of Troy* must be nearly a thousand miles away by now. What a lad you are, Golly! Walking about on the Atlantic! I wonder you didn't lose yourself. Did you carry a compass? And how is Captain Aikness and all the merry men of the lugger?"

He heard Golly sigh deeply, and knew that something nearer to the truth was coming.

"There's no use in lying to you, Mr. Wade, you've got eyes like a hawk. It is me and that's the truth. The fact is, I run away!"

John Wade shook his head reprovingly.

"Deserted your ship? That's an offence, Golly."

"No, run away from the missus. I've never been to sea," said the little man breathlessly. "Between you and me and the gate-post, Mr. Wade, she's a difficult woman to live with, and I couldn't stand much more of it, so I up and told her that I was going away. She didn't believe me, and naturally, when she found I'd gone, she didn't want no scandal and put it about that I'd gone to sea."

There was a possibility of truth in this that might have convinced one less sceptical than John Wade.

"How do you know she put that about?"

"I've heard it," said Golly quickly. "I'm living private now and I've got a good job, in—in a tea warehouse."

John looked at the navvy clothes and sneered.

"Shovelling tea or excavating coffee? Golly, I've always known you to be a liar, but I never gave you the credit for such quick lying. I've been mistaken in you—you've what I call an immediate intelligence. Men like you keep an alibi up each sleeve. Where are you living?"

For a second Golly hesitated.

"Nowhere particular. I'm living at a lodging house at the moment."

"And the flowers, I presume, are to decorate your cubicle?" said John. "No, sweetheart, that story won't do! Besides which, the tea warehouse story won't bear investigation. I know the job you've got." He pointed an accusing finger in Golly's face. "You're a footman," he said.

The man was staggered.

"A what, sir?"

"A footman," repeated John. "You ride on the box of motor-cars and sing little songs—you can't sing for sour apples, but you try. And you accompany crazy females from the Thames Valley to London."

He heard the quick intake of the man's breath, but Golly recovered himself immediately.

"I'm blest if I know what you're talking about, Mr. Wade. I've been doing regular work. If you go to my wife she'll tell you——"

"But your wife doesn't know where you are," said the remorseless John. "You're so anxious she shouldn't know that you've shaved off your moustache and gone into fancy dress."

He waited for Golly to flounder, but the little man was too wise to make a second mistake.

"If I've done anything wrong, you can take me round to the station," he said recklessly, "and you can charge me! Go on—I dare you to do it! What have I done? Nothing! Is running away from my old woman a crime? Is cutting off me moustache a crime? Is buying a few flowers to decorate the garden a crime?"

John patted him gently on the shoulder.

"Spill it, Golly," he said gently. "Tell papa all the news, and get a little comfort from an understanding heart. You went to Cookham to bring a lady back in a car—where did you take her?"

But Golly shook his head.

"I don't know what you're talking about," he said sulkily. "I've got alibis and affidavits——"

Wade's attitude instantly changed.

"Then you'll take a walk with me," he said roughly.

He took Golly's arm and led him a little way along the street. He had no intention of charging the man; indeed, there was no offence with which he could be charged. Golly was well aware of this, apparently, and when Wade fell again into his persuasive mood the little man was scornful.

"You can't bluff me, Wade. I know just how far you can go."

"You're not going to be sensible?" asked John. "I was going to be such a good friend of yours."

"I'm not wanting friends," said Golly scornfully, "and if I did I shouldn't go to a rozzer."

"Rozzer's vulgar, Golly," said Mr. Wade. "So you're not going to be good and tell me the true story of your low amour? All about the woman you ran away with——"

"I didn't run away with no woman!" snarled Golly.

His irritation was justifiable, and John Wade expected some such outburst. But he was not wholly prepared for the most unexpected ferocity in the little man's voice. He had surprised him into the revelation of a Golly he neither knew nor suspected.

John Wade relied considerably upon an eighth sense, a something which underlined impressions. But for the moment he was too staggered at this new and startling view of Golly's character to offer his usual flippant comment. He had always regarded this little man as the henpecked husband of a woman who was infinitely more clever and infinitely more dangerous than he. He was a figure of fun, rather pitiable, certainly not a factor in the operations which had their headquarters at or near the "Mecca."

Golly must have sensed the effect of his tone, for he instantly became his old apologetic self.

"Mr. Wade, you're barking up the wrong tree, as the saying goes. I've done nothing to nobody, and it's a wicked shame to 'ound me from pillar to post."

John nodded.

"We'll let it go at that, Golly," he said.

He walked as far as the corner of the street and stood under a lamp-post watching the grotesque figure fade into the night. Grotesque it was, for one of the straps about his legs had come unfastened and the trousers were much too long for him. The sound of his nailed boots grew fainter. John Wade turned back the way he had come, a little perturbed and more than a little curious.

Golly would expect to be watched, and would go to some trouble to throw a pursuer off the track. This in a sense was an advantage. Five minutes later Wade saw a detective and gave him a description and instructions.

"Pick him up and tail him to where he lives. It will probably be a lodging-house, and the real tailing will have to start to-morrow."

He went back to his little cottage with certain problems to solve. Why did Golly Oaks venture forth in disguise to buy flowers? That was an odd thing for him to do—to risk discovery for the sake of a few pansies. He remembered that Golly was something of a flower lover and had made many efforts to raise a garden along the wharf, but obviously the flowers were not for the "Mecca."

The old ex-policeman, Henry, who acted as his servant, knew Golly rather well.

"That's funny," he said, when John Wade had told him. "Golly's not much of a gardener. It's all over Wapping that he's run away from his wife, and most people think he's gone to sea. Perhaps she does too."

There was an excuse here to visit the "Mecca." The question as to whether he might be making mischief between husband and wife did not greatly concern John Wade. It was so small an issue that in any circumstances he would not have given it consideration. But he had an idea that his news would not be news to Mrs. Oaks.

He ate a frugal supper and went out towards the "Mecca." He frequently went alone at nights, though Wapping would never believe this, and left him unmolested. The river thugs who hated him credited him with an armed bodyguard, and the legend that he walked under the surveillance of innumerable detectives, each clutching the butt of an automatic in his hand, saved him from a great deal of unpleasantness.

The outer door of the "Mecca" was closed when he arrived, and it was Mum Oaks who opened it to him. He observed what he had not noticed before, that the hall lamp was tilted forward so that its full light shone on any new-comer, and was so shaded that the passage was in a state of gloom.

Mum Oaks peered at him, and he thought he detected a look of alarm in her eyes. Nevertheless she asked him no questions, but, closing the door behind him, walked ahead to her sitting-room.

Lila was there, sitting forward on the edge of an arm-chair, a book on her lap. She looked up as John entered, and sprang to her feet. He thought she was a little paler than usual. There was no doubt about the concern in her face.

"Run away, Lila; I want to talk to Mr. Wade."

For a second the girl stared at him and he read in her eyes an urgency of warning which he could not mistake. She opened her lips to speak, but changed her mind, and would have gone but he stopped her.

"Hallo, Lila! Studying the classics, or are you preparing for your French school?" he asked.

Before she could answer, Mrs. Oaks pushed her towards the door and stood between them until the door was closed.

"Well," she asked, a hint of defiance in her tone, "what brings you here, Mr. Wade?"

"I've come to have a chat about Golly. Have you had a radio from him?"

She did not answer, but he saw her lips tighten. If she had been a good actress, or if she had been ignorant of Golly's presence in London, she would have shown some surprise, but she was so obviously on the defensive that he was certain that Golly's adventure was well known to her.

"What's his first port of call?"

"Look here, Mr. Wade"—she was quite calm—"you've seen Golly to-night. He telephoned to me. It's no good beating about the bush. Naturally I don't want everybody to know this little skunk has run away from me. He did have the decency to ring me up and tell me you'd recognised him. I can't tell you any more about him than you know. I'm finished with Golly."

"This is very sad," said John soothingly.

"There's nothing to get fresh about, either. I don't know what my private troubles have got to do with you, but, if you want to know, Golly and I don't get on well together, and, what's more, he's too fond of these river rats to please me. He's always getting the home a bad name through buying stuff from those fellows. I told him I wouldn't stand any more of it."

This was an unusually mild and righteous Mum—so unusual that John Wade was unimpressed.

"I suppose he didn't leave his address?"

"No," she snapped. "I tell you, I'm not interested in Golly. And anyway, you'll know it. I suppose you've put a couple of busies on to watch him?"

John Wade's restless eyes were roaming round the room. There was nothing worthy of note, and Mum's attitude told him little except that Golly had left with her consent and as the result of some pre-arrangement.

"How is his lordship?" he asked blandly.

"I don't know what you mean—oh, that fellow who came the other night? I've never seen him since."

"And Anna, now—where is Anna?"

She shook her head.

"I don't know anybody named Anna, except a girl I once had, and she was a pretty beauty."

John Wade smiled broadly.

"You lost a great opportunity, Mrs. Oaks. You should have told me that Anna was the girl that your flirtatious husband ran away with."

He rose from the chair where he had seated himself without invitation and stretched himself.

"I'm a tired man. I've been to Maidenhead to-day, looking for the girl that Golly took away in a motor-car numbered X.P. 1102."

He did not know the number of the car, but he guessed that she didn't know either. For a moment he saw consternation in her face.

"I don't know anything about motor-cars," she said doggedly.

All the time he could see her mind working quickly, and, had he the gift of telepathy, he would have known exactly where that car was garaged.

"A big machine," he went on. "Golly sat by the driver, and was recognised, of course. If anything happens to Anna"—he kept his steely blue eyes fixed on her—"suppose, for example, she were taken out of the river dead in a day or two, it would be extremely awkward for your husband. I don't suppose you are sufficiently interested in him to care whether he is hanged or not."

It was a line of attack which the moment had suggested. It was based upon the bluff of the number. In spite of her amazing self-possession she blinked.

"Nobody's going to kill her——" she began huskily, and stopped suddenly.

He walked across to the woman and stood staring down at her.

"Mrs. Oaks, you're playing a very stupid game," he said, "and you're more deeply involved than you imagine. You know Golly went to Maidenhead to get that woman; you know he brought her up here, either to 'Mecca' or somewhere in London; you know she was taken without her consent, and you know why she was taken. I repeat, if her body is fished out of the Thames to-day, to-morrow, any day, your husband and you will find it rather difficult to explain away your connection with the—murder." He said the last word deliberately. "And you might find it also very difficult to dissociate yourself from the India-Rubber Men, who have done several little murders."

She swallowed something.

"If you know where the car is——"

"I don't. I don't even know the number. I invented it—I'll make you a present of that information, because I saw you make a mental note of it, and by to-morrow you would discover that I had bluffed you. I am not inventing the fact that your husband was seen on this car, and I am certainly not inventing the fact that I shall arrest him on suspicion at the first excuse I get."

For a moment she was desperate, and then some thought which had come into her mind brought her comfort. The cloud passed from her face.

"Was that all you wanted to see me about—Wade?" she said, with a return of her old insolence.

"That's all," he said cheerfully. "Don't bother to show me the way out: I know it."

Through the door of the sitting-room she saw him go up the passage, and was, John Wade guessed, still watching until he slammed the door behind him.

He was half-way up the path to the little iron gate when he heard something strike the pavement behind him. He heard the ringing tinkle of steel, and, turning, took his lamp from his pocket and threw a beam upon the pathway. He saw a small key, one of those cheap, useless things that are fitted to every jerry-built wardrobe. Attached, by a thread he afterwards found, was a piece of paper tightly knotted about the middle.

He had only time to retrieve this and to slip it into his pocket when the door opened and the path was flooded with light. It was Mum Oaks standing in the doorway.

"Mr. Wade," she called, and he went back.

She was most conciliatory.

"I hope you won't report about Golly," she said. "What I have told you is God's truth, and I don't want my name dragged in the mud. I'm going to see if I can get hold of him to-night and tell him to come and see you to-morrow morning. If he knows anything about the motor-car, he'll tell you. If you like, I'll bring him here and you can see him yourself."

"I'll think it over," said John Wade.

He was tempted to stop under the first street-lamp and read the paper attached to the key. He had no doubt that Lila had thrown it to him. She had told him she slept in an attic room in the front of the house. But he overcame the temptation: he did not know, but could guess, that he was under observation.

Henry, his servant, had one fault: he was a very sleepy caretaker, and unless John had his own key it was very often difficult to waken his slumbering man, who had a disconcerting habit of falling asleep over his supper.

John had not got his key, he discovered to his annoyance, and after he had rung the bell several times, he decided to go to the back of the house and wake Henry by tapping on the scullery window.

All small London houses are built on identical lines. There was, for example, the same barrier door separating the back of the house from the front as he had found at the villa in Langras Road, but this was a stouter kind. To his surprise, however, as he was preparing to climb over the top, the door yielded to the pressure of his knee. This, again, was not remarkable, for Henry performed the locking-up at eleven o'clock every night and made it something of a ceremonial.

He pushed open the door and went through. He had taken two strides when his toe struck against something and he almost went sprawling. It was not a very heavy obstruction, for his foot moved it. Taking out his lamp, he switched it on and examined the obstacle.

"Suffering Moses!" said John Wade softly.

What he saw were two tightly packed boxes full of pansies. They had been laid side by side along the garden wall, and against them were two brand-new spades. Farther along, also against the wall, lay a long steel crowbar. Nor was this the only remarkable discovery he

76

made. Close to the kitchen door was a circle of wood made of stout planks screwed together. The planks were new, the work was neatly done.

At first he thought that, unknown to him, Henry had been arranging some repairs to the house. How long they had been there he could not guess, but obviously the flowers had been recently deposited. He could have sworn that one of the boxes was that which he had seen under Golly's arm.

"Curiouser and curiouser," said John Wade.

Going to the lighted windows of the kitchen, he knocked. Through a chink of the curtain he could see his servant sprawling in a Windsor chair, his chin on his breast. It took five minutes before he was awakened, and then another few minutes before the dazed man returned from the front door, which he had gone to open automatically. At last the back door was unbolted and John was admitted.

"I'm very sorry, Mr. Wade, but I didn't get much sleep last night——"

It was the invariable excuse, but Wade cut it short.

"What's this stuff in the side passage?" he asked.

"Stuff?" Henry was now wide awake. "I don't know what you mean."

He followed John into the open and examined the flowers and tools, a very bewildered man.

"Looks like a lid of something." He tapped the wood with his knuckles. "They must have made a mistake and delivered it to the wrong house. It's a funny thing I didn't hear 'em——"

"That's the only thing that isn't funny," interrupted Wade.

He went into his own room, took the key from his pocket and unfastened the thread which bound the paper. There were a few words scrawled in pencil on a piece of thin white paper which had evidently come from a dress box.

Please be careful, it ran. *Watch the grating in your room. That is what they talked about. I am terribly worried.*

There was no signature, but, though he did not recognise the writing, he could guess who had sent the warning. Grating? What grating?

He went up to his room, which was as familiar to him as the back of his hand, and looked round helplessly. Suddenly he remembered, and pulled the bed into the middle of the room. In the wall, on the floor level, was a square iron ventilator. His father, who had built the house, had had this put in, being a lover of fresh air, and having a very excellent reason for wishing his windows to be closed in a neighbourhood which did not greatly love him. For John Wade's father had also held a position in the Metropolitan Police.

Stooping, John tried to peer through. He had never looked at the ventilator before, but he knew that there was a corresponding grating outside, let into the side of the house. The aperture was too small to admit anything bigger than a cat. Moreover, he slept well above this level.

To make sure, he went outside the house and threw out the beams of his lamp. Then he saw that the grating had been removed, and there was a square, irregular hole in the wall. The removal had been recent; he found the grating itself standing by the garden wall, and on the stone flags there were lumps of mortar which had been dislodged when the ventilator plate had been taken down.

Going back to the house, he examined the bolts and the window fastenings, and then called Henry into consultation.

"Your sleep is very often disturbed, isn't it, Henry? At night, I mean?"

"Yes, Mr. Wade," said Henry. He was a stout, red-faced man, with a bristling, iron-grey moustache, and, being police-trained, he was suspicious.

"It's going to be disturbed to-night," said John Wade. "In fact, I think you are either going to have the most sleepless night, or else you will be waking in Heaven."

He had a telephone installation; he took up the instrument, intending to call the local station, but the telephone was dead.

"Can't you get 'em, sir?" asked Henry anxiously. "Funny—I've been on the phone to-night to a friend of mine."

"I think the wire's cut," said Wade quietly.

"Cut?" cried the startled man. "Who do you want, sir—the station? I'll run round——"

"If you do, it may be the last time you will ever run, Henry," said the detective grimly.

He opened a locked drawer in the desk of his little study, took out a heavy-calibre Browning, emptied the magazine and carefully examined each cartridge. In the one little spare room the house could boast was a box containing war relics that he had collected in France, and one or two articles of equipment that he had acquired as souvenirs of a very strenuous time.

"Now I think we'll go to bed. You can go out and lock the doors, put out the lights in the kitchen, and I'll make an artistic retirement in my own room," he said, after he had given Henry necessary but rather baffling instructions.

The time was 12.30 when the last light in the house went out. There followed an hour of complete and trying silence. John Wade sat on his bed, not daring to smoke, whilst Henry, as wide awake as any man who feared death, kept watch in the little room, the windows of which overlooked the leads of the kitchen.

The hall clock chimed the quarter before two when the first sound came to the detective's ears. It was the sound of something scraping against the outside brickwork; very soft—not loud enough to have awakened him had he been asleep. Indeed, he would not have heard it had not his ears been strained for any unusual noise. Then—

S-s-s-s-s-s-s-s-s-s-s-s!

It came from the ventilator, and was noisier than he had expected. He made a swift adjustment and stepped noiselessly to the floor. The hissing sound must have continued, though now he could not hear it.

Ten, fifteen minutes passed, and, stooping down for the third time, he saw that the ventilator was no longer obliterated by something that had been placed outside. He could see the faint light of night through the perforated steel plate, and, stepping to the door, he opened it noiselessly, closing it after him, and went down to join his companion.

Henry did not hear him come in and jumped when John Wade laid a warning hand on his arm. Side by side they stood, and presently an indistinct mass appeared over the edge of the kitchen building. Then another, until three men stood on the flat roof. By their height and peculiarity of movement John knew they were Chinamen.

One came forward, touched the window near the catch, and seemed to be drawing a large circle. In another second that circle of glass came away; a hand came in and pulled back the catch, and the sash was gently raised. One by one the three men stepped into the room and pulled the blind down after them. As they did so John Wade switched on the light.

The first of the three stared through his mica mask, and then his hands went up. The third made a dash for the window, but Henry caught him by the throat and flung him to the ground. The second man accepted his fate philosophically.

"If you make a sound I'll shoot you!" shouted Wade. It was necessary to shout, because all five men were wearing gas-masks.

Two pairs of handcuffs fastened the three prisoners back to back, and they were pushed ungently down the stairs to the floor level. Wade left Henry in charge of them and, going back to his room, he opened all the windows gently. Whoever was outside must have been expecting this, though he himself could see no sign of life.

Going downstairs, he opened the front door noiselessly and stepped out into the little forecourt. A man who was standing by the gate came quickly towards him.

"Is it all right——" he began, and then he saw the height of Wade and knew that he had made a mistake.

He turned to run. Wade leaped the low railings and, gripping him by the collar, swung him round. John saw a faint gleam, dropped his hand in a flash and knocked aside the pistol as it exploded dully. He heard the bullet whiz through the bushes that fringed the path to the door, and the smack of it as it struck the wall.

He released his right hand and struck. The man dodged under his arm and flew up the street with the speed of an athlete. The first impulse of the detective was to follow; then the realisation of his danger made him turn—and only just in time: a dark, stunted figure had appeared from nowhere; somebody threw a knife. It missed him and fell with a clang to the pavement.

Only for a second did he hesitate: he had all the policeman's dislike of firearms, but now he realised that the danger was very real. He fired at the nearest man to him, and at the sound of the explosion there was a wild scamper of feet and his assailants fled in all directions.

The street was honeycombed with little passages and entries, and at the end nearest the cottage two narrow alleyways led to the twisted thoroughfare lined with warehouses which formed the river front. He heard a police whistle blow, and then another, and presently he saw a policeman running towards him.

Doors and windows were opening. It almost seemed as if this unsavoury street were sitting up expectant of the tragedy that had been planned, for instantly the pavements were alive with half-dressed people.

"No, nobody's been hurt," said John, as he stripped off his gasmask. "Blow your whistle and bring some men here, and don't venture inside that door if you value your life."

By this time the poison gas which had been poured through the grating had been rolling down the stairs. He adjusted the mask carefully before he went through the front door, which was opened by Henry. The three prisoners, terrifying spectacles in their masks, were huddled together at the foot of the staircase, and on the arrival of police reinforcements they were pushed into the street. The police formed a cordon and pressed back the curious sightseers, for, though the gas was dispersed as it floated out of the house, it was strong enough to be extremely unpleasant for those who breathed it even in its diluted form.

Day was breaking before the cordon was relaxed, and it was possible to move in and about the house without a protective mask.

The instrument by which the gas had been introduced had been discovered at once: a steel cylinder with a nozzle and rubber cap, and a light bamboo ladder on which the operator had worked, were found to the north of the house.

But the most important discovery came with daybreak. At the end of the garden was a deep well, and the garden bed had been broken and the mould dropped into the deep cavity. The new well-lid had been rolled down to the vicinity, and close at hand were the two boxes of pansies.

The thoroughness with which the murder had been planned excited John Wade's admiration. Even the pansies which had been planted by Henry in the flower bed had been carefully matched, and the new flowers were intended to replace those rudely disturbed by the midnight workers.

"You and I, Henry," he said, as he sipped the hot coffee which his servant had prepared, "by rights should be at the bottom of that well, and nobody would have known where we had gone. They sent a fake wire from Dover to explain my absence from town."

Henry shook his head.

"It's the flowers that beat me. Get the man who bought those flowers and you've got——"

"Exactly," said John Wade, and went out to look for Golly Oaks.

CHAPTER VIII

Day had just broken, and there were very few people in the streets approaching "Mecca." John Wade had turned the corner of the street which led to the club when, from a dark, narrow entry which ran down to the worn river stairs, he heard his name called urgently and turned back.

"Don't go any farther, Mr. Wade. They are waiting for you."

He had passed the entry when the warning came, and, swinging round on his heels, he ran back. It was Lila.

"What on earth——" he began.

And then something struck him in the leg and he half stumbled and was half dragged into the entry. Lila's arm gripped his coat with frantic strength and dragged him on.

"They knew you would come alone . . . they said you'd come alone," she breathed.

He was dimly conscious of her deshabille. She wore a man's old coat over her nightdress; her feet were bare. He tried to pull back from her, but she was in a frenzy of fear and would not release her grip. He allowed himself to be dragged to where the slimy stone steps ran down to the water. The river was shrouded in a thin mist, through which the riding lights of tramp steamers showed dimly.

He felt curiously weak, and when she pushed him into the little boat he almost fell out on the other side. In an instant she had followed him, cast off the painter and was pulling with long strokes into the middle of the river.

The entry through which they had come was indistinguishable. The street lamp which usually gave light had been extinguished.

"Why did you come? Why did you come?" she sobbed, as she tugged at the oars.

He was looking back, and suddenly saw two white pencils of light; there was no sound except two dull "plops." Something struck the gunwale and went buzzing away like an angry bee. And then, coming slowly up-stream, he saw and recognised, even in the mist, a police launch, and, raising his voice, hailed it. Again somebody shot from the entry, and he saw a ribbon of water leap up where the bullet struck.

Lila also had seen the launch, which had now accelerated speed and was coming towards them. In a few seconds they were alongside.

John Wade knew he had been shot before they lifted him into the launch. His boots were red and glistening. But his only thought was of the girl. By the time she had been taken into the launch she was in a state of collapse.

The police boat turned down river and made for the nearest station at full speed, and here hot coffee and brandy revived her. She was shivering from head to foot, despite the heavy blankets which covered her, and her face was as white as chalk when John, who had had the calf of his leg roughly dressed, looked in to see her. But she had recovered something of her self-possession, and when he urged her to tell him all she knew she shook her head.

"I don't know. It's been like a dreadful nightmare. . . . I can't tell you, I mustn't tell you. Only I was so afraid for you that I ran out to stop you . . ."

"Somebody knew I was coming to the 'Mecca' and coming alone: is that what you were going to say?"

She did not answer.

"And they arranged a little ambush for me. Mrs. Oaks knows all about it?"

She shook her head.

"I can't tell you," she said, and began to weep softly.

Even when she had recovered, she refused to make any statement except that she had had a bad dream.

Elk came down from head-quarters and interviewed Mrs. Oaks, who had anticipated the inquirers by going to the police station to ask for news of the girl.

"Unless your Lila talks," he told John Wade when they came back from the cottage, "there's not a single shred of evidence to connect the 'Mecca' people. Half a dozen of the boarders say that they heard nothing in the night, and one of them swears that Mrs. Oaks didn't leave her room till this morning—though why he should know I can't tell you. Anyway, there's no sense in raising a scandal."

"She heard something. She knew they were coming to my house," said John.

Lila had been taken to the house of a detective-sergeant and had been placed in the care of his wife, and it was hither that Mrs. Oaks came after a disagreeable hour of cross-examination by Inspector Elk, for that weary man had a knack of asking uncomfortable questions.

She was more than annoyed to find John Wade sitting by the girl's bedside; a little disappointed, too, for again the rumour had run round Wapping that John Wade had been "caught" by the India-Rubber Men. It was a little unnatural that the woman's first inquiry should be directed toward John.

"A flesh wound, my dear sister," said John Wade cheerfully, "It looks serious, but it isn't. I'm hobbling around on both feet. I wish you'd tell all inquiring friends that I hope to be very active in a day or two."

It was then that Mrs. Oaks remembered her auntly duty, though her first words were of reproach.

"Whatever made you run away in the middle of the night, Lila?" she asked, in her shrill, complaining tone. "You gave me a start and it's made a perfect scandal in the neighbourhood. I've never been so upset in my life!"

She was upset now; those basilisk eyes of hers were almost red with fury as she glared down at the girl.

"Lila was walking in her sleep," said Wade, in his most cheerful manner. "A distressing disorder, as you probably know. Did Golly ever walk in his sleep?"

But she ignored his banter.

"You'll have to come home straight away. I've got a cab——"

"And I've got a doctor's certificate," interrupted John Wade quietly. "She is not to be moved for three days, either in a cab or an ambulance—or by any of your Chinese friends."

The woman was quivering with anger but, with that extraordinary self-command which John had noticed before, she smiled, and shrugged off her fury, and became almost good-humoured. More than this, she appeared to be greatly interested in Mr. Wade's personal affairs.

"What's this story I hear? It's all over Wapping," she asked; "about your house being broken into? What a nerve these fellows have, to burgle the house of a famous detective! They'll be burgling me next—though heaven knows I've got no money. . . ."

John Wade listened, watching the woman, intent only that she should not by any sign or look shake the decision of Lila Smith. He was a master in the art of outstaying, and after a futile effort to obtain an interview with the girl, Mrs. Oaks left and was accompanied to the door by the detective.

"She'll be three days here, eh?" said Mrs. Oaks, thoughtfully. "Well, I suppose it can't be helped. Why she went out at all I don't know—*must* have been walking in her sleep! It's a mystery to me."

It was a mystery to John Wade too, for Lila had offered no explanation of her presence in the street that chilly morning, clad only in her night-clothes and a man's old coat. It was a mystery to which he was determined to find a solution, though up till now the girl's condition had not been favourable to very searching inquiries.

When he came back to her, the police officer's wife was with her, feeding her hot *bouillon* out of a tea-cup. He waited patiently till this was over, then nodded to the woman to await him outside the door.

He saw the ghost of a smile in the girl's eyes as her nurse went out, and grinned in response.

"You're feeling better?"

"Not well enough to answer questions," she said quietly. "And you are going to ask questions, aren't you?"

"That is how I earn my living—I'm the world's interrogation mark," he said, as he pulled up a chair to the bed.

"You're going to ask me why I was in the street, why I dropped that note when you left the 'Mecca'—oh, and a lot of other questions—and I'm not going to answer them," she retorted.

It was an unpromising start, but she modified her determination.

"I can't tell you without running the risk of getting all sorts of people into trouble. Mrs. Oaks . . . I don't like auntie terribly, and I don't like Uncle Golly either. But I've been terribly mean, listening through the floor-board. . . . Honestly, I didn't hear much—only a mention about the grating in your house . . . and——"

She hesitated, and he knew instinctively that she was thinking of some conversation she had heard before she had fled in a panic from "Mecca" to warn him of his danger. John Wade was in a dilemma. He might have shown the same consideration to another girl, and refrain from questioning her, but he was the more tempted to persuade Lila to speak because she was Lila.

He got up and sat on the edge of the bed, and took her thin hand in his. She neither resisted nor attempted to release his hold.

"My dear, I'm in two minds about you. You see, I'm really very fond of you."

The colour came to her face and she looked at him with a quick, intense eagerness as though she were searching his face for confirmation of his words. For a moment he was taken aback, and then the heavy lids fell and he heard her say:

"Very fond of me? . . . How funny!"

He was merciful enough not to pursue the subject.

"Because I'm fond of you I am putting you first—before my duty as a police officer. You heard something that made you run out into the street; you thought somebody was going to kill me. Was it Golly you heard?"

85

She stared at him, startled.

"Golly . . . Mr. Oaks? I thought he was at sea . . . isn't he?"

He evaded the question.

"You never know what Golly is doing," he said lightly. "Anyway, you didn't hear his voice—not even raised in song? And I presume you've not heard anything of Anna?"

He was watching her closely as he asked the question; but apparently Anna had no significance for her.

"She is a woman for whom I'm searching. I thought she might have finished her journey at the 'Mecca'," he explained. "Now what about Lord Siniford; do you know him?"

Siniford had for the past few days been the object of John Wade's especial attention.

To his surprise she nodded to his question.

"Yes, I've met him. Isn't it wonderful, Mrs. Oaks knowing a real lord? He has known me for a long time——"

"Who told you so?" asked John Wade in surprise.

"Mrs. Oaks said so. And then she corrected herself and said he hadn't. Of course I knew then that he had, though I've never seen him before. He was very nice"—she hesitated—"yes, quite nice, but——"

"But what?"

She shook her head.

"Really very nice. He's been most polite to me and kind."

"When did you see him last?"

"Some days ago." She shook her head. "I don't know when. He was there last night——"

She stopped suddenly, pressing her lips tightly together as though to arrest any further indiscretion.

"He was there last night?" suggested John.

"I can't tell you." And then the hand which she had withdrawn was impulsively thrown forward and clasped his. "I'm frightened—terribly frightened," she said breathlessly. "There's something dreadful happening and I don't know what it's all about . . . it's against you; that worries me."

She was silent for a moment, and then asked, with that oddly whimsical smile of hers:

"Do you like my being worried about you?"

He nodded.

"I mean, do you have the same feeling as I have when I feel that you are being unhappy about me? . . . I know you are sometimes."

"Lots of times," he said, and his voice was strangely husky. For the moment he forgot all his duties, the necessity for securing some sort of information from her. It was she who brought him back to an understanding of his lapse.

"Who is Anna? . . . There was a woman who came one night. She cried—I heard her, and I wondered who she was. We very seldom have women in the Home. The last time it was the wife of one of the officers who came; she made an awful scene, and Mrs. Oaks said that he had another wife—wasn't that a dreadful thing?"

"Terrible," said John mechanically.

The police-sergeant's wife came in at that moment, a good-humoured soul who had once been a hospital nurse.

"This is where you get off, Mr. Wade," she said with a smile. "This young lady is going to have no more questions put to her till I ask her how she slept."

John Wade drove back to the police station by taxi. He boasted of hobbling about, but in truth he had little discomfort and practically no pain from the clean-punctured wound through his calf. The bullet had in reality passed through two sets of muscles without injuring either, and the doctor had promised him that, if he would lie up, the wound would be thoroughly healed in two or three days. But he of all men could not spare the time.

Every spare detective in the metropolis had been drawn to the neighbourhood, and there was in progress a systematic visitation of lodging-houses frequented by Eastern sailors. No ship worked by a Chinese crew had come in in the past twenty-four hours, and all the Chinese residents in the district could be accounted for—with few exceptions they were men with good records, known to be law-abiding, as is the average Chinese citizen in a foreign country. The *tong* is not recognised by the police in England. But there were certain known leaders of the Chinese colony who were in a position to give information, and who could be trusted. When such inquiries were made, they knew that the police would waive such little irregularities as an illegal game or even the discovery of a new opium house, and, with the knowledge of this indulgence, the chiefs were very frank. They could offer no explanation for the appearance of a Chinese gang or for the attempt on Wade's life.

Elk, who was personally superintending the search came up to the station door as John Wade's taxi stopped. He was, he admitted ruefully, full of useless information.

"These Chinks came from some other quarter—must have belonged to the same crowd as the fellow who was killed the other night," he said. "There's no ship in the Pool which has a Chinese crew, and none of the headmen of the colony have heard a word about this business last night."

87

"And if they did they'd lie," said John cheerfully, but Elk shook his head.

"Old San Yi is a pal of mine—a low man who would have been in bad trouble with the police years ago if everybody had his due, but he's been a good citizen for I don't know how long, and I've helped him once or twice. In fact, this poor, simple yaller man looks upon me as a brother. Naturally these fellows have to lie sometimes, but I always know when San Yi is trying to put it across me."

John Wade bit his lip thoughtfully.

"Then where the devil did they come from? If the *Seal of Troy* was in the Pool I shouldn't ask, but she's well away."

"She's well away," agreed Elk calmly, "but is the crew well away? Is Captain Aikness well away? Is Raggit Lane——"

"He's here all right," said John Wade shortly. "He was the fellow superintending last night's little surprise party."

Wade had telephoned to the Borough Engineer's office, and whilst he was talking to Elk there had arrived a large envelope, which he carried into the inspector's room and opened. Inside was a rough plan of a building, with one or two sketches of sectional elevations on tracing paper.

"What's that?" asked Elk curiously.

John Wade was examining the plan, whistling softly.

"Don't you recognise it?" he asked at last. "It's the old building that stood on the site where 'Mecca' is. There's the brew house—a bit of that building still remains—and there"—he pointed—"are the cellars."

"Cellars?" repeated Elk, and twisted the plan round to see it better.

"They cover the whole area of the building, and there's room there for half a battalion of Chinese thugs. I've seen one cellar—Golly used it as a woodshed. I've been down inside the place—but it's pretty small."

He looked up from the plan.

"By the way, have you found Golly?"

Elk shook his head mournfully.

"We are, to use a term highly popular in the press, scouring London for him. Three squads are combing the district, and I've set another to look at the Surrey side."

Only at this moment did it strike John Wade as strange that Mrs. Oaks had made no inquiry about her lawful husband, and had shown not the slightest concern as to the consequences of the part he had played in the attempt of the previous night. That she was well aware of Golly's act, Wade had no doubt whatever.

CHAPTER IX

A detective, confronted with half a dozen problems simultaneously and all associated with the same central problem, will not only naturally but properly follow the easiest line of inquiry; and that which presented itself instantly was a more careful search of "Mecca." Matter must occupy space; Chinese criminals must be bedded and fed, and the possibility that beneath "Mecca" was an extensive cellarage had always been present in Wade's mind. For the moment, however, a raid on the Home was inadvisable. Nothing was more certain than that police activities were being closely watched, and a move towards the Home would be signalled and his prey escape before he could get his men in position.

It was much more intelligent a plan to leave "Mecca" till the night and switch his inquiries into another direction and, being what he was, he chose that avenue which bristled with almost insurmountable difficulties. But he was determined to find the source of Siniford's income and discover why this penurious man had suddenly found himself in a comfortable position with money to burn. There was just a chance that his unpleasant lordship was being subsidised by the India-Rubber Men; there was certainly a line of communication between them, but how long this had existed Wade had to discover.

A police officer can do many things, and the magic of his name will carry him completely to his goal, always providing that his line of inquiry does not extend to a bank and the private business of its customers. Banks have very rigid rules, and John was too wise a man to attempt to make a direct approach. He knew the bank where Lord Siniford kept his money, but unless he took the authority of a magistrate, which he knew would not be given, it was impossible to examine the man's account. It was equally impossible to discover the source of Siniford's income.

But there were other methods of approaching the problem than through a stony-faced bank manager, and Wade had already set inquiries in motion which that day had produced an important clue.

On the first and the fifteenth of every month Lord Siniford received a heavily sealed envelope, and he made a point of being at home when it arrived. That morning the man who had been watching Siniford reported that his lordship had paid in a banker's draft, and the draft was obviously the contents of the sealed envelope that had arrived that morning, for when he endorsed it at the bank counter the watching detective had seen him draw it from its cover.

This day Siniford had done a stupid thing—he had probably done it before but he had not been under observation. After the draft had been paid in and he had drawn a cheque for a substantial sum, he crumpled the envelope and threw it on the floor. The watcher waited his opportunity, secured the envelope, and this was brought to John Wade whilst he was still at the police station.

There was no name printed upon it, but the flap bore a heavy boss of red sealing-wax on which a steel stamp had been pressed. Save that the edge was broken this was intact when it was brought to John Wade in the inspector's office. There were four initial letters—L.K.Z. and B.

Though there are isolated instances where quadruple names appear in a business, they are most commonly found amongst solicitors. Procuring a Law List, he began a careful search amongst the L's. If they were lawyers they could easily be checked, because "Z" was an unusual initial. In a few seconds he found what he had been looking for—the eminent firm of Messrs. Latter, Knight, Zeeland and Bruder, of Lincoln's Inn Fields. He jotted down the address, and late in the afternoon he drove westward, calling in at the office of a solicitor friend to discover something of the standing of the firm.

"They're big people," he was informed. "Latter and Knight are dead, Zeeland has retired, and old Bruder runs the business. He's as close as an oyster, but, like all these Chancery people, full of common sense. If you tell him what you want, very likely you'll get it."

He was fortunate enough to find Mr. Bruder in his dingy little office, and, after some delay, was ushered in. The lawyer was a tall, thin man; all of his head that was not bald was sandy. He looked at the detective through his thick, concave glasses, and from John to his card.

"Sit down, Mr. Wade," he said with a faint smile. "It's a long time since I saw a police officer in my room—my mind is free, because I'm perfectly sure none of my very respectable clients has been getting into trouble!"

"Lord Siniford is a client of yours?" suggested John, and, to his surprise, the lawyer shook his head vigorously.

"No," he said emphatically; "he is—er—well, he isn't a client."

He looked at John thoughtfully for a moment, and as plainly as words could speak his eyes told the detective that he was quite prepared to hear that Siniford had got into any kind of trouble.

He motioned John to a chair, the springs of which were broken, and folded his hands on the littered table.

"Now, Mr. Wade, what do you want?"

John had an inspiration. Even as he spoke, he knew just how dangerous was the ground on which he trod, that there was an official reprimand waiting for every sentence he spoke.

"I'm going to put my cards on the table, Mr. Bruder," he said. "I'm engaged in a search for the India-Rubber Men about whom you may have heard."

The lawyer inclined his head.

"Even I have heard of them," he said.

"Naturally I must investigate every leader I find on the main thread," John went on. "I have discovered that Lord Siniford is an associate of people who are suspected of being in close touch with these crooks. I do know that up to a few years ago he was a very poor man, but that recently his fortune has changed and that he receives an allowance from you. When I say I know, I really mean, with regard to the latter statement, that I'm guessing. But he's getting money from somewhere, and it's very important to us that we should know the source of his income."

The lawyer looked at him, his lips pursed thoughtfully.

"His income is a perfectly legitimate one," he said. "It is quite true that he receives certain funds from us. Whether he gets any other money is outside my knowledge; but, as I said before, we are not his lawyers, but are acting for certain executors."

John must have shown his disappointment, for the lawyer smiled.

"I'm afraid I've spoilt an interesting theory."

"Well, no," Wade hesitated. "It wasn't exactly a theory. Of course, if he's inherited money——"

"He hasn't exactly inherited money," interrupted the lawyer carefully; "there is a certain trust fund from which he draws, as it were, an interim income. In a year's time the whole of the money will go to him."

He smiled again as he saw John's perplexity.

"I'm being mysterious, I'm afraid. I see no reason why I should not tell you what you could ascertain for yourself by a search of records at Somerset House. A client of ours, who was a relation of Lord Siniford, died five years ago and left a very large fortune—an extremely large fortune," he added emphatically. "The money would ordinarily have been inherited—um—elsewhere. I don't think I can tell you more than that, except that the trust money was settled upon an individual who is dead, but cannot be distributed until the twenty-first anniversary of that person's birth.

"I can't tell you very much more, inspector." Bruder leaned back in his chair, his finger-tips together, his sceptical eyes fixed upon the detective's. "But I don't think I have told you any more than I should."

"Can you tell me the name of the testator whose affairs you're handling?"

The lawyer thought for some time, and in his whimsical way John Wade thought he was not ill-named.

"Well—as I've remarked before, you could find particulars of the Pattison Trust at Somerset House. The most I can do in propriety, is to tell you that Lord Siniford draws his income from what is known as the Pattison Trust, which administers the affairs of the late Lady Pattison, the grand-aunt of Lord Siniford."

He rose from the chair, stood frowning for a moment at the desk, and then:

"I don't know why I should not go a little farther: I've had rather an unpleasant experience with Lord Siniford lately. He has been here making inquiries which seemed to me to be unnecessary, and we had an unpleasant exchange of words. I have since written advising him to consult a lawyer—frankly, I would rather do business through a brother solicitor than with his lordship. So that you may say I'm not exactly friendly with him."

"Would it be indiscreet to ask what the quarrel was about?"

Again the lawyer cogitated.

"I suppose it would be in any other person than a police officer, who may be pardoned a little overzealousness. Lord Siniford asked for certain deed-boxes that are really the property of the trust, and will be the property of the trust until the estate is handed over to him. I refused him access, rightly or wrongly, and advised him as to the course he should pursue. He was a little abusive—I rather think he was the worse for drink. And that's all I'm going to tell you, inspector."

He jerked out a long, bony hand and gave John's a feeble shake; followed him to the door and closed it upon him when he went out.

A very mundane and commonplace dead end to his inquiries, thought John Wade, as he strolled back to Scotland Yard. But if Siniford was the heir to a large property and was for the moment the recipient of a respectable pension, why on earth should he bother himself with the India-Rubber Men, or spend a night on the *Seal of Troy* with Captain Aikness?

He was passing through Bedford Row when he took a sudden decision, and, calling a cab, drove to St. James's Street. The hall porter told him that his lordship was at home, had just come in.

There was a little cubby hole in the vestibule, and a small table, one of the few articles of furniture it contained, was piled high with long, flat, cardboard boxes. A name caught Wade's eye and he went closer to inspect it. It was on the label of a fashionable dressmaker, and, lifting the box, he saw that the second also contained a woman's dress.

Scrawled on the second label was a pencilled note.

Une couturière viendra essayer les robes de la jeune demoiselle Mercredi soir.

Evidently an instruction by the saleswoman.

Who was the young lady to be "fitted"?

"What name shall I give his lordship?" asked the commissionaire, poising the telephone plug.

"Wade," said John after a moment's thought.

There was just a chance that Siniford would not see him; but it was a remote chance. If his guess was right, Lord Siniford was in a position where he dare not refuse an interview for fear of arousing suspicion. His surmise was right, for the answer came:

"Show Mr. Wade to the apartment."

It was a large, bright room overlooking St. James's Street. His lordship was standing with his back to the little fire. He was a very alert, attentive man, entirely on the defensive. This John observed, and used one of the oldest tricks of his trade: he put his hat carefully on a chair, slowly and deliberately took off his gloves. It was an action which had very frequently disturbed the equilibrium of a man who had a story all cut and dried.

Siniford wrinkled his little nose apprehensively.

"Well, well," he asked with some impatience, "what do you want, Mr. Wade? I can give you exactly three minutes."

"I require exactly four," said John Wade coolly. "You're a friend of Captain Aikness?"

He sprang the question without preamble, and saw the man flinch.

"Aikness? The sea captain? Yes, I know him. He was an old friend of my father's many years ago, and recently I had the pleasure of renewing his acquaintance—he is in South America now."

John Wade nodded.

"A friend of your father's? Then you'll be able to vouch for his integrity, Lord Siniford?" he said, not taking his eyes from the red-faced man.

His lordship wriggled uncomfortably.

"I can't vouch for anything," he snapped. "My dear fellow, be reasonable! I knew—er—my father knew Mr.—Captain Aikness. Surely it was an act of civility to pay him a visit on his ship. A very nice man, charming!"

"And Miss Lila Smith? Do you find her charming, too?" asked the other suavely.

Lord Siniford started at the mention of Lila's name.

"I've met her, yes. Good lord, inspector, what is the idea? You come here to a gentleman's flat and cross-examine me—him, I mean?"

"You're very much interested in Lila Smith?"

John Wade had him at a disadvantage and knew it.

"I know the girl—she's very nice. I'm not more interested than I am in——" Lord Siniford shrugged—"any girl."

"Interested enough to buy her a complete outfit?" suggested Wade.

Lord Siniford's face went red and white, then purple.

"What the devil do you mean by watching me? You be damned careful, inspector, or I'll have your coat off your back! I'm not the sort of man who'll stand for that kind of thing, and don't you forget it! I'll buy anything I please, for whom I wish. As you're so beastly curious, let me tell you that the clothes were not for Miss Smith, far from it——"

"For Anna?" suggested Wade.

Siniford swallowed something.

"I don't know whom you mean," he said sullenly.

"I mean the woman who was staying in your house at Maidenhead and who was brought to London in a closed car the night the Oxford Street bank was held up. You did a little clothes-buying there, if I remember aright, Lord Siniford." He walked closer to the man. "I've warned Golly; let me pass on the same warning to you. If this woman Anna is taken out of the Thames in the clothes you bought, you'll have a very unpleasant hour when you meet the coroner."

The man was shaken; he made no attempt to deny his knowledge of Golly, though he might well have known Mr. Oaks by another and more dignified title. Evidently the warning had not been passed on. He blinked at the detective, and for the time being was incapable of speech.

"I guess I know what you're thinking," John Wade continued. "You're saying to yourself that nothing can happen to this woman, and at the same time you're realising that it is quite likely something *may* happen. Anyway, you'll be in a rather embarrassing position if this woman turns up, dead or alive."

Lord Siniford was not a good actor; the prospect was frightening. His heavy face twitched spasmodically for a second or two.

"I really don't know what you're talking about." His lordship's voice was surprisingly mild. "I think you must have been dreaming, inspector. I know nothing of Anna—was that the name?"

Here Wade drew his bow at a venture.

"Does Anna benefit under the Pattison Trust?" he asked.

The arrow struck. Siniford's brown eyes opened wide in amazed horror.

"Pattison Trust?" he repeated shrilly. "What do you know . . ." He stopped, out of breath.

"I was just wondering, that's all."

Wade took up his hat, stick and gloves.

"What do you know about the Pattison Trust?"

"Everything," said John Wade in his blandest manner, and left on that note.

It occurred to him as he was driving to the Yard that he might not have been very discreet in his reference to Lila Smith; but he was satisfied that the clothes were for her. There might be a very simple explanation for this "shopping" of Lord Siniford's. He was, if report could be credited, rather generous in his gifts to young ladies who interested him. That Lila Smith should interest the man at all rather worried him. Why was Siniford so frequent a visitor to the "Mecca," and what was the attraction which brought him to this unsavoury neighbourhood? An answer to these questions might possibly be found that night, though for his own part he had little faith that the raid on the "Mecca" would produce any instructive results.

He found Elk in his dingy little room—Elk had a faculty of creating dinginess, for he was an inveterate smoker of other people's cigars, and he hated fresh air. The gaunt detective was writing slowly and laboriously, but put down his pen when John came in.

"I've got everything set for to-night's little visit," he said. "Three of your launches will patrol the river and close the wharf on signal. Thirty-five picked men will surround the house and assist in the search for a dangerous criminal who was seen making for the wharf half an hour before the raid started." He stroked his stubbly chin. "I don't know what the dangerous criminal had better be—a murderer? No, that would get into the newspapers. Better be a man wanted by the police—that means almost anybody. No search warrant; everything to be done in a gentlemanly manner by kind permission of the owner of the house."

John nodded.

"That seems good to me. Is there any news of Golly, by the

way?"

"None whatever. The well-known ground has opened and swallowed him up. If he stops before reaching his proper destination he'll be lucky. But I guess he won't sink so far."

"The Chinese inquiry?" suggested John.

"There's nothing to it. The very last Chink is accounted for this side of Tilbury. The Chief's put you in charge of to-night's surprise party. Are there any further instructions?"

John hesitated.

"No, I don't think there's anything. I'd have been a bit worried if the girl was there, but fortunately she won't be——"

"The girl being that young woman Smith?" suggested Elk.

John Wade was irritated.

"That young woman Smith, as you call her, doesn't come into consideration," he said tartly.

Elk sighed.

"If we could only stop good-lookin' detectives from fallin' in love!" he said, and Mr. Wade did not pursue the subject.

"Golly must be found," he said. "He is the key that will open a lot of cell doors."

Every police station in London had been furnished with a description of Golly. The lodging-houses, superior and small, had been diligently examined, but without result. The police suffered from the disadvantage that Golly had no "haunts." He was a notorious home-lover, and seldom strayed from the quiet of the dingy wharf which ran before the "Mecca." He had no known friends, visited no hostelry, and the whereabouts of such men as these invariably presents an insoluble problem to the police, especially if the man for whom they seek has the intelligence to lie hidden.

"He's at the 'Mecca.' If I was a betting man I'd bet on that," said Elk. "Personally, betting means nothing to me. I've a pretty good tip for the three o'clock race to-morrow from a publican in Lambeth. By the way, you might remind me to-morrow. I've seen more houses ruined——"

Wade cut short his moralising.

"Elk, do you remember, on the night of the big bank robbery in St. James's, the India-Rubber Men escaped on a fast boat?"

Elk nodded.

"You missed it," he said.

"I missed it," said Wade, "because it was lying on the shore side of the *Seal of Troy*, and was in all probability swung inboard when I was going in the direction of Greenwich. It never occurred to me till now that I got most of the information about that boat from the ship.

It wasn't a big boat, and a couple of derricks could have put it under hatches in ten minutes. It's probably on the ship now, unless they've thrown it overboard in mid-ocean. I've cabled our South American agent to inspect the ship the moment she touches port."

Elk filled a strong, foul pipe and lit it. He puffed for a long time.

"Lila Smith's the mystery," he said, "not the *Seal of Troy*. It was plain to any amachoor that the *Seal of Troy* is the biggest receivers' den that the world has ever known. I'll bet she's got workshops on board—here, I'll show you something you've never seen before."

He opened a drawer of his desk and searched its untidy interior, muttering condemnations of the man who was responsible for its untidiness. After a while he drew out a sheet of paper, in the centre of which was pasted a cutting from a newspaper.

"The Record Department dug this out of a Lancashire paper three years ago. One of those local *Timeses* that are published weekly."

John Wade took the paper.

A friend of George Seeper, the jeweller, who was sentenced to eighteen months' hard labour for extensive frauds, and who will be remembered kindly by the people of this town despite his lapse and his misfortune, recently saw him in Buenos Ayres. He is now living down his past and has a good position with a steamship company. He has made several voyages to England. We are glad that Seeper is making good. His work in connection with the Young Men's Recreation Room can be set against his unfortunate lapse. . . .

"And here's another one," said Elk, producing a second paper bearing the rubber stamp of the Record Department. It was an advertisement:

Working jeweller required for South America. Excellent opportunity for man who requires fresh start or who wishes to rehabilitate himself.

"I've checked them up. The *Seal of Troy* was in London when the advertisement appeared, and was in Buenos Ayres when Mr. Seeper met his friend. How many replies do you think they got for that princely salary ad.? Thousands! And how many of those fellows were Dartmoor old-timers?"

Wade rubbed his chin thoughtfully.

"It seems a pretty dangerous proceeding. If Aikness is the head of the Rubber gang, he'd hardly place himself at the mercy of an old lag."

Elk smiled pityingly.

"A fellow who'd shoot policemen wouldn't think twice about keeping these fellows under lock and key. We've been making inquiries, especially about Seeper. He's got some relations in Peebles, and they've never heard from him since they got a letter saying he'd been offered a good job. He's been once or twice in England, hasn't he? Well, he's never been seen by mortal eye or heard from except one, though his old mother gets a money order regularly. He's got a lifer, that fellow, and if he ever touches his princely salary he will be lucky. You can bet that every bit of jewellery that's taken aboard that ship is broken up before it's there an hour."

CHAPTER X

It seemed a fantastical idea that the India-Rubber Men, who planned and accomplished great coups, should bother themselves with jewel thefts. But when he refreshed his memory with data from the Record Department, the reason for such expert assistance was obvious. John traced fourteen big jewel robberies, where gems to an enormous value had been stolen, and which crimes were attributed to the India-Rubber Men.

It rained heavily that evening, clearing up towards night, and possibly it was the weather which made his wound smart, though it was more likely, as the police doctor pointed out to him, that his activities of the day were responsible. He made most of his arrangements by telephone, and when darkness fell on the river he went down to the "float" and gave his final instructions to the officers in charge of the three launches that were moored to the edge of the landing-stage.

They were carrying extra crew, and each man was armed. In the bow of the larger boat was an unusual piece of equipment—a small Lewis gun, which John Wade had begged for. Scotland Yard is very averse from placing firearms in the hands of policemen, and it took a lot of persuasion before they permitted the introduction of a machine gun. Their experience of the India-Rubber Men, however, had taught them a lesson which they were not likely soon to forget, and the little gun had arrived from the Tower of London, camouflaged—lest Wapping should see and wonder—and had been put in position.

There was half an hour's council of war, when all the details were settled, and at nine o'clock John Wade went down and took his place in the fastest of the launches.

The land party were to arrive in a closed lorry, of a type that frequently passed "Mecca" on the way to the docks, and would be no unusual phenomenon at that early part of the night. The three launches were supplemented by a roving patrol that would hold the middle of the river whilst the raiding boats closed the wharf.

An old Thames policeman who knew every phase and mood of the river gave them a piece of information just before the boats pushed off.

"There will be a very high tide to-night—we've had the tip from Gravesend, and the land police are warning riverside people to watch out!"

The night was unusually fine, and the three boats moved off in single file and swept across the river to the Surrey side. Once clear, the first of the three increased its speed until John judged they had given it sufficient start, when he moved on. As they neared Wapping the three craft slowed. John glanced at the illuminated dial of his watch; it wanted five minutes to the hour, and he signalled with his lamp to the boats to turn to the north shore. From where he sat in the launch he could see the upper windows of "Mecca"; two of them were illuminated; the third, which he knew was Mum Oaks's room, was dark.

He was half-way across the river when he heard his sergeant's fierce whisper.

"Something coming away from the wharf!"

This police officer had extraordinary sight. He could see in the dark what was invisible to most men, and for a long time John Wade himself could see nothing moving. Then he saw a black shape sidling across the river. It was a boat of unusual length, and although it was scarcely fifty yards away when he sighted it, he could hear none of the sounds which are associated either with a motor-boat or a steam launch, except a dull purr which was only now distinguishable. A powerful electric launch, he decided, and swung his own boat to meet it. It was only as he did this that he realised the extraordinary speed at which the launch was moving. Almost before he knew what had happened, the flying craft was on him. He saw the wide V-shaped wake and shouted a warning . . .

It was no accident; the straight bow smashed into his stern and, had he not been clutching at the gunwale, he would have been thrown into the water. Instantly the engines of his own machine stopped, and the launch lurched over.

It all happened in a second. The dark boat flashed past; he glimpsed the face of a man who was sitting, only his head visible, below the well deck . . .

Aikness!

Captain Aikness, who at that moment was on the high seas. He had no time to wonder; already the police launch was down by the stern.

"Holed," said a voice breathlessly. "She's sinking."

There were keen eyes on the other launches, and as the boat sank beneath him, the nearest police launch came roaring up and grappled

100

the sinking craft. In a second he had jumped the edge of the boat, and his companions were in safety almost as soon.

John looked round but could not locate the black boat. It had vanished in the shadows, and the crew of the rescuing launch had been so intent upon picking up their comrades that nobody had noticed whither it had disappeared. But instantly signal lamps began to flicker, and from up and down the river came agitated responses.

"Close shore, sir!" said a warning voice.

A green signal lamp was winking from the wharf of the "Mecca." The raiders had arrived, and the two boats moved towards the foreshore, came under the moored barges and made fast to the slimy face of the wharf. John Wade forgot his feet were wet and that the legs of his trousers were clinging to him unpleasantly.

The tide was high and running strongly—the water was within a foot of the "Mecca" wharf top when the launch came alongside. He leapt ashore and gripped a dark form that came racing along the wharf towards safety. The man struggled wildly, and for a second John thought that it was Golly, until somebody focused the prisoner in a circle of light and John Wade gazed upon a familiar face.

"Why, Sniffy, you're getting into society!"

"I've done nothing," whined the man. "You can't say I've done anything, Mr. Wade . . . naturally I run when I see the busies. You never know what lies they're cooking up about you."

"Take him," said John, and ran towards the house.

Despite the perturbation suggested by the hurried flight of Sniffy, there was an air of unruffled quietude about the "Mecca." The only police officers in sight were Elk and his assistant, though in the dark of the street he saw a number of men who were obviously policemen in plain clothes.

Elk was standing in the passage-way with Mrs. Oaks, and John thought her unprepossessing face was unusually pallid. Another peculiar fact, which was significant to him, was the woman's attitude. She neither stormed nor raged at the intrusion upon her quiet. Possibly the seriousness of the raid was responsible for this. She gave one quick glance at John as he came into sight, but immediately returned her attention to his comrade.

"The only thing I ask, Mr. Elk," she said, in an even tone, "is that none of my boarders shall know anything about this raid. It may ruin the Home, and I've quite enough to put up with as it is. What do you want to see? You can have the keys of every room in the house."

"We would like to see the cellars, Mrs. Oaks," said John.

He saw the involuntary droop of her eyelid. She looked at him quickly for a moment, and again fixed her eyes upon Elk.

"I'd like to know who's in charge of this business," she asked, and for the first time there came a tremor of anger to her voice. "I've got to know who's responsible, because naturally I'm not going to sit down under this kind of treatment. There's going to be trouble, and I want to be sure who the trouble is coming to."

"I'm responsible," said John quietly. "Will you give me the key of the cellar?"

She stood as stiff as a ramrod, her hands lightly folded before her, and made no movement to comply with his request.

"There is no cellar," she said steadily, "only the wood cellar, and we don't keep that locked. We're not so afraid of thieves as some people are, and, what's more, we don't grudge the poor a little bit of kindling wood."

Wade smiled broadly.

"That's exactly what Golly told us to-night," he said. There was no flicker of eyelid here.

"Indeed?" she said calmly. "Then Golly spoke the truth for once in his life."

She had called the detective's bluff, and he had played the game long enough to know that she had no fear for Golly's safety. She must have seen him that night, he thought, and probably the little man was in the house at that moment, or, if not in the house, within call.

"Who has been here to-night?" he asked brusquely. "No, I don't want the names of your lodgers—I want to know all about your visitors. What time did Aikness come and go?"

She looked at him, a little bewildered.

"Aikness—you mean Captain Aikness?"

He nodded.

"Of the *Seal of Troy*?" She shook her head. "No, I haven't seen him for weeks."

"He's been here to-night," said John. "Now, Mrs. Oaks, this is a matter too serious for you to pretend you know nothing. Aikness was here to-night; that doesn't mean that he's done anything wrong or that you've done anything wrong by entertaining him."

A sour little smile played at the corners of her thin lips.

"I don't know who's done wrong and who's done right," she said shortly. "I've not seen Captain Aikness."

There was nothing to be gained here. He sent her in search of the keys, though he suspected they were in the little wallet she carried suspended from the leather belt about her waist. She came back with them and dropped them into his outstretched palm.

"There's no key to the cellar—I told you that before. Do you want me to come with you?"

John had no such wish. He and Elk went along the wharf, and with the aid of their torches found the short flight of stairs that led to Golly's coal cellar. At the bottom was a fairly wide space, stone-paved, where, out of sight though not out of hearing, Golly was wont to chop wood—his only regular occupation. The door was a very old one and heavy, its face warped with age, and it was pierced with a square hole in which was a rusty grating. Wade expected to use all his strength to push it open, for these ancient portals are as a rule rustily hinged. To his surprise, the door yielded instantly and noise-lessly.

He could have pushed it open with the tips of his fingers, he re-alised, and going round to investigate, he found that the hinges were clean and shining with grease. This was interesting. He returned to the face of the door again and inspected that very carefully. There was an old and rusted lock which had not been used for years, and it looked as though this was the only fastening until, putting his lamp up and down the thick edge of the door, he saw a small triangular hole, and, examining the lintel, he discovered another triangular de-pression that corresponded. Obviously there was a concealed lock here, but it was a long time before he discovered the keyhole. It was very cleverly hidden on the inside of the door, under a drooping and rusty knob and a broken bolt—a tiny slip in the wood, just large enough to admit a patent key. There was no keyhole on the outside, so that the door could only be locked by somebody who was in the woodshed.

"Interesting," murmured Elk, a fascinated spectator. "Some-body's gone to a lot of trouble for no apparent reason!"

The cellar had one electric globe which dangled from the centre of the vaulted roof. They found the switch of this and turned on the light. There was apparently nothing here for investigation. Round three sides of the vault heavy logs of wood, old ship's timbers, sawn off to exact lengths, were neatly stacked, and above them smaller bundles of kindling wood. . . . In the left-hand corner there was a cir-cular iron bin, rather like a heavy ash-can. Opening the lid of this, Wade discovered nothing more romantic than silver sand of the type that is used for scouring purposes. The receptacle was half full of this material.

With the assistance of one of his men, he pulled down enough of the stacked wood to enable him to examine the wall. He found noth-ing but greenly discoloured brickwork. When he tapped the wall, however, it gave a hollow sound, by no means the sound it should have made if his information was correct and the rest of the cellarage was filled up. He tried another wall, with no better result, and whilst the detectives were restacking the wood he made an inspection of the floor.

It was covered with heavy flanged stone; there was no sign of a trap.

"Why the sand?" asked Elk suddenly. "And the answer is, because it's heavy!"

He tugged at the bin but it did not move.

"Because it's darned heavy!" he repeated. "But not so heavy that I oughtn't to be able to lift it. Give a hand here, Wade."

The two men pulled at the bin but it was immovable. Taking off his coat, Wade bared his arm and groped down through the sand. At first he felt nothing, but presently his fingers touched a metal projection, rather like a candlestick in shape, which evidently ran up from the bottom of the bin. It was situated in the exact centre and refused to yield to his tugging. Feeling left and right, his fingers suddenly touched another iron object, shaped rather like the handle of a corkscrew. He pulled at this and it yielded immediately. He heard the hollow clank of steel against steel.

"What's that?" asked Elk curiously.

The other thought for a moment, and then:

"Give me a hand with this bin," said John Wade quietly. "I think it will move now."

It moved so readily that he was almost sent sprawling. The bin swung round on an invisible pivot, situated, he guessed, somewhere in the region of the handle. It had been placed upon a circular steel plate, in the greasy centre of which he saw a bolt end. He had no time to examine this, however, for as the container swung round, the corner walls opened inwards, revealing a narrow doorway.

"Gosh!" gasped Elk.

The piles of wood, so artistically stacked, had vanished also. They were most artistically and immovably fastened to the wall, and so were the logs on either side of the door.

Flashing his lamp before him, John stooped and passed through the queer little doorway, Elk following.

"There's a switch here," said the latter. "Electric light and all modern conveniences."

There was a click and the inner room was revealed. It was a long apartment, evidently running the full depth of the "Mecca." Walls and roof were of ancient bricks, all bearing the green stain of ancient water, though the cellar seemed dry enough. In some places the brickwork was in a considerable state of disrepair. Near the door they had entered was a steel lever which came up from the flagged floor.

Elk stopped to give a few instructions to the detective he had left in the upper cellar, and, coming back, pulled the lever. Immediately the two "leaves" that formed the corner of the wall swung into place.

"That's fastened it," said Elk. "I guess it has pushed up the bolt into the sand bin."

Wade was making a careful search of the room. There were two tables placed end to end, and a dozen chairs. There was nothing there to indicate that it had been recently occupied, but under one of the chairs he found a piece of paper rolled up into a ball, and, smoothing it out, discovered that it was a page from a vernacular Chinese newspaper. More than this, he found near one of the walls a small inkpot and brush such as Chinamen use when they are writing.

From the long cellar led a door, which was ajar. Pushing this open, he found himself in a small cell, furnished with a bed and a table. Hanging behind the door on a nail was a woman's coat—a cheap but fairly new article of wear, which bore on the tab behind the collar a significant label. Embroidered on the tag was the name of a Maidenhead outfitter. This, then, had been the home of Anna, thought John Wade.

How long had she been gone? Not long, he guessed, for the bed was untidy and had recently been slept in. There was a half-filled glass of water on the table and a small, unlabelled bottle containing white tablets. The water was fresh, and the picture newspaper discovered amongst the disorder of bedclothes bore that day's date.

He turned over the pillow and found a woman's handkerchief. A more important discovery came when Elk pulled the overlay from the bed, for between that and the wire mattress he found a knife. It seemed of Chinese manufacture, and on the imitation jade handle were roughly carved grotesque figures of dragons; but when Elk examined the weapon he pronounced it pure Birmingham.

"They sell these things in the junk shops to Chinese sailors. What do you make of that?"

"Anna's first and last line of defence," said John promptly. "She had intelligence enough to know she was in some kind of danger, and managed to get the knife and hide it. Which means that she was taken away rather suddenly and unexpectedly."

He picked up the bottle of tablets and shook them, then sniffed.

"Mr. Raggit Lane has been here. I presume he was the doctor. That man should change his pomade."

A prolonged search brought to light nothing new. The underground cellar was well ventilated—a little too well, for it was as draughty a place as any John could remember.

"There's a big open ventilator somewhere," he said. "Our Mr.

Aikness, or our Mr. Raggit Lane, whoever the master of ceremonies is, is a devil for hygiene, and it looks as if there had been water in the cellar at some time—look at the green stain—it runs up to the roof! Let's go."

They went back to the lever and Elk pulled. The lever apparently had stuck, and though Wade lent his weight it would not move.

"Whom did you leave outside?" asked Wade sharply.

Elk considered.

"Martin and Scance," he said. "They've probably been monkeying about with the——"

At that moment the lights in the cellar went out. Instantly Wade drew his torch from his pocket and turned it on.

"Try the door," he said, but though they put their shoulders to the corner of the wall they might as well have pressed at any other face of it. Elk rapped on the walls to attract the two police officers outside, but there was no answer. He himself had observed and marvelled at the thickness of the "door."

For a moment John was silent.

"Was it an accident?" he said at last.

He heard Elk's quiet chuckle, and a cold shiver went down his spine, for Elk never laughed unless he was in very serious trouble.

"I guess not," drawled the older man. "Let your light so shine, brother, that friend Chink can't come up behind you and jab you one—I'm going to have a look at the electric light attachments."

John kept his face towards the far end of the room, and sent a fan of light travelling along the darkened chamber.

"That's it," said Elk after a while, as he heard the click-click of a useless switch. "There's a control outside. I wonder what's happened to them two officers—pardon my bad grammar, but when I'm upset I always get common. Do you notice something about this room?" he asked suddenly.

John Wade nodded. He had seen the green-tinted walls, and now he began dimly to understand.

"I think I know why they all cleared out to-night, too," he said quietly. "It wasn't because we were coming."

His ear caught a strange sound; a rustling and a confused squeaking; and then, into the focus of his lamp, he saw come running first one and then two queer little brown forms. They stopped, fascinated by the light, and, even as he looked, the two had become six. Something brushed against his feet.

"I'm not ladylike," said Elk, and his voice sounded a little agitated, "but if you don't mind we'll stand on that table. I'm very fond of animals but I never could stand rats."

They got on to the table. The floor was alive with rodents, running aimlessly from side to side, squeaking, scurrying, leaping vainly and senselessly against the wall. They were in a panic, terrified by some unknown danger. Their beady eyes glinted in the light of the lamp. Elk found half a dozen had climbed the legs of the table and were running over his feet before he could kick them away.

"Notice the ventilation's stopped?" he asked.

John Wade had noticed that. The air in the room had grown heavy; it was an effort to breathe. But presently he felt a cool breeze, and almost instantly, from the far end of the room, came a strange gurgling sound, and the squeak of the rats grew fiercer.

"Water," said Elk. "Remember what that copper of yours said? A very high tide to-night. It'll be too high for us, I'm thinking. Look at those devils swimming."

Already the chairs were floating in three feet of water, and each was thick with rats, clinging like marooned sailors to bars and legs. In an incredibly short space of time the water overlapped the top of the table and was up to their ankles. Elk reached down and yanked a chair, scattering its squealing crew.

"That bar for us," he said.

Across the brick-vaulted roof, immediately above their heads, ran a rusted iron bar, probably placed there to strengthen the roof in some bygone time. Each section of vaulting had the same support. He reached up, John steadying him, and caught the bar, and with some difficulty his companion followed. Instantly the chair and table rolled away under them, and they were left hanging waist-high in water.

Their lanterns were gone now. John saw the dim glow of them on the floor of the cellar. They were watertight, but their light was so faint under the flood that they gave no illumination to the room. In the darkness John felt furry little figures clawing at his coat. He shook his shoulders with a shudder, to free himself of the unseen things that in their terror were clinging to him.

"The river must be terribly high," he said, "but it can't be as high as this."

He made a rapid mental calculation. Even supposing the water had risen above the level of the wharf, it should not be higher than their waists as they stood upon the table.

"The Metropolitan Police are going to lose two very good officers," said Elk calmly. "Who'll get your promotion, John? That fellow Stanford will get a step—I never liked the man. I'm almost sorry I'm going to die."

"Shut up!" snapped John savagely.

The water was up to his neck. Presently it touched his uplifted chin. He was no longer interested in his little four-footed companions. The fact that they were squealing in his ear caused him no concern. The water was above his chin. His face was flat against the brick vaulting above.

Lila Smith . . . she was safe, anyway. He wished he could have got to the bottom of that Pattison Trust, and he'd like to have had one crack at Aikness, and——

He felt a shock, but could hear nothing, for his ears were beneath water. The whole building seemed to shake. And then, with extraordinary rapidity, the water began to descend, first to his shoulders, then with a rush to his waist.

"What's happened?" gasped Elk.

The mystery was susceptible of only one solution; a portion of the wall had collapsed under the pressure, and the water was rushing somewhere else, finding a lower level.

John touched the table, felt it sinking beneath his hand as the flood fell.

"Drop into the water," he advised Elk. "We must find the breach."

He swam along the wall until he felt his legs sucked from under him, and, bracing himself against the brickwork, he groped down. Presently he found the hole; a section of the wall four feet wide and three or four feet high had burst under the pressure of the water, but whither that led he could only surmise.

The movement of the water had ceased. The level had been reached, and a few minutes later it began to rise again, but by this time they were little more than breast-high, and both men were touching the floor with their feet.

Diving to where the glow revealed their presence, John Wade retrieved the lamps and made an examination of the aperture.

"There must be a deeper level there," he said. "One of us will have to see where it leads."

"That one will be you," said Elk.

Wade made a mental plan of the neighbourhood. Adjoining "Mecca" was an old warehouse occupied by a firm of provision merchants. He knew the place; it had a deep cellar in which a former occupant had erected a refrigerating plant. He had once paid a visit to the cellars in company with a river thief to identify stolen property.

With the watertight lamp in his hand, he dived again, struggled through the hole and came up on the other side. His feet no longer touched bottom. Treading water, he threw the light of his lamp round the roof. It was evidently an older portion of the building. The roof was raftered and supported on great oaken pillars, and, floating thickly on the surface of the black water, were a number of small wooden cases.

Now he knew where he was, it was only necessary to find the exit. Diving back through the hole, he told Elk what he had found.

"This is evidently the limit of the 'Mecca' cellar, and the water has dropped on to the deeper floor of the warehouse. There must be a way out of that."

The two men dived through the hole and came back to the vault of the warehouse. They made slow progress, pushing their way between the floating cases. Their progress was made more difficult by the fact that it was impossible to use the lamp except at intervals, but after ten minutes swimming through the floating debris, John saw a sight that gladdened his eyes. Within a few feet of him a flight of steel stairs led out of the water to a small door. Presently they were dragging themselves up the steel stairs and reached an iron door.

To John Wade's relief and surprise it was not locked, and, sliding it aside, he found a short flight of stone steps that led to a large room, obviously on the street level. He was unbarring this when an authoritative voice hailed him. It was the night watchman, who held in leash a ferocious-looking Alsatian.

"Police, are you? Let's have a look at you," said the sceptical man.

It took some time to convince him, and then he explained what, to Elk's orderly mind, was the supreme mystery of the evening, why the iron door into the warehouse cellar had been unlocked.

"I knew the floods were up and I've just sent a message to the fire brigade," said the watchman. "I left it unfastened for them in case they wanted to do some pumping, but, Lord! it'll be hours before the river goes down. They're flooded out at the 'Mecca' by all accounts, and a couple of men who were down in the wood cellar were nearly killed. The water came over the top so suddenly. What they were doing down in the cellar I don't know."

John could have explained, but did not. The watchman let them out through a wicket door and they went back, ankle-deep in water, to the club, in time to arrest the activities of a rescue party which was preparing to force its way into the cellar in a last despairing hope of getting the two men out alive.

A launch carried them back to one of the police boats, and as they were changing their clothes, after a hot bath, Elk was loquacious.

"No, I'm not scared—I was, though," he admitted. "I've ruined a perfectly good suit, and who's going to pay for that? There was a rat in each pocket and they were both dead. That's the first time I've had a rat drowned in my pocket, and I'm thinking of writing a book about it. What worried me at first was the thought that these Inja-Rubber boys had caught me. I see now it was an act of Providence."

"Was it?" asked John Wade quietly. "There was somebody there to close down the ventilating shaft and put the light out—you'll probably find a control in the house. I'm going back to do a little investigating. And it wasn't the weight of the water that kept those doors shut—they open inwards. Providence is not the name I should give to the India-Rubber Men."

CHAPTER XI

By the time he reached "Mecca" the river had sunk well below the level of the wharf coping. The raiding party, some of them wet through to the waist, had been relieved by another and better equipped body of men drawn from the police reserves. Three throbbing fire engines were standing in the street, pumping out the flooded basement of the warehouse, and the wood cellar had been pumped dry. The little room was now an indescribable confusion of logs and sodden kindling wood.

John opened the secret door and examined, with a little shudder, the place of his imprisonment. He had already decided that this was not the first time the cellar had been flooded. The place had been under water before, as he guessed. One of the detectives had been told by Mrs. Oaks that four years previous the water had come into the cellar and reached the roof.

The floor was littered with dead rats. In support of his view that the failure of the lights was due to human agency, they were now shining again. Apparently the water had had no effect upon the connections. He drew Elk's attention to this fact.

A careful scrutiny of the walls showed the ventilator shaft through which he had felt the breeze. It came from above the bed where, as he guessed, Anna had been sleeping when she was aroused and taken to a place of safety. She was probably one of the crew of that black boat which had run him down.

The ceiling here was higher than in the rest of the vault, and above was a slit in the brickwork about four inches deep, which communicated, as he found, with a narrow *cul de sac* which ran for a dozen feet between the warehouse and the "Mecca." The ventilation had been cut off by an iron shutter, which was kept in place by means of a chain and a hook, and this had obviously been lowered by malignant hands. Why the electric light had gone out was more difficult to discover; in the lobby of the "Mecca" he found three controls, but had no time to make any further investigation.

Mrs. Oaks was in her room, he was told, "terribly upset" by the ruin which the floods had brought. There was an excuse here, for the water had swept through the house and done an extraordinary amount of damage in the very short time the river had been up. The floor of Mrs. Oaks's private room was grey with river mud. The carpet before the fire-place had been swept aside, and it was the presence of the mud which betrayed a certain hiding-place. John saw a rectangular line of tiny bubbles, and, sweeping the mat aside with his water boots, he saw the outlines of the trap. Mrs. Oaks had given him her keys, which he had transferred to his pocket, and one by one he tried these in the little lock until at last he found a flat key that fitted, snapped back the lock and pulled the trap open.

"This looks like Mum's private safe," he said, groping in the interior.

At first he thought the receptacle was empty, but after a while his fingers touched a small, square, iron box, and this he drew to light. It was unlocked, and he turned back the lid curiously. If he expected to make a sensational find he was doomed to disappointment; there was nothing here but a flat book, and this he opened.

The book contained four pages of careful writing, and consisted of girls' names arranged in alphabetical order.

Ada	*Rita*
Bertha	*Sara*
Clara	*Moira*
Dora	*Pamela*
Emma	*Ursula*
Freda	*Ada*
Gloria	*Bertha*
Hilda	*Clara*
Ina	*Dora*
Jenny	*Emma*
Kitty	*Freda*
Lena	*Gloria*
Moira	*Hilda*
Nita	*Jenny*
Olivia	*Ina*
Pamela	*Nita*
Rita	*Olivia*

Sara	Kitty
Theresa	Theresa
Ursula	Zena
Vera	Yolande
Wenda	Vera
Yolande	Lena
Zena	Wenda

On one page was hastily scrawled in pencil:

Pamela
Rita
Jenny
Bertha
Ursula
Olivia

He studied the book for some time, put it back in the little box and went to find Mrs. Oaks.

Mum Oaks was in a condition bordering upon hysteria. The strain of the night was telling upon this woman, bending that iron nerve of hers. When John Wade saw her, she was in turn tearful and defiant. He was not unaccustomed to the threats she babbled: they were the concomitant of such a situation.

He produced the little tin box.

"I've rescued something of yours, Mrs. Oaks," he said. "You might at least be grateful."

At the sight of the box her face changed.

"There's nothing in there except private papers," she said shrilly, and made to snatch the box from his hand.

"Also a code." He held the box out of her reach. "A number of girls' names, which mean other girls' names. A cumbersome little code, I think. Each name stands for a letter of the alphabet. I see you've scribbled down 'Pamela, Rita, Jenny, Bertha, Ursula, Olivia'—that means 'danger,' doesn't it?"

She did not reply.

"To whom have you cabled—or wirelessed—in the last three months?"

She was quite calm by now.

"I don't know what you're talking about. That's a list of young ladies' names that I got out for a friend of mine who wanted to find a name for her baby."

"To whom have you cabled?" persisted John, and then, in his old blarneying way: "Come across, Mrs. Oaks. It's going to be easy to recover all your wires from the post office and to decipher them."

"Then do it," she said promptly, and he knew, without further explanation on her part, that such telegrams as had been sent were in some other name than hers, and that the difficulty of associating her would be wellnigh insuperable.

"Is that all you want to see me about?" she asked, dropping into her more truculent manner. "If it is, I'll be glad if you'll clear out! I've had enough trouble with the flood—I don't know which is the worse, the river or coppers."

John smiled.

"Coppers are the worse," he said flippantly. "The waters of justice never go down. I've only one further question to ask you—when did they take Anna from the cellar?"

Her eyebrows rose at this, but her manner of surprise was not convincing.

"Anna? I don't know what you're speaking about."

John Wade's eyes were fixed upon hers, and he saw her mouth twitch.

"You mean the woman about whom you asked me before? I've never seen her."

John Wade nodded.

"She was in the cellar, in the smaller room. I've just collected a coat of hers, which is going to Maidenhead to be identified. I've warned you once before, Mrs. Oaks, it will be a very serious business for you——"

"If she was ever here, I should know it."

The woman spoke rapidly; she was thrown for a moment off her guard.

"We leased the cellar—at least, Golly did—to some people who wanted a place to store their things. I've never been in the cellar . . . don't know how to get in. Golly knows; he attended to all that kind of thing. They paid us a pound a week. Golly used to give me the money."

Her eyes were fixed upon the black box in John's hands.

"That's my property," she said. "I'd like to have it."

"You'll know where to find it," said Wade carefully, and gave her no other satisfaction.

He deposited the box and its contents in the safe at the police station before he went home. This time he was accompanied by two armed detectives, and found a policeman on duty in front of his house. It was hardly likely that the India-Rubber Men would attack him in his own little stronghold again—at least, not for a spell—and he had a feeling that affairs were moving rapidly to some sort of climax.

The house still smelt faintly of that devastating gas which had been loosed, and his man told him that a little pocket had been found by the chemical experts in the coal cellar and had had to be pumped out. His own district had not escaped the consequence of the floods; the water had been up to within a few feet of his own house, and the small back gardens on the other side of the street were under water.

He was called on duty after three hours' sleep to deal with some of the consequences of the erratic tide. A barge had broken from its moorings and had fouled a steamer lying at anchor in the Pool before it had drifted to a derelict wharf on the Surrey side, where it had been made fast and looted in an incredibly short space of time by some of the Rotherhithe rats.

The launch carried the weary police officer on his rounds from barge to barge. Sometimes these craft were left entirely without crew, but in the majority of cases there was somebody on the deck to report "All's well."

He came at last to the two long barges moored opposite the "Mecca," and here his interest quickened. He had seen that there was a watchman on board, and this man might give him some information about the movements of the black launch.

As dawn was breaking he hailed the solitary figure that stood by the tiller, smoking a short clay pipe.

"All right, guvnor, nothing wrong here. . . ."

"I'm coming aboard," said John.

The launch drifted to the waist of the barge, and with the assistance of the watchman's huge hand he jumped on board. It was the left hand he extended; the right he kept in his pocket—a circumstance which did not at the moment strike John Wade as peculiar. Many of these watchmen were injured men who had lost the use of a limb, and his first impression was that this was one of them.

The bargeman told him more than he expected. He had not only seen the black boat cross the stream, but had been a witness of the collision.

"No, it didn't come from the 'Mecca' wharf." He was emphatic as to this. "I saw it pushing downstream on the Middlesex shore a long time before it turned to cross the river. I had an idea at first that it was a police boat watching the launches on the other shore—they was yours, wasn't they? Anyway, I was surprised he could move so fast, and the river was certainly doing a bit of moving on its own! I meant to ask who it was, but I've seen nobody since last night."

The watchman was unknown to John, who asked a few questions.

"Me? I come from Grays. I don't often work up as far as this, but these barges have a cargo of machinery from Belgium—electric machinery for some works up at Oxford—and they've hired me to go up with her."

"Have you hurt your hand?" asked John.

The man laughed softly and took his right hand from his pocket.

"A bit," he said. "The flood made the barges bump into the 'Mecca' wharf, and I fell over the tiller." He had ricked his wrist painfully, and went on to speak of the black boat. "It's funny the things you see. I found a feller hiding on this barge—feller named Sniffy, according to all accounts——"

"Whose account?" asked John quickly. "You said you'd spoken to nobody."

"Only the police—the river police. They've been dodging about all the night. Never seen so many river police in my life—regular Sherlock Holmeses they are!"

John could not miss the covert sneer in the man's voice; and knew that, for some reason or other, the river police were as unpopular with watchmen as they were with thieves.

"What was Sniffy doing on board?"

The man shook his head.

"I never know why thieves go on board barges," he said ironically.

As the launch pulled away and vanished in the grey morning mist, the watchman stooped and lifted two black-painted cylinders that lay in the scuppers. They were heavy, and, depositing them under a canvas cover, he walked slowly to the hatch that led to his quarters. He turned his back upon the hatchway and did not move when a voice called him softly from the depths behind him.

"Wade," he answered. "I thought he might come below—and then I thought he was after a search. I'd have gunned him and bombed the launch—it would have been easy."

He heard the grunt of agreement and grinned to himself. Captain Aikness invariably signified his approval with such a grunt.

CHAPTER XII

It was nearer eight than seven when John Wade went back to his bed, and he woke to the sound of children playing in the street, a sure indication that it was late afternoon. He had had his bath and was dressing when Elk arrived.

"No, there's no news, except that the Aylesbury police arrested a man they thought was Golly. It wasn't him, though."

Elk was portentously solemn, and John guessed that behind the bald information that nothing had happened he had serious news of a kind.

"I've just been to see that young lady, Lila Smith. She's O.K., and the doctor says there's no reason why she shouldn't go back home. And his lordship called this morning."

"Siniford?" asked John, in surprise.

Elk nodded.

"With bouquets," he said sardonically, and made a sweeping movement with his hands intended to indicate the size of the floral offering.

John made a little grimace. The activities of Lord Siniford brought to him a sense of uneasiness. Here was a mystery as profound as the mystery of the India-Rubber Men and even more inexplicable.

The India-Rubber Men needed no explanation. Their object was self-evident. They represented the rarest of phenomena, an organised criminal confederacy engaged in wholesale robbery. But Siniford's attentions to Lila Smith. . . . There was a distinct association between the three factors—the Rubber Men, Siniford and the girl.

Aikness was in London; there was no possible chance that he had mistaken the man he saw when the black launch had shot past in the darkness. Below in the cockpit where Aikness had sat was a green light, possibly an indicator light on the engine board, and in its faint glow the face had been plainly visible.

"I'll see Lila," he said at the end of a long silence.

Elk grunted something that might have been agreement.

Ten minutes later John Wade was on his way to the girl's temporary lodging. There was a colour in Lila's face that John Wade had not seen before; her eyes were brighter, and it seemed that there was a confidence in her voice which was altogether novel. Her old attitude towards him had undergone a subtle change, and he was a little baffled.

His first alarmed impression was that she was feverish and light-headed; that, in the past twenty-four hours, Lila Smith had tidied the chaos of her perspectives and had placed him of all people in the immediate foreground, was not to be imagined.

Yet this had happened in those hours of the night when the sound of a ticking watch brings a sense of companionship.

Old clients of "Mecca," returning recently from long voyages, had seen remarkable developments in Lila Smith. She herself had been unaware of those changes until that night when she found herself laughing softly at the clear-cut problems which in their vaguer shape had been a little terrifying—certainly distressing. And, grading those problems in the order of their importance, she had placed John Wade in the first position. To a woman it is essential that a man shall have certain enigmatical qualities. To be obvious is to be uninteresting. Lila Smith had decided that she alone of all women held the key to this particular enigma. Which was proof of her development.

She could meet his gaze without embarrassment, could, from the dais of her sudden understanding, experience a pleasant sense of superiority. In the expectation of his visit she had taken considerable pains to make herself unusually presentable—far greater trouble than she had taken over the furtive dinner parties of Captain Aikness. He expected to find her in bed: she received him in the little parlour of her temporary lodging, sitting before a small fire. There was a book on her knees and a pair of horn-rimmed spectacles on her pretty nose.

"Why, Lila, I didn't know you wore glasses," he said as he shook hands.

She motioned him to a chair; the unexpectedness of the gesture was rather disconcerting.

"I wear them when I read," she said, closing the book and putting it on the table by her side and as deliberately removing the glasses. "I sent for them last night."

Her calm scrutiny of him was uncanny. He was used to bantering her, treating her as a rather overgrown child interested in lollipops, dolls perhaps. Now he was uneasy in her presence and tongue-tied.

"The floods were up? Mrs.—I forget her name, the woman who is looking after me—I call her Alice—told me. Poor Mrs. Oaks! We had a flood years ago. The water filled the cellar and covered the ground floor. It was a terrible business. Why didn't you come to see me this morning?"

He was staggered by this peremptory demand.

"I was asleep," he said disjointedly. "Up all night—floods and all that sort of thing."

She nodded.

"I thought you might be," she said.

There was an awkward pause—awkward for him. She was enjoying his embarrassment, finding a queer joy in her newly discovered superiority.

"You've got powder on your face," he said suddenly, and she laughed.

"Of course. Everybody uses powder. How silly you are!"

Nevertheless she opened her little handbag—it lay on her lap and he had not noticed it—and scrutinised her face with the assistance of a tiny mirror.

"How is your leg? It wasn't a serious wound, Alice told me." She shivered. "It seems now like a horrible nightmare. Horrible!"

She had come back to unpleasant realities and was in danger of losing her sense of exaltation.

"Why do they hate you so?"

"Who?" he asked.

She hesitated.

"Mrs. Oaks and—and—everybody. Why do they?"

There was a note of desperation in her voice. She knew there could be only one answer, yet dared ask the question in the faint hope that he might supply a comforting response. And, when he did not speak:

"They are bad—all of them? Mrs. Oaks too? How bad, please? Tell me, John—do you mind if I call you that? I suppose it is Jack really?"

Here indeed was a new Lila Smith. There showed no evidence of confusion. Never once did those big grey-blue eyes leave his.

"Jack—anything you like, my dear. Yes, they're all pretty bad. I don't know how bad, but I can guess. Listen, Lila—have you ever heard them speak of the Pattison Trust——"

"Trust?" she repeated quickly. "Yes—what was it called?—Pattison? No, I've never heard that. But they spoke of the Trust. The lord—what is his name?"

"Siniford?"

She nodded.

"He spoke. Golly—Mr. Oaks—was there, and Mum and another man. I think it was Lane. He scents himself abominably. I was listening. I've been terribly mean about listening. It is you—I mean, I wanted to hear about you, because——"

"Because?" he prompted when she paused.

"Oh, I don't know—just because. The Trust? It was something to do with a bank—the Medway Bank. I heard Lane say 'Medway Bank'—I think he was writing it down. It is in the City, in one of those odd streets with odd names—Luffbury——"

"Lothbury," said John quickly.

"That may be it," she said, nodding. "The Trust has something to do with that. I heard Lane say something about 'the engravers'—does that mean anything?"

He shook his head.

"Not to me at the moment."

She put her hand over his and laughed.

"Shall I become a detective in time?" she asked.

It was the friendliest, most confident of gestures, but he felt a thrill that he had never felt before, and caught her hand in his tightly.

"If you marry a detective," he said, and his voice was husky.

Very gently she drew her hand away. She was not frightened; never had he seen her so self-possessed. She was astonishingly in control of the situation.

"I *am* worried about things," she said. "The 'Mecca' and the people who come there. It isn't disloyal to tell you. I can't be on both sides, can I? It is because I've been trying to be on both sides that all this has happened. What does this man want?"

She indicated with a little gesture the big bunch of flowers that lay in a basin on the wash-stand.

"Siniford? I don't know."

She nodded wisely.

"He wants to marry me," she said with the greatest calmness. "Isn't it absurd? But he does—I should be Lady Siniford of Siniford. Where is Siniford? It isn't in the railway time-table."

He was staring at her in an amazement induced not so much by Siniford's offer as by her cold-blooded reception of it.

"Of course I'm not going to marry him. He's a dreadful man—he drinks. You can tell—a long way off."

John shook her hand gently.

"Just stop, will you, Lila? He really wants to marry you, and Mrs. Oaks agrees? She does, does she? Are you going to marry him?"

She smiled at the question.

"Of course not! I'm going to marry—well, anybody who is nice."

"Like me?"

It did not sound like his own voice; it was oddly husky and

120

strange. Her eyes were fixed on his, serious eyes full of confidence.

"Like you," she said quietly.

John Wade went out of the house an hour later, a strangely new man. Life had suddenly become unreal, people and things had assumed new values. He could never afterwards remember what happened in the walk between her house and his.

Elk was waiting for him outside the house and came half-way up the street to meet him.

"A man named Pouder or Wouder or something rang you up—wants to see you. He's a lawyer——"

"Bruder?" asked John quickly.

"That's right—Bruder. He had one of those Oxford voices which makes almost every word sound like anything you like. It is very important. He's staying at his office till you come."

Mr. Bruder had phoned only half an hour before, but Wade lost no time. He had intended seeking an early interview with the solicitor of the Pattison Trust and the opportunity was welcome. A taxi brought him to the lawyer's office as the clocks were chiming seven, and he found Mr. Bruder immersed in the study of a brief.

The solicitor got up and closed the door behind his visitor.

"I wished to see you in relation to the Pattison Trust," he said, "and with special regard to Lord Siniford. But I am in rather a quandary, Mr. Wade. If the information I could give you were incidental to an inquiry you—um—might be making, my difficulties would disappear. If, on the other hand, I were calling you in for the especial purpose of initiating an inquiry—well, that would be awkward."

John smiled.

"In other words, you don't wish to 'start something.'"

"Exactly," said the other. "I should not be justified in calling in the police—I feel justified in furthering investigations which have already begun."

He began to pace up and down the little room, his hands clasped behind him.

"Lady Pattison, as you probably know, was the wife of Lord John Pattison, the third son of the Duke of Soham. She was a very rich woman—very rich," he added emphatically.

John waited. He knew in a dim kind of way that there was such a person as the Duke of Soham, but as to what part he played in national affairs he was ignorant.

"The present Duke of Soham is a poor man," Bruder went on as though he read his visitor's thoughts. "All the money in the family came to Lord John through his mother and through Lady Pattison.

They had a son who married. Within two years of their marriage they were both killed in a motor-car accident leaving one child, a daughter."

John caught his breath—a daughter! But instantly the lawyer destroyed his wild dream.

"She also died—it was a terrible tragedy. She perished in a fire at Lady Pattison's house in Belgrave Square. It broke the old lady's heart and, I fear, deprived her of her reason—though as to this," he went on hastily, "there is no suggestion that when she created the trust she was anything but *compos mentis*. Certainly she harboured the delusion that Delia Pattison was alive and to that end deferred the distribution of her wealth until a date which would have corresponded to the child's twenty-first birthday."

"Lord Siniford is the heir-at-law?" asked Wade.

Mr. Bruder nodded.

"Yes. He is, in a sense, the heir-at-law."

John Wade thought quickly.

"There is no doubt that the child was killed?"

"None. She was in the house when the fire occurred—it destroyed the building—and she was alone. All the servants were out; her nurse—she was three years old—had left her, it is believed, to meet a young man at the corner of the street; she undoubtedly lost her reason, and it was probably due to her ravings and queer delusions that Lady Pattison made her will as she did——"

"What was the nurse's name?" asked John eagerly.

Bruder considered this.

"Atkins," he said after a while.

"But her Christian name?"

The lawyer rubbed his bony chin and frowned heavily.

"Let me see—the name is very familiar to me—um—I can't think of it for the life of me. Mary? No. Alice?"

"Anna?" suggested the detective, and Mr. Bruder started.

"Of course—Anna! That was it—how stupid of me! You know, then——"

John Wade had suddenly lost the power of speech. Delia Pattison was alive—she was Lila Smith! It was easy enough to see: Delia had become "Lila."

After a while he found his voice and interrupted the lawyer, who was talking of Anna's antecedents.

". . . very respectable young woman——"

"Why did you want to see me? What has happened since I was here last?"

Mr. Bruder had resumed his seat at his desk. Now he swung

round in his swivel chair.

"My office was entered last night," he said, "and the deed-box relating to the Pattison Estate was opened and searched."

He got up and walked to the end of the room opposite the window. Here was an iron rack filled with deed-boxes, some shiningly new, but the majority inscribed with names in fading print. He pulled out one box. It was labelled "P.T. & E."

"Pattison Trust and Estate," he explained as he put the box on the table. "Look!"

Wade examined the lock; it had been forced and was now unusable.

"They came through that window. I found that a pane of glass had been cut and the catch forced back. Curiously enough, I did not notice this until I had occasion to go to the box this afternoon."

"Has anything been taken from the box?" asked John, looking into the interior, which was half filled with bundles of papers tied with red ribbon.

"Nothing," was the reply. "These are leases and deeds of little value to anybody. The intimate documents are at my bank."

Wade examined first the lock on the box and then the window. The work had been done by a craftsman: the hole in the glass was an exact circle, and the piece removed was still lying on the window-sill.

"No, nothing was taken," said Binder again. "We have a check on all documents—a rather complicated system of double entry as it were."

"Was Lord Siniford here yesterday?"

"The day before. I think I told you that he had been rather unpleasant. He wanted to see the contents of the Pattison deed-box—even though I told him that there was nothing in the office which could interest him."

"Would the contents of the other box interest him—the one at the bank?"

Mr. Bruder took time to consider the question.

"Possibly. In the other box are articles personal to Lady Pattison and her granddaughter. There is a portrait of the child——"

John Wade heard a smothered exclamation behind him and spun round.

Lord Siniford was standing in the doorway. His face was pale, his round eyes starting from the sockets. He stood open-mouthed—a ludicrous picture of consternation.

For a second Wade was so dumbfounded by the unexpected apparition that he could not speak.

"Well, Lord Siniford, do you wish to see Mr. Bruder?"

The man shook his head.

"No—no!" His voice was shrill. "Not at all. Sorry I came. . . . See you another time, Bruder."

The door slammed behind him and the two men were left looking at one another wonderingly.

"Funny devil, what scared him?" asked John.

"I'm blowed if I know," said Mr. Bruder, becoming vulgarly human. "Bless my life, he gave me a start."

Wade smiled.

"But not the start that we gave him."

He looked at his watch. He had arranged to meet Elk at eight.

"I gather that you don't wish me to make a report of this burglary." Mr. Bruder shook his head vigorously. "If I do, it will be left to the local inspector. I shall have to make a confidential report, of course. When can I see the other box?"

"To-morrow at eleven; I'll get it from the bank."

Bruder looked apprehensively at the door.

"You don't think there is any personal danger to myself?" he added nervously. "You wouldn't think, for example—well, that the India-Rubber Men, as they call them, had anything to do with this business?"

"Why do you say that?" demanded Wade sharply.

For answer the lawyer pulled open the drawer of his desk and drew out a glove. It was of thin rubber and designed for a left hand.

"There it is," he breathed heavily, as though a weight were lifted from his mind.

Wade picked up the glove and examined it curiously.

"When did you find this?" he asked.

Mr. Bruder settled himself into his chair. He experienced that pleasant thrill which can only be known to the Chancery lawyer whom fate has led into the more exciting by-ways of the common law.

"I did not notice the glove until my clerk drew attention to it this afternoon. It was lying under my desk. The thief had evidently taken it off to make an examination of the paper——"

"That is the time he would have kept it on," smiled John. "No, he took it off to write; one of the things that no man can do well is to write in rubber gloves. He used his own fountain pen and he was making a note of the contents of the box. Probably the second burglar was reading over these titles. Did you notice that your blotting-paper was new this morning?"

Mr. Bruder frowned.

"Yes, I did—now that you mention it."

The lawyer's writing-pad consisted of half a dozen sheets of thick blotting-paper. Wade removed the drawing pins.

"That was the sheet?"

Mr. Bruder peered down and nodded.

"Yes—there's my date-stamp. I always test it on the pad. You see yesterday's date," he pointed out.

John was scrutinising the blotting-paper. Evidently it had been in use at the office for many days, and it had the advantage that Mr. Bruder was not the careless type which utilises a blotting-pad to fill up the empty spaces of thought.

"Is that your writing?" asked John.

He indicated a long, narrow column of words which stretched diagonally across the sheet. The solicitor shook his head.

John procured a mirror from the outer office and examined the writing.

"That was a good guess of mine," he said. "I gather this is a list of the documents in the box."

The lawyer's careful inspection confirmed this view.

"There's nothing we can do to-night," said John. "By the way, you can give me your private address and telephone number in case I want to communicate with you later. But in any event I shall be here at half-past ten, and if you would have what you call the intimate box ready for me I should be obliged."

Wade paused at the door, deep in thought.

"There is no doubt at all in your mind that Delia Pattison is dead?"

"None," said the lawyer.

Wade was half-way down the stairs when he remembered a question he ought to have asked, and returned.

"When is Delia's twenty-first birthday?"

"On the twenty-first of this month," was the reply.

"After which the property will be handed over to Lord Siniford?"

"A long time after; there are certain legal formalities to be gone through, but to all intents and purposes the inheritance is transferred on the twenty-first or the twenty-second."

CHAPTER XIII

Wade went straight back to Elk's room in Scotland Yard, where they had arranged to meet, and briefly told him of the lawyer's experience. He added his own private views, and Elk made a little face.

"Your romantical notions I can't stand, and anyway, the long-lost heiress is one of those comic figures that belong to the movies. Who was the woman again—the mad grandmother?"

"She wasn't mad," said Wade, annoyed by his colleague's scepticism. "Lady Pattison."

Elk's eyebrows went up into shaggy arches.

"The emerald woman! Good lord, I remember that fire——"

"The emerald woman?" said Wade quickly.

"She had hundreds of 'em," explained Elk; "kept a small museum in her house. The one thing we could never find out was, whether they'd been pinched. The house was burnt from garret to basement, and a few of the stones were found, or what remained of 'em. But the old lady was so upset about her granddaughter's death that she wouldn't give us any information about 'em. Humph!"

He crouched back in his chair, his bony hands clasping and unclasping, his eyes fixed on his desk.

"The emerald woman," he muttered. "Of course! It's one of the doubtful cases in the India-Rubber Men's file! All this happened before we knew these birds as well as we know 'em to-day. The only thing we could find was that the servants had been got out of the house with theatre tickets, and the maid who was in charge of the child was lured by a telephone message to meet some feller who had taken her fancy. It looked like a well-planned job at the time, I remember, but as I say, we couldn't get the old lady to talk."

"The body of the child was found?" asked John anxiously.

Elk pursed his lips.

"Well," he drawled, "I don't want to go into gruesome details, but you couldn't find *anything* after a fire like that—anything you could swear was human. Why, the fire was so fierce it burnt the brickwork into dust! Long-lost heiress, eh?" He was not sneering now.

Suddenly he got up to his feet.

"We'll take the chance of looking foolish. You'd better post a couple of men on Tappitt's house, and see that nobody interviews your young lady—that is, nobody but me. I'm going to see her to-night, and find out what she can remember about her past."

"I could do that——" began John.

"You could do nothing," said Elk calmly. "You're sweet on her, and that means that you've lost your judgment and your fine police touch."

On their way they called at the police station, and intercepted Sergeant Tappitt, Lila's host, just as he was coming off duty. He demurred to Elk's suggestion that two men should be posted at his house.

"The missus won't like that," he said. "She'll think it's a slight upon her. And I don't think there's any danger. If it was an isolated cottage like Mr. Wade's, there might be, but we live in a block of flats with people coming and going all the time—anyway, come along and see her."

His home was situated within a stone's throw of John Wade's house, a block of artisans' apartments, recently built. His own flat was on the first floor, and he let them in with his key.

The tiny hall was in darkness.

"My old lady's getting economical," he said, as he switched on the light.

Leading from the hall was a narrow passage; he led them down this to the end and opened the door of the kitchen, where he knew his supper would be laid. This room also was dark.

"That's queer," he said, and his voice was a little troubled.

He turned on the lights. The table was laid for three. There was a cup half filled with cold tea, but nothing else on the table had been used and the kitchen was empty. John knew that Lila's room was that immediately opposite, and he tapped on the door. There was no answer. He tapped again, and finding that the door yielded under his hand, he pushed it open.

"Lila!" he called softly.

There was no reply. He groped for the switch and found it. The room was empty; the bed had recently been occupied, but there was no sign of Lila, while her coat, which, he remembered, was hanging behind the door, had gone.

CHAPTER XIV

"My wife must have gone out."

There was something in Tappitt's tone that sent a cold shiver down the detective's spine. All the man's sudden panic had communicated itself to him, and he knew that if there was one thing which the police sergeant did not believe, it was that his wife had left the house of her own free will.

"I'll just look in her room."

He turned the handle of the door, but it did not move.

"Put on the hall light, somebody," he asked sharply. "It's near you, Mr. Elk."

Elk found the little lever and turned it down. The sergeant was calling his wife by name, gently rapping at the door. Then suddenly John Wade saw.

"The key's on the outside," he said.

In another instant Tappitt had snapped back the lock, thrown open the door and gone into the room. They saw a sudden flood of light, heard his startled exclamation, and, going in behind him, John Wade found himself in a cosily furnished bedroom.

Lying on the bed was a woman, apparently asleep. He recognised her instantly as Lila's custodian. She lay on her side, so still that at first they thought she was dead. Tappitt shook her by the shoulder.

"Mary!" His voice was shrill with fear. "My God, she's——"

"She's all right, she's breathing," said Wade.

He turned the woman on to her back and lifted her eyelids gently. The glare of the light made her face twitch painfully.

"Open the window and get some water."

Remembering how completely unconscious she had been her recovery was amazingly rapid. In five minutes she was sitting on the edge of the bed, still dazed, looking wonderingly from one to the other.

"What's the matter?" she said at last. "I've been to sleep. Is Lila all right?"

She recognised John and smiled faintly.

"You live here, Mr. Wade," she said, and put up her hand to her

128

head. "Why did I go to sleep?"

They took her into the kitchen and made her some tea.

"Don't empty that cup!" said John sharply.

The sergeant was on the point of throwing the half full cup of cold tea into the sink.

"I may want that."

Tappitt looked from the cup to his superior.

"You mean it's doped?"

He set it aside carefully.

John knew that it was useless at the moment to question the woman, and possibly dangerous to administer a shock. But this quick-witted ex-nurse realised that something was wrong, and it was she who raised the question of Lila.

"Not there?" she said incredulously. "But I left her a few minutes ago—what time is it?"

They told her it was half-past eight. She stared at them in amazement.

"But it can't be. It was five o'clock when I was in the High Street—I went out to buy her a pair of slippers. I left Mrs. Elford, the woman who lives opposite, to look after her; then I came back and made myself a cup of tea——"

She paused.

"Do you remember anything after that?" asked John.

She shook her head slowly.

"No, I don't."

Mrs. Elford, the neighbour who lived on the opposite landing, offered a solution to the mystery. She had been called in to play caretaker in the flat while Mrs. Tappitt went out to get the slippers, and she had been there for a little more than ten minutes. While she was there, and soon after Mrs. Tappitt left, a man had called with a note for Lila. She did not remember what he looked like, except that he seemed a seafaring man. There was an answer, according to the messenger, and she had left him at the open door and gone into Lila's room——

"During which time a second man slipped into the flat and hid himself in the kitchen. Is there any place here where he could hide?"

In the kitchen was a door which led to a tiny scullery. It was still ajar though Mrs. Tappitt was certain it had been shut and bolted.

"This is the place," said Wade. "Do you remember making your tea, Mrs. Tappitt?"

She nodded.

"After it was poured out, did you leave it for any time?"

She considered.

"Yes, I did go out for a second or two. I went to ask how the slippers fitted."

"Then you came back and drank your tea? And that is all you remember? They gave you enough stuff to knock you out, carried you into the bedroom and locked the door on you."

The three men conducted a careful search of Lila's bedroom, but the only discovery of any moment they made were her shoes behind an arm-chair.

"They couldn't find these in their hurry," suggested Elk. "What were those slippers like, Mrs. Tappitt?"

"Red leather ones," explained the woman. "She had them on when I left her. They were rather expensive slippers, but Mr. Wade told me I was to give her anything she wanted."

Leaving the woman in the care of her husband, the two detectives hurried from the flat and began their inquiries on the spot. In this neighbourhood, where children play in the streets till late at night, and women make their doorways centres of gossip, it was almost certain that somebody would have seen the party leave. In five minutes, working independently, they found two independent witnesses. From these they learnt of a taxicab which had driven up to the door; four people had come from the flat, two women and two men. They had got into the cab and driven off. Nobody had seen them arrive at the building: they must have come one by one.

There was no other information. Apparently the girl had gone willingly; there had certainly been no outcry, no struggle. From John's point of view the failure of the testimony was that nobody recognised either of the two men; its value was that the identity of the second woman was established.

"To-morrow we shall probably find somebody who can tell us more," said John. "The second woman was Mum Oaks—Lila would have gone with nobody else."

"Then we'll try the 'Mecca,'" said Elk.

The club wore an air of bland innocence. The house had been tidied and the hallmarks of the flood removed. Mum Oaks received them in her sitting-room, and was neither surprised nor alarmed at the visitation.

"I haven't been out this night," she said shrilly. "What new charge are you cooking up for me, Wade?"

"I want to see over the Home," said John shortly. "Lila's room particularly."

She glowered at him.

"Have you a warrant?" she demanded.

"The old warrant hasn't expired," Elk put in. "Don't give a lot of

130

trouble, ma'am."

The lips of the woman curled.

"You won't find Lila here——" she began.

John turned on her in a flash.

"Why should I?" he asked harshly. "How do you know she's left the place I put her?"

For a moment the woman was disconcerted.

"I never said I did."

John walked to her slowly and stood glaring down at her. She had never seen him like this before, and involuntarily she shrank back.

"You went to Sergeant Tappitt's house to-night accompanied by two men," he said, "and you induced that girl to leave."

The challenge was there; the danger of its acceptance did not seem very pressing. Her assurance, her hatred of the man, led her into a supreme error that was to cost her her life. Unable to forgo the momentary triumph which the opportunity offered her, she threw away discretion.

"Suppose I did? She's in my charge, ain't she? You've no more right to detain her away from her own lawful home than you have to detain me! There's no crime in going and bringing my own niece away from undesirable company, and you know it, Mister Wade."

"And that is what you did?" he asked gently. "You don't deny that? I'm not telling you that you were recognised, because you weren't."

"That is what I did," she said defiantly; "and if you want Lila you'd better find her. She's in good hands. I admit it was me and some friends——"

He saw her jaw drop, and a look of fear come into her eyes. Too late she had recognised how completely she had placed herself in his power. There was a detective watching "Mecca" day and night. The man had reported on the threshold of the club and had told him nothing unusual. John beckoned him in.

"Place this woman under arrest," he said. "I will come to the station and charge her later."

"Under arrest? Why—what have I done?" she quavered. "You can't charge me with anything——"

"Conspiring with others to administer a dangerous drug to Mary Tappitt," said Wade. "You forgot that little part of the abduction."

He left her with the detective and a slatternly and tearful housemaid, collecting the necessities of toilet for a night in the police cells, and he and Elk conducted a quick search of the house. Lila's room had not been occupied.

"It ain't likely they came here," said Elk. "The officer would

131

have seen the cab drive up——"

"They would not have come by cab. The India-Rubber Men's approaches to 'Mecca' are by water."

"Why come here at all?" asked Elk. "There must be a dozen bolt-holes——"

"Mrs. Oaks came here," interrupted the other impatiently. "Let's have a look at the wharf."

With their hand-lamps they made a quick survey. There was no boat tied to the rotting face of the wharf. The two barges which had been moored were no longer there. There was a wide space of water entirely clear of any kind of craft.

They were on the point of leaving the deserted front when something red came into the swinging rays of Wade's lantern. He walked across to it and Elk heard his sharp exclamation of surprise and joined him.

"Don't touch it," warned John.

It was a red slipper, and it lay right on the edge of the wharf.

CHAPTER XV

"How did it get there?" said Elk wonderingly. "She must have stood on the edge."

"Or it was thrown up from a boat deliberately," said John. "There's no mud on the heels and practically none on the sole. The boat came here to land Mum Oaks, after that it went on to another destination. Lila took advantage of the woman's landing to throw up the shoe, knowing that we would probably find it."

He lifted the slipper with a wild hope that in some way she might have scribbled a message on its shiny surface.

"There's no mark here. Get this woman up to the station: we may make her squeak," said Elk, and then, suddenly: "I suppose there's nobody in the rat-hole?"

He pointed to a pile of bricks which stood near the sunken entrance to the woodshed. Evidently workmen had been repairing the breach in the wall, for scattered about was a litter of other building material.

"In a hurry to make that place habitable," said Elk thoughtfully. "Can you spare a minute?"

Reluctantly John Wade followed him down the steps to the door of the woodshed. It was not fastened and they passed into the wood store proper. Elk put his lantern into the steel container.

"New sand and everything," he said.

Groping down, he found the handle and pulled it. The door swung open. As it did so, they saw that the interior was lighted. John passed the other into the long room where he had suffered the greatest fright of his life. As he did so, something stirred at the far end of the room. For a second there appeared a figure near the door of the little chamber which had once housed the mysterious Anna. He had just a glimpse of an arm and shoulder as they disappeared.

"Come out, you!" he cried sternly.

There was no response. He challenged again, and leaving Elk in the doorway, walked slowly into the room towards the sleeping place. He heard a scramble and ran forward, arriving in the room just in time to see the soles of two feet disappearing through the small ventilating shaft. Turning, he raced back to where he had come from, leapt past Elk up the steps and on to the wharf. He knew the position of the ventilator and hoped to meet the fugitive in his flight. Quick as he was, however, his quarry was faster. Something came flying past him towards the end of the wharf. He reached out to grab him but missed. In another second the figure had leapt into the water and swam with swift overhead strokes out of the range of vision.

John came back breathlessly, and the detective met him at the head of the cellar stairs.

"Golly, or I'm greatly mistaken," he said. "A surprising little fellow. I didn't even know he could swim."

"Can't you pick him up?"

Elk peered into the water ineffectually.

"There isn't a launch within miles," said John. "We'll leave him. You might phone the Yard for a flying squad. This girl has got to be found—to-night. If Mrs. Oaks doesn't talk, Siniford will."

Driving westward, John went over the points of his interview with the lawyer and of his talk with Lila.

Lila was in the hands of the India-Rubber Men—yet he felt no sensation of horror—scarcely feared for her. She had always been in their hands. Elk was more perturbed than he, and, as the police car flew westward, jerked in one anxious question after another.

"I hope nothing happens to that girl. Listen, Johnny, suppose them India-Rubber fellers——"

"Oh, shut up!" snarled John.

His imagination needed no stimulant.

"I think by half-past ten to-morrow I'll have Siniford under my thumb. No, I'm not worried about Lila: the plot is so obvious. Siniford wants to marry her, and for some reason Aikness is helping him—for a consideration. Lila is Delia Pattison, which means that nobody is going to hurt her. What will happen after the marriage is quite another matter, but the ceremony has got to be performed properly. Siniford will take no risks."

"What do you expect to find in this private deed-box—by the way, where is that box?"

"At Bruder's bank."

"And where is that?" asked Elk.

John realised that he had not asked.

"I'm only wondering," said Elk, "because, if I remember rightly, this young lady told you that she'd heard some talk about a bank and an engraver's—where was it?—Lothbury, wasn't it?"

Wade leaned out of the window.

"Pull up at the first telephone booth," he instructed the driver.

"I'm going to telephone Bruder," he explained. "I was a fool not to connect the Lothbury bank with the story Lila told."

He got straight through to Mr. Bruder, who had a flat in Portman Square, and it was the lawyer's voice which answered him.

"The Great Central Bank," said Mr. Bruder. "The Lothbury branch."

"Lothbury?" exclaimed John. "Tell me, Mr. Bruder, is there a firm of engravers anywhere near that bank?"

He thought he heard the lawyer gasp.

"Why——" he began.

"Tell me," said John impatiently. "It is very important."

"Yes, there is a firm of engravers. They occupy the top floor of the bank. As a matter of fact, the engraver, an elderly gentleman who, by the way, is one of my clients, is a freeholder of the property, and he only allowed the bank, which originally occupied the ground floor, to rebuild the premises on the understanding that he should have the top floor for carrying on his business. It has, of course, a separate entrance."

"That is all I want to know, thank you," said John, and abruptly cut him off.

He was in something of a dilemma.

The City area of London occupies a peculiar position: it has its own police force, its own detective service and its own police administration. There could be no difficulty in obtaining co-operation, but the knowledge that he might be encroaching on their preserves prevented his calling Scotland Yard direct.

He returned to the car and reported to his companion.

"Did you call the Yard?" asked Elk, and, when John Wade replied in the negative: "Silly idea, isn't it?"

"It is a City job anyway, and I don't want to look silly in Old Jewry."

Old Jewry is a thoroughfare in the City of London which houses the head-quarters of the City Police, a curiously independent body over which Scotland Yard exercises no control.

"We'll have a look at the bank. Policemen are as thick as flies near the Bank of England, and if there's any trouble we'll have all the help we want."

Lothbury was deserted. They saw a policeman turn the corner and walk away as they went into the thoroughfare. The bank occupied the end premises, a new stone-fronted and rather narrow building. As they approached, Wade saw a tall man standing outside the premises: he faced them as they alighted and thrusting his head forward, scrutinised the two men.

"Isn't that Inspector Wade?" he asked. "My name's Cardlin, a detective-sergeant of the City Police."

"Is anything wrong?"

The man did not answer immediately, but smoothed his short black beard.

"That is what I'd like to know," he said. "I don't want to get a lot of uniform policemen round here unless I'm absolutely sure. Sergeant Topham promised to join me, and I badly want somebody to telephone to the sub-manager—a fellow named Wilson—who lives just off Holborn."

"I'll do that for you. I saw a booth near the Royal Exchange. What brought you here, sergeant?"

The bearded man considered the question before he answered. He was evidently the kind of man who attached an especial value to his spoken word.

"Nothing brought me here exactly, only I thought I saw a light in the engraver's, and I went back to Old Jewry and got the duplicate keys. I haven't been up yet. But by the time I came back the light was out."

He gave them a telephone number, and in a short time John was talking to the sub-manager and discovered that they had met a year before on some rather unimportant business.

"I'll come round and bring the keys. Is there a burglar inside?"

"That is what we want to discover," said John.

He returned to find Cardlin and Elk walking up and down on the opposite side of the road.

"The manager will be here in five minutes. Which is the engraver's?"

Cardlin pointed upward to the top floor.

"If you fellows will go up, I'll hang on here. I've got a gun and if anybody is there they will have to come out by the front door."

Crossing the road, Wade fitted a key in a side door and opened it, and went in, Elk following.

Behind the door was a narrow passage which ran by the side of the bank premises. At the end was a small electric lift, around which wound a narrow stairway to the top of the building.

"There will be so many City policemen here that nobody will escape. Any burglar trying to get through would be crushed to death in the crowd. What is it to be—the lift or the stairs?"

John had decided on the stairs, and, removing his shoes, he went up noiselessly, Elk close behind him. They were both armed, but they met no opposition, and reached the top landing, which was also the elevator head, without adventure.

Two doors led from the landing, both half panelled with glass, on which was painted the name of the engraver. John fitted a key, turned the lock noiselessly and stepped into a large work-room, which, save for a glass-panelled office in one corner, covered the whole of the floor. Here was a number of benches littered with the paraphernalia of an engraver's trade, as they saw when the lights were put on.

"Nobody is here," said Elk. "The place hasn't been disturbed."

Across the ceiling ran a number of steel girders, which had been painted white to harmonise with the ceiling. Looking round the work-room, John saw a bar of steel hanging from one of these. It was fastened to the girder by wire, and he wondered what particular purpose this dangling bar served an engraver.

The bottom part of it was hidden between two benches, and, going forward to make a closer inspection, he discovered the secret. Immediately beneath the bar a great jagged hole had been torn in the concrete floor, and on one side of the hole lay a crowbar, a powerful motor-jack and a steel cone. Attached to one of the solid legs of the benches was a rope ladder, which disappeared through the hole into the darkness beneath. He had seen such an instrument as this in a German criminal museum and understood instantly what had happened. The steel bar, having been suspended, was braced against the girder; the cone placed point downward on the floor, and between had been inserted the motor-jack. A few turns of the screw would have made the "jack tight," and the pressure applied by this instrument would be sufficient to drive a hole through the floor which the crowbar could enlarge.

He took all this in in a second. Gripping the rope that held the end of the ladder, he squeezed through the hole and descended into the room beneath. It was a big office; line after line of desks ran across the room, and obviously he was on the bank premises. He found a door, the lock of which had been cut away bodily, and beyond this a narrow spiral steel staircase that took him to another office floor.

He heard the sound of a door opening below and jerked his pistol from his pocket, but there was no necessity for defence; the bank manager had arrived and had admitted Cardlin by the main entrance. He found them on the ground floor and interviewed the bank official.

"It is extraordinary they should have broken in here. We carry no large reserves of bullion—we're too near the head office," said the manager.

"Have you a deposit vault?" asked John, and in a few words revealed his suspicions.

"Yes, there are a number of deed-boxes deposited here," said the manager, "but they couldn't get at those without forcing this door, and it hasn't been touched."

He indicated a great steel door set in the wall in the small inner office where ordinarily he himself sat. The door was fast, but a superficial examination of the lock showed that it had been tampered with. There were scratches on the paint and later they found, hidden beneath the desk, a kit of delicate tools and a powerful blow-lamp. Producing a bunch of keys, the manager turned the lock and swung open the door.

The sub-manager's office was a small, lofty apartment leading from the main public offices. It was almost like a strong-room itself, John noticed, and the bank official explained that it had been used for that purpose.

"We have a number of clients who are members of the Stock Exchange, and in the old days, before the vault was built, this room was used to keep scrip and documents that we wished to get at without a great deal of trouble. The under vault was built subsequently.

"Somehow," said the sub-manager with satisfaction, "I never thought they'd do anything with this door."

Evidently he was very proud of his new vault. The door was of chrome steel, he explained, and was the very latest invention of the most efficient maker of bank safes Wolverhampton has produced.

"Are you sure there's no other way into the vault?" asked the bearded Cardlin.

The manager smiled.

"Unless somebody has found a way of eating through ten feet of concrete, there's no way in," he said emphatically.

He asked them to stand a little way back whilst he spun the dial, then inserting first one and then another key, turned back the lock. There was the faintest of clicks and the door swung open on its great crane hinges. He turned a light-control which flooded the interior and passed his hand down the flange of the thick safe door before he descended the six steps that led to the concrete room.

"Here are the deed-boxes," he pointed to row upon row of black japanned boxes. "And there"—he indicated a steel grille which separated this apartment from an inner—"is another vault, but we keep our books and a little cash there."

"Which of these belongs to the Pattison Trust?" asked Cardlin.

The manager touched a box which was smaller than its companions, and Cardlin pulled it out; and then, to John's amazement, he inserted a wedge-shaped instrument between the lid and the box. There was a sharp crack; the lid flew open, and, putting in his hand, Cardlin drew out two small bundles of papers and thrust them into his pocket. And then as calmly he turned and walked towards the stairs.

Only then did John recover from his astonishment.

"What's the idea, Cardlin?" he demanded.

He took two steps after the bearded man and stopped. Cardlin was facing him, and in his right hand was an automatic pistol of large calibre.

"Don't move, any of you birds," he said. "I don't want to shoot in case a copper hears me; that might spoil my getaway and a week's good fishing."

CHAPTER XVI

John for the first time realised that the man was an American. He was dimly conscious too that he had heard the voice before, only it was not American then. Why he should realise details so unimportant he could never afterwards understand.

The man went back up the stairs, reached the top, withdrew slowly into the room; still covering them with his pistol, he stooped and felt down the flange of the door.

"My God! He's shutting the door on us!"

It was the manager's voice, thin with terror.

"——feeling for the safety bolt. We shall be smothered——"

It was at that moment that John Wade jerked out his pistol and fired. He heard a cry of pain and the clatter of the bearded man's automatic as it fell to the floor. The great steel door was closing slowly. In two strides John Wade was up the steps and had wedged his shoulder between door and lintel. At the first move towards the stairs the bearded man had turned, run from the room, slamming and locking the door behind him.

"The alarm bell!" gasped the manager. "Let me."

He pushed past Elk, sprawled over the desk and groped underneath. Presently he found the little steel trigger, and instantly the quiet of the street echoed ponderously to the clang of the alarm.

It was a City policeman who relieved them. In his hurry the thief had left the outer doors of the bank wide open. The policeman reported that a car had passed him just as he turned the corner of Lothbury. By the time John left the building, the street was filled with uniformed men, and a few minutes later the chief of the division came.

"Cardlin? No, I don't know any such name in our force," he said. "What did he look like?"

John described the bearded man, and again the police chief shook his head.

"There isn't such a man, not in this division at any rate, and if he were a sergeant I should know him."

Half an hour later two very depressed police officers drove along the Embankment.

"The laugh is on us," said Elk gloomily. "At the same time, it would all have happened if we hadn't turned up. He didn't expect me, but he was pretty quick on the uptake. I'd give a month's salary—almost anybody's salary—to lay my right hand, or even my left, on Mr. Whiskers."

John said nothing; to him that adventure spelt neither ridicule nor waste of time. For the bearded man had unconsciously offered him the one clue that he needed.

Their first call was at Mr. Bruder's flat, and he was waiting up for them. Though he was concerned to learn that the contents of the deed-box had been stolen, he did not seem to regard the loss very seriously.

"My recollection is that there was nothing of any value, from a lawyer's point of view, though I dare say there is much of sentimental interest——"

"What was in the box?"

"Birth and marriage certificates, a number of letters written by Lady Pattison's young son, a few photographs, mainly of the child Delia." He hesitated and thought. "A statement made by the servant Anna, concerning the—um—conflagration. There was nothing more. Lady Pattison was most anxious that these things should be kept separate from her other papers. That is why I put them in the bank, though it hardly seemed worth while."

"Who knew they were at the bank?" asked John.

"Nobody," replied the other promptly. "I did not even tell Lord Siniford——"

"Yes, you did," said John quietly. "You were telling me when he was in the room last night. You remember he came in, looking like a wet ghost, and bolted out again?"

"They knew before then," said Elk. "Didn't the young lady hear about Lothbury and the engraver's shop days, perhaps weeks, ago? It might have been the first time Siniford knew, but if what you tell me is right, he was more upset by the idea of your seeing the papers than knowing where they were."

From the lawyer's flat John put through a call to his lordship, but there was no reply. He called up the hall porter, who had a separate number.

"His lordship came in and went out again," said the man.

"Did he come in alone?" asked Wade.

The man did not reply, and John repeated the question.

"No, sir, he came in with a small gentleman—I don't know his name. They went out together."

John called alone at the flat in St. James's Street, but the hall porter could give few further details.

"Was the little man white or Chinese?"

"White, sir. Rather a common-looking man—he came here once before. His lordship had run out of whisky and I took him up a fresh bottle. I think the little gentleman must have had something to do with the sea; he was saying how cold the river was that night. I've got a pass key to all the flats, and I happened to go in as he was saying this. I suppose that's no use to you, Mr. Wade?"

"Just that, eh?" said John, interested. "The river was cold."

"Well, not exactly in those words. What he said was: 'I've never known the river feel so cold'—and then I came in and he stopped."

John nodded. So Golly was the visitor! And he had been to the flat before. That was a link in the chain.

Weary as he was, he had to return to Wapping to formulate his charge against Mrs. Oaks. He found that lady in her most conciliatory mood.

"I don't know why you should persecute me, Mr. Wade," she said. "I've always been polite to you, and I certainly have done you no harm. The charge is ridiculous—administering drugs! And as for Lila, I haven't seen her since yesterday. That girl's more trouble than she's worth—I wish somebody would take her off my hands."

She was looking steadily at John as she spoke.

"She's not a bad-looking girl, and there's a bit of money goes with her. My poor, dear sister left nearly a thousand pounds. She's very young, but she'd make some man a good wife——"

"Me, for example?" said John brusquely. "Is that the bait you're holding out? Well, I don't rise to it. And as for your poor dear sister, if you ever had one, I'm quite sure she was neither poor nor dear—that story doesn't wash. Lila Smith is Lila Pattison."

He saw her blink at this and the colour come and go from her face.

"I—I don't know what you mean, Mr. Wade," she stammered. "It's all a mystery to me."

John nodded to the sergeant and briefly stated the charge.

"You'll give me bail, won't you, Mr. Wade?" She was almost tearful. "You wouldn't keep a woman of my age and respectable character in a dirty police cell all night?"

"The cells at this station are both clean and healthy," said John coldly. "And besides, Mrs. Oaks, who would bail you?" And then, suddenly: "Yes, my good friend I'll accept your husband's bail if he'll put in an appearance. You had better send for him."

She was taken aback at this.

"I don't know where Golly is—you know that. I haven't seen

142

him——"

"You spend your life not seeing people," said John wearily. "You ought to have met him to-night. I found him in your wood cellar. The last view I had of him he was swimming towards London Bridge. I hope he doesn't suffer from rheumatism."

Her face was set; the old mask he knew so well. She shot one venomous look, opened her lips as if to speak, then changing her mind, turned on her heel and followed the matron down the passage that led to the cells.

Wade returned home that night dead beat and was asleep before he knew he was in bed. He woke after five hours of sleep to find the lank form of Inspector Elk by his bedside.

"No, I never sleep," said that imperturbable man. "It's a great waste of time."

"What do you want now?" grumbled John, as he sat up, yawned and stretched. "I suppose you've brought a first-class kick from the Yard?"

Elk sat on the bed, and deliberately lit the stub of cigar before he replied.

"No, that will come in due course. I thought you'd like to know that your river coppers took the body of a man from the water at daybreak—found him floating close to the Middlesex shore."

John stared at him.

"Who was it?" he asked.

Elk blew a cloud of smoke to the ceiling.

"The late Lord Siniford," he said.

John gasped.

"Siniford—dead! Drowned?"

Elk shook his head.

"Knifed," he said. "A very neat job. The doctor says he never knew what killed him."

CHAPTER XVII

The contents of the pockets of the dead man lay neatly arrayed on a plain deal table at the police station. A gold cigarette case, a watch and guard, a tiny gold box containing a powder in a state of solution, which was to be chemically analysed, but which John Wade knew was cocaine; a small silver knife, a platinum ring, keys, and a packet of patent medicine universally known as a specific against sea-sickness, comprised the property. There was no pocket-book, no paper money, no document by which the body might have been identified, although it was fairly certain, as Elk pointed out, that the keys and the cigarette case would have been sufficient to establish an identity.

The fatal wound was hardly visible, as John had seen when he examined the body. Siniford had been stabbed in the neck from behind. The blow, skilfully delivered, had severed the vertebrae and death had been instantaneous.

"I've seen one or two murders like that," said Elk. "Original fellows, these Chinese. What do you make of these?" He waved his hand to the table.

"Nothing, except that he was a bad sailor and that he was going to sea. The murder took place between midnight and six o'clock when he was found: therefore it occurred somewhere in the region of Westminster."

He took down from a peg the heavy-looking waistcoat the dead man had worn.

"This is proof that he expected to go to sea. It is padded with fibre, and is the sort of thing worn by nervous passengers; it would act as a lifebelt. They didn't realise he'd float. The watch stopped at 1.17, five minutes before the tide began to ebb. That means the murder occurred six hours from Greenwich. The tide had turned just as the body was found."

Elk beamed.

"Reg'lar little Shylock Holmes you're becoming, Johnny. What's this?" He picked up the ring from the table and looked at it curiously. "Bit small for his finger, wasn't it?"

"It was in his waistcoat pocket," said John quietly. "It was never intended for his finger—it is a wedding ring."

Elk whistled.

"He was going to be married, eh?"

He put the ring down on the table, and then he caught a glimpse of Wade's haggard face.

"You're getting rattled, Johnny," he said kindly, and dropped a huge paw on the other's shoulder.

Wade nodded.

"I'm rattled terribly," he said. "All my ideas and pet theories are knocked sideways. I thought the scheme was to marry Lila to this fellow, and I've been counting on this to be a respite for her. It lessened the danger, but now——" He made a despairing gesture.

Elk left him soon after, and had only been gone an hour when he telephoned through asking Wade to come to Scotland Yard. Weary of mind and body, sick at heart, Wade obeyed the summons.

Elk was in the superintendent's room in consultation, and the burly chief was studying a radio message, when John came in. He pushed the paper across the table.

"Here's the end of the *Seal of Troy*," he said. "Acting on instructions from the Admiralty, one of our cruisers picked her up as she was nearing the Brazilian coast—here's the report."

It was a long message covering four sheets of paper.

Acting on your XF.43/C/9A1/95142, I intercepted "Seal of Troy" latitude X. longitude X. and made search. Ship carries cargo agricultural machinery and motor-cars. Manifests in order. Master Silvini, Chief Officer Thomas Treat of Sunderland. Neither Captain Aikness nor Chief Officer Raggit Lane on ship. In cabins 75, 76 and 79 on fourth deck below water line I found three men, two English and one American, who stated they had been detained on the ship six years and were employed in the melting down of the settings of stolen jewellery. Each man made an independent statement to the effect that the ship was mainly utilised for the reception of stolen property. In the cabin behind the panelling I found a small strong-room which was opened by artificers and found to contain 1,250 carats cut diamonds, 750 carats emeralds, many of a considerable size, 17 small ingots of platinum, 55 ingots of fine gold. The ship has three refrigerating chambers, one of which was found to contain a number of negotiable bonds to the value of £83,000, and as far as can be ascertained £184,000 in bullion and currency notes. One of the jewellers stated that these represented the proceeds of six robberies, including a bank robbery. Am proceeding. . . .

The two lines after this were in code and unintelligible. Then the message went on:

145

Statements from the men have been taken and will be verified before magistrates and forwarded you. "Seal of Troy" proceeding in charge of her own officers.

Here the message ended.

"This will be sad news for Captain Aikness, not to say Mr. Raggit Lane," said Elk.

John shook his head.

"Not so sad as you imagine. My own opinion is that Aikness knew the game was up and allowed the ship to go to sea, expecting it would be held up. The loss will not hurt him very much. Somewhere in South America he has a pretty large sum cached. This won't hurt him—always providing he can follow up, which he won't."

Elk looked a little dubious.

"Aikness? Humph! What is Golly doing in that galley? Poor little devil—he's roped in with the rest of the crowd. I rather like Golly—even though he did buy pansies! But he's an instrument."

"A double-edged one, I think," said John.

He had an appointment at the police court and found an unusually large number of Mrs. Oaks's friends and members of the neighbourhood. There wasn't a river rat from Tilbury to Barking Creek who did not know Mum Oaks or had not partaken of her furtive hospitality.

The grey rats and the black rats and the Rotherhithe crowd and the Wapping lot—they knew that tumbledown old wharf, where in the darkness of the night they had conducted many hurried and profitable bargains. That chamber behind the wood cellar had once held twenty thousand pounds' worth of silk that had vanished between sunset and daybreak from a foreign steamer lying at anchor in the Pool. The captain had had his cut, and the purser, but the biggest cut of all came to Mum Oaks.

The crowd of loungers that stood with their hands thrust in their pockets, lit cigarettes drooping from their mouths, scowled at John Wade as he passed, or gave him a sycophantic greeting. He saw Sniffy there, and the sight of those unprepossessing features reminded him.

"Didn't I take you the other night, Sniffy?"

"Yes, sir, but there was no charge owing to the goods," smirked the river thief.

"What were you doing at Mum Oaks's? Putting a little money in soak?"

Sniffy was amused.

"I went there on purely a personal and private visit," he said unctuously. "A gentleman calling on a lady—is there anything wrong

146

about that?"

"When you're the gentleman, yes," smiled John. "I haven't had you through my hands for a long time, sweetheart."

Sniffy beamed.

"That's more like yourself, Mr. Wade. And you won't have me through your hands either: I've dropped all that low hooking. I've had the offer of a regular job. A man like me, who knows the river backwards—I'll bet there ain't another man in this room that's followed the river to Gloucester—oughtn't to loaf round this dog-hole."

It was perfectly true that Sniffy was one of the few Cockney rivermen who knew the stream in its more pleasant moods: the long, silvery reaches that wound between the wooded hills, the old mill-streams, the green-grey locks, the tiny hamlets that cluster round the banks of the river where it narrows.

"I've jumped across the Thames," said Sniffy complacently. "I'll bet there's few people who can say that—jumped from one bank to another. I know the river better than any pilot; I know the landlord of every pub from here to Oxford."

He stopped suddenly, and John was conscious of a mighty inhibition. It wasn't that he wanted to change the subject: he was talking too much, as the detective realised.

"What are you going to do with Mrs. Oaks—that's persecution, if you like. A more innocent woman never drew the breath of life. There's a lady!"

John was moving on when the man caught his sleeve.

"You'll find a pretty tough lot round here to-day, Mr. Wade," he said in a low voice. "I shouldn't wander about alone if I was you."

"All friends of Mrs. Oaks, eh, Sniffy?" said John, and passed on.

The warning was not necessary, though Wade saw it was well justified. There were strange faces here, men who did not belong to his "manor"; gaunt, brute men who stared at him with expressionless eyes as he passed, and glanced quickly at one another but uttered no word.

He saw Mrs. Oaks in the small waiting-room adjoining the corridor. She had evidently slept very little, but she was calm and practical. She asked if he had been to the Home, and, when he said he had not, relapsed into silence. And then:

"I hope you're going to settle this business to-day, Mr. Wade. I don't see how you can bring any charge against me, much less prove it. I've got the best lawyers that money can buy, and if they don't tie you in knots I'll be surprised. I don't want to make you look foolish in court, Mr. Wade—if you'll withdraw the charge, I will say no more about it and I'll bear no malice."

He shook his head.

"The case has gone forward to the Public Prosecutor and I shall ask for a remand," he said, and saw two unruly spots come into her cheeks and her eyes blazed again.

"All right, you'll see what I can do! I've got some friends, you know, Mr. Wade. Lord Siniford will—"

"Lord Siniford is dead."

John Wade spoke coldly and deliberately, watching the woman. She went scarlet, and then the colour faded, leaving her face peaked and grey.

"Dead?" she whispered.

He nodded.

"When—when did he die?"

"He was murdered last night," said John. "His body was found in the river."

She was standing stiffly before him as she asked the question. He saw her knees bend, and as she swayed forward, he caught her and sat her in a chair. She had not fainted; those round eyes of hers were glaring dreadfully. Her voice was a croak.

"They killed him—the lord was going to marry her—why did he let him do it?"

The answer came from John's lips as an inspiration. He had never before thought of that solution.

"Because he wants to marry her himself," he said, and she raised her hand as though to ward off a blow.

"No, no!" she wailed. "He couldn't do that—he wouldn't do that. My God, he wouldn't do that!"

The detective laid his hand on her shoulder and patted it lightly.

"Mrs. Oaks, you're not so much a driving force as a cog in the machine," he said. "I'm going to drop all pretence with you—why don't you talk? Take your chance as a King's witness. Aikness means money to you, and we know all about the *Seal of Troy*, all about Lila Smith."

She was silent.

"I'm not trying to bluff you. I only say I'd like to help you. I've only just understood how unimportant a help you might be."

She raised her eyes to his, and he was startled at the mute agony he read in them.

"I don't know—I don't mind the remand—and I shan't want bail. Perhaps I'll see you to-morrow or the next day."

She came into court, a drooping, listless figure. Her solicitor, with whom she had a short interview, communicated her decision to the eminent counsel who had been briefed overnight to represent her, and when she did not ask for bail, there was only one person in the court who knew why she preferred Holloway Prison, and that one person was not John Wade.

"That's the dame," said one of the strange-looking men who had appeared in the neighbourhood that day. "Looks kind of nutty to me."

His companion chewed on something and offered no comment.

"Say—ain't these courts a laugh? They don't call um judges—magistrates. What's the difference, anyway? And everybody so darned Ritzy—'Yes, y'r worship,' an' 'No, y'r worship' . . ."

The second man chewed on and said nothing. Once he thought they were being followed, and made sure that the gun on his hip was drawable, but apparently he was mistaken. After a while he broke his silence.

"Yuh—that's the dame. Say, do you think it's O.K., Jakey? Listen, I've never pulled one like 'at."

They discussed the ethics of their task more fully when they reached their lodging.

CHAPTER XVIII

The secret of the *Seal of Troy* was a secret no more. Somebody on the ship had wirelessed a protest to the Government of Brazil. The British Government promptly issued a statement to the afternoon papers, and side by side with the tragedy of Lord Siniford, and an inaccurate account of a raid on a City bank, appeared the story of this romantic treasure-ship and a list of the depredations of the India-Rubber Men.

Later came an account of the police court proceedings, and the fact that the portrait of Golly Oaks appeared in all the newspapers as one of the wanted men, had its piquancy in the arrest of his wife, on a charge which seemed to have no connection with the more sensational story, for nobody knew about Lila Smith, and her name did not so much as appear in print.

It was a day of conferences, and John Wade had to appear before the dread Big Four, who are not ready to accept excuses or to forgive errors. They took what he thought to be a charitable view of the bank episode.

"They're clever, those fellows," said the superintendent. "They'd evidently tried the safe and knew they couldn't open it—it was a stroke of genius to send for the bank manager, and of course your being there and his knowing you was a bit of luck. One of the City police had seen Cardlin, as he called himself—not a bad name that—and he produced a Scotland Yard card! No, we're not blaming you, inspector, but we want Aikness and Oaks very badly."

"I knew Oaks very well twenty years ago," said one of the four. "He used to be the cleverest fence in the East End of London and must have made a fortune. A clever little devil—he speaks five or six languages."

John stared at him in amazement.

"Oaks?" he said incredulously. "I've always regarded him as illiterate."

"Not he," said the other. "He's only got one weakness; he thought he had a voice, and spent hundreds, probably thousands, of pounds in having it trained. Oh, yes, he's a Cockney all right, ungrammatical, drops his h's, but they tell me he speaks French and German like an educated man."

This was a new aspect of Golly, a novel presentation which so impressed John Wade that he made a call that afternoon at the "Mecca." He knew Golly's room, and had once made a superficial survey of it. It occurred to him that it might pay to make a closer inspection.

It was a large room immediately over the coal cellar, and rather dark, for it only had one small window to admit light and air. A small iron bed and a large book-case, filled with paper-jacketed volumes, an old standard lamp and a well-worn sofa, were the principal furniture. John noticed that in no case was the title of a book visible. They had been enclosed in carefully cut jackets, and either the man knew their positions by heart or he must have spent exasperating minutes searching for the volume he required. The little library was, he found, methodically arranged. The first of the volumes was a New Testament in Greek, and this discovery was his first shock. There were half a dozen volumes dealing with strategical practice in war, and these had evidently been read and re-read, for in the margins were innumerable pencil notes, mainly indecipherable, or else referring to some other page where similar or divergent views had been expressed.

Quite a number of the books dealt with the theory of music. There was a thick volume on singing, and the rest of the library was made up of travel and philosophical works in German, Spanish, French and Italian. Cæsar's Commentaries in Latin were there, and a Magyar primer that had been well used. The tiny desk in the corner was spotted with ink, as was the floor round about it. Evidently Golly was an untidy writer, but wrote often.

Searching the drawers of the desk, John made another discovery. The astonishing Golly was a dabbler in the occult: there were astrological charts, half finished horoscopes, and he was not uninterested to discover his own name at the head of one of these.

Evidently Golly was without the necessary accurate information to complete this chart of life, and John now remembered an occasion when the little man had been tremendously interested in the date and hour of his birth. A curious and surprising person.

There was no evidence as to his financial position; no bank pass-book, nothing to indicate the extent of his possessions. If he had been a rich man twenty years before——

John shook his head. Golly was the greatest puzzle of all. He pulled up the carpet, and went carefully over the floor space, tried the walls, but could find no secret place.

He had made one find which was destined to lead him far along the road of understanding. It was a small book, gilt-edged and platitudinous, that bore on the flyleaf: "Presented to G. H. Oaks by his employer, William Deans. 'Well done, thou good and faithful servant.' "

John could have laughed at this if he had been in a laughing mood. The book was one very popular in the eighties—"Christie's Old Organ"—and the character of Deans's business was unexpectedly revealed, for between two of the pages, used as a bookmarker, was an ancient billhead, "Deans & Abbit, Surgical Instrument Makers," whilst along the bottom was a printed advertisement line: "Deans' Patent Rubber Gloves, for all surgical work." Was there an association between rubber gloves and rubber masks?

The remainder of the day was restless and unhappy. The police of four counties were conducting a diligent, painstaking search, but no news of Lila Smith had reached head-quarters. That evening he paid a visit to Mrs. Oaks in Holloway Prison; she was morose and uncommunicative, and the talk ended in a storm of abuse, the woman flying into a fury which cut short the interview.

He himself stood in greater danger than he had at first realised. He was constantly meeting, in the course of the next few days, the strangers he had seen outside the police court when Mrs. Oaks was charged. He had an extraordinary memory for faces and knew he was not mistaken. They appeared in the neighbourhood of his cottage; he met them on his way to duty; once, when he was engaged in a special patrol of the river, he passed three of them in a boat, two rowing and one sitting in the stern, steering. They did not so much as look at the police launch as it passed, which in itself was a suspicious circumstance. He met them again the same afternoon; they were coming up-river as he was going down, and they obviously altered their course to pass him at short range. Fortunately there was another police boat on the other side of the river, and this he signalled to close with the suspicious craft. No sooner did the rowers see the manœuvre than one of them stopped, and, picking up something from the floor of the boat, dropped it into the water. A minute later, John's launch was alongside.

"What did you throw overboard just now?" he demanded.

The stroke of the boat rested on his oars and stared at him insolently.

"Ground-bait," he said. "We're fishing. Is that against the law?"

"Fishing with Mills bombs is forbidden," said John, "and if they weren't Mills bombs you dropped over the side, I've never seen one."

He took the boat in tow to the nearest river station. The three were unprepared for this, and were, moreover, embarrassed by the fact that the second police boat had come alongside. As they landed, one of the men surreptitiously dropped something, as he thought, into the river. It fell on the landing-stage and a policeman picked it up—a Browning pistol with one cartridge still in the chamber and nine in the magazine.

"Have you a licence for that?" asked John.

"Sure—a dog's licence!" grinned the man.

He was a peaky-faced, undersized individual, who looked like an Italian, but was, he claimed, an American citizen. His passport was in order—he had been in the country three weeks. His domicile was the city of Chicago. The two other men were also from the United States, and the indications on their passports showed that they had arrived in the same ship on the same day. One of them, the steersman, also carried a pistol.

"No Sullivan Act here, is there?" he asked as they took the gun from him.

"We'll tell you all about it," said John.

Who had brought these men into the country? Their antecedents he could guess. They all had foreign-sounding names, and Scotland Yard sent an urgent cable of inquiry to Chicago; two hours later a reply was received:

Three men well known gunmen here. Riccini and Orlvitch twice convicted murder. Our information is large number of bad men gone London last two months

"There's a whole lot of coincidences floating round," said Elk, after the cable had been read. "We've had messages up from three tough districts of London that the local police have spotted a number of foreigners—Russians and Finns mainly; they've all arrived in the last few weeks. We pulled in a couple the other day, and what the Riga police said about those fellers is nobody's business!"

"Is anything known about Golly Oaks? I mean, has he any earlier history?" asked John, and the other nodded.

"He had a conviction in '15 for stealing from his employers—sheet rubber." His eyebrows went up. "Sheet rubber?" frowned Elk. "That's funny."

"The servant didn't remain good or faithful," said John grimly. "Anything else?"

"There was a charge of receiving, which was not proved. He ran a boy gang in Wapping when he was a kid—they used to fight the Brick Lane gang—but he never came into our hands over that. Then he went to Birmingham and organised a gold-stealing business. Birmingham's full of jewellers, and gold-stealing used to be pretty easy. You just substituted an alloy for the amount of gold you pinched, and it's surprising how easy it is to get away with three or four pounds of gold and not even the testing office know the difference."

John tried to recall his earlier impressions of Golly Oaks. They were difficult to recover. He had certainly regarded this man as a petty thief and receiver, and he knew that Golly was respected by some of the worst characters on the river—and good men are never wholeheartedly respected by bad men, whatever the story-books tell you.

A meek man, who submitted to the nagging of his wife without protest—it was difficult to believe that he ever organised as much as a gang of rabbits.

"Has he had any convictions?"

"None," said Elk. And then thoughtfully: "It's funny how old Golly settled down to be a respectable citizen and chop wood. I used to think it was Mum Oaks who tamed him, but maybe he never was tamed."

"That's my bet, too," said John. "I'm beginning to get new ideas about Golly."

CHAPTER XIX

Lila Smith was getting new ideas, too. She had been alone in the luxurious little cabin where she had been taken after she had been hurried from the Tappitt home. What kind of ship it was she did not know, for she had suffered the indignity of being blindfolded soon after Mum Oaks was landed at the Mecca wharf. She was not afraid; her first emotions were of intense curiosity. Fear never really came until the night of the fire.

It was not like any ship's cabin that she had ever seen; it was broad, low-roofed, and, though it was beautifully furnished, the walls panelled with polished grey ash and the fittings of silver, there was no porthole, no outlook upon the world. Somewhere near the cabin she could hear the hum of a little engine which served to ventilate and light her quarters. There was a beautiful bunk bed, a writing table, and on the walls pictures, some of which, she guessed, were veritable old masters. A broad, low fire-place with an electric fire gave warmth in the chilly evenings.

The only person she saw was the Chinese servant who brought her meals and put her bath ready. Nobody had ever troubled before to fill Lila's bath, and this experience of service was rather exciting; and the little room, with its shallow marble tub and its tiled walls, though somewhat restricted and innocent of any but artificial light, added to her sense of comfort.

The ship was moving slowly most of the time. She could hear feet pattering on the deck above, and several times at intervals she heard a peculiar rumbling like thunder somewhere overhead. The ship was still in the river; she could hear the sirens blowing, and had heard a church clock strike ten.

She heard other things, and awoke in a fright with a woman's scream ringing in her ears. It must have been fancy—or she was dreaming, she decided. For the rest of the night, her first on board, and despite her anxiety, she slept like a log, and woke to find the Chinese servant arranging a small wicker-work table by her bedside. It was odd and a little alarming to be waited on by a man, but she got used to his presence. He spoke little English, smiled easily, and anticipated most of her wishes.

She could lock the outer cabin door, and that was a comfort. On the other hand, it was bolted on the outside, and she had no opportunity of exploring this ship or of discovering in what company she was. She quite thought Mrs. Oaks was on board, since it had been Mum who brought her from her safe asylum. She was even more sure that John Wade would be looking for her—she preserved a faith in the police that amounted to fanaticism.

The coming of Golly was an event. She liked the little man; suspected he was associated with all kinds of rascality, but looked upon him as a rather blunt instrument. She was sitting at breakfast when the door opened and he came in, an amused little smile upon his uncomely face. He usually wore hats which were slightly small for him or caps that covered his ears. He wore a high-crowned derby now, and it had the appearance of an ill-fitting crown. His gold-rimmed glasses, the little ginger moustache, the very vulgarity of his shabby clothes, made him an incongruous figure in this elegant setting.

"Why—Mr. Oaks!" she said, rising from her chair.

"Sit down, my dear. I'll have a cup of tea if you've got one to spare."

It was only then she noticed that two cups were on the tray. He took off his hat and put it on the floor, rubbed a handkerchief over his thin hair.

"What a life this is, eh! As the well-known Socrates says——"

He said something that sounded gibberish to her. Never did she imagine he was spouting authentic Greek. He could read many languages and speak them fluently, yet his quotations were the well-worn tags that are familiar to most schoolboys and adorn the back pages of the cheapest dictionaries. Of these he had an inexhaustible store, for his memory was amazing.

"Comfortable, Lila?"

She hesitated.

"Yes, I'm comfortable, but where are we going, Mr. Oaks?"

He looked over his shoulder towards the door, and lowered his voice.

"Lord knows," he said. "Nobody knows where anybody's going any day. I thought I'd be at the 'Mecca'—dis aliter visum!"

She was staggered at this.

"Is Mrs. Oaks on board?"

He shook his head.

"She couldn't come," he said. "She's got a lot of business to attend to—what a woman, Lila!" His little blue eyes were watching her. "What a lady, what a tartar! What a helpmate for a man!"

Again he said something in a language she did not understand, though she did not dream it was a language understood by anybody but Golly. She remembered now: he was in the habit of saying these incomprehensible things.

"You'll be all right, Lila." He leaned over and patted her hand. "Don't you worry; nothing's coming to you but luxury and 'appiness. Jools, di'monds, carriages and Rolls-Royces—everything the 'eart can desire."

She gazed at him in astonishment.

"When, Mr. Oaks?"

He tapped the side of his nose cunningly.

"In good time, my dear."

He looked round the cabin with a certain air of pride which was surprising to her. She thought he might feel a little uncomfortable in these gorgeous surroundings, but his air was almost proprietorial.

"That's a Tintoretto," he pointed, "in what I call his second style. He must have been getting a bit long in the tooth when he painted that. A lot of these so-called Tintorettos are pupils' work. That black-and-white thing over there behind the pianner was drawn by Sansovino; that other picture is Bellini—not much of a one, but he wasn't what I call in the front rank. Personally, I'm all for the Venetian school. You can have your Florentine."

She listened open-mouthed. This little man, whom she had regarded as something of a family butt, who had, so far as she was aware, no interests outside his daily newspaper, his pipe and his interminable wood-chopping, was laying down critical laws with the assurance of a Chelsea student.

"Benvenuto, he was the man for my money. Ever read his book? Laugh! I've split me sides over that book. But not a painter—statues! Ever seen the Medusa? I went to Florence once and had a look at the model.... And there's a couple of salt-cellars he made for the King of What's-his-name—France, was it?—and a dish arrangement in the Loove."

He looked at the pictures again and smacked his lips.

"There's nothing better than them in England," he said.

"Why, Mr. Oaks, I didn't know you were such an authority upon art," she said, smiling.

He smiled complacently.

"I know a bit; but music's always been my 'obby. Ever heard Tetrazzini and a canary singing together? I have! I don't suppose anybody else ever heard it. I'm supposed to have a voice like Caruso's."

He made this outstanding claim without a smile, and instinct told

157

her that if she supplied the missing hilarity she might be making a terrible mistake.

"I—I've never heard you sing, Mr. Oaks——" she began.

"Uncle Golly," he corrected. "What's all this 'Mr. Oaks' about? Yes, you have heard me sing." He looked at her wistfully. "Haven't you?"

She shook her head. She was lying: she had heard him sing many times, and had closed the windows to shut out the dreadful sound.

"What about the aria from 'Faust'?"

She shook her head again, not daring to speak. To her amazement, he walked across to the little piano, sat down and began to play. Was she dreaming? He was playing like a master. And then he began to sing.

He had the most extraordinary falsetto voice she had ever heard. Hitherto, distance had robbed it of its terrors; but now, close at hand, in this confined room, the howl and squeak of it were almost insupportable. He sang in Italian, swaying to and fro on the piano seat, his head thrown back, his eyes closed ecstatically. His voice went from shrill to harsh; the din of it was overpowering. If she had only the courage to put her hands over her ears! But she lacked this, or else that inner instinct of hers warned her against adopting this means of protection. After an eternity, as it seemed, he stopped, and beamed round on her.

"Well?"

"Marvellous," she gasped. "I—I didn't know—you could sing."

To her intense relief he closed down the cover of the piano and came towards her, his hands in his pockets, his chest thrown out, curiously sparrow-like.

"Few people do," he said—"very few people."

Was he mad, or did he really believe that this fearful caterwauling bore the remotest relationship to singing? He answered that question instantly, as though she had put her thoughts into words.

"I don't sing in the modern style, I admit that. People who've got no taste or judgment don't like me as much as they like some of the singers, but in ten years' time my voice will be the kind that will be all the go."

She hastened to change the subject by asking him the name of the ship.

"The *Rikitiki*," he answered promptly. "She was an Indian ship. The captain bought her for a song—one of the fastest boats in the world."

"Where are we now, Mr. Oaks?"

"Uncle Golly," he admonished her reproachfully. "Where are

we now?" He looked at his watch with great deliberation. "Off Gravesend, or maybe not so far down. We're waiting for the pilot."

For the first time her nerve began to fail her.

"Pilot? What, are we going to sea?" she asked in alarm. "Where are we going, Mr. Oaks—Uncle Golly?"

He shook his head.

"Nobody quite knows."

"Why am I being kept here?"

"For your own good, my dear."

He sat down and drank his tea in large, noisy gulps.

"For your own good. There are all sorts of people after you. That man Wade"—he shook his head solemnly. "What a rascal! What a villain unhung! One of the trickiest men in Wapping. Lives on graft—the India-Rubber Men have paid him thousands."

She could not believe her ears, but Mr. Oaks was very serious. He was almost convincing, too.

"I'm telling you," he said solemnly. "I wouldn't be surprised if he isn't one of the India-Rubber Men himself—the police are in all these swindles. Haven't you read the papers lately?"

"But Mr. Wade couldn't do a thing like that," she said indignantly.

"Oh, couldn't he?" demanded Golly with a sarcastic smile. "You never know what a fellow like that will do. What's his pay—a beggarly five pounds a week. Do you think he can live on that? No, my dear, he gets lashings of money from people who've got to keep him sweet—gambling-house keepers, and places you'd never dream existed. He was after your money."

"My money?"

He *was* mad, then.

Mr. Oaks recovered himself with a chuckle.

"That's what I call a figure of speech. He wants somebody who'll be a sort of servant to him—bake and iron and wash and keep his house for him—for nothing. A beggarly fellow like that naturally would want a cheap kind of wife. He couldn't afford——"

"But you said he made thousands by dishonesty," said the girl.

Mr. Golly Oaks coughed. He had fallen into error again.

"In a manner of speaking," he said vaguely, and, wiping his mouth on a not too clean handkerchief, he got up. "Plenty of books here—books that will amuse you. Pity you can't read foreign languages; that's where all the literature is."

He indicated a very well-stocked bookshelf, at which the girl had not yet looked.

"Look after yourself. I'll send the captain to see you."

"The captain? You mean Mr.——"

"Aikness his name is," interrupted Golly. "Never mind what you called him before. The gentleman that used to take you out to supper."

He was examining her through narrowed lids.

"Nice feller, isn't he? More like a father than anybody you've ever met, I'll bet. Fifty-eight—that's how old he is. If he tells you he's fifty-two he's telling a lie."

With this piece of information, he went out with a cheery wave of his hand.

CHAPTER XX

He left her with plenty of food for thought. The Mr. Oaks she knew had gone for ever; this was a new man, fantastical, unreal. And all that was left of the old Mr. Oaks served to emphasise how fantastical was the new. She was not really afraid; less afraid, now that she knew Golly was on board, than she had been in the first unpleasant hour. Somehow she preferred him to his wife; they had always been excellent friends, and Lila had been the receptacle of his troubles. And he played the piano like a master, and sang like——

She shuddered. The ship was very still, scarcely moving. She thought, earlier in the day, that something had bumped against its side—probably a tug, but it must have been a powerful tug, for the whole structure of the vessel quivered.

She went to bed early that night and woke at four to hear a curious sound—the lowing of a cow. Most ships carried cows, she remembered, for the service of the passengers. Then came another and a deeper sound—a second cow. And then she heard a cock crow, and a sweet bell sound the four quarters of the hour. Cows and chickens and village chimes did not accord with Mr. Oaks's statement that they were lying in midstream at the mouth of the Thames. The sound of the cow came from close at hand. And then distinctly she heard the creaking of a cart-wheel, but no sound of iron tyres.

She determined to ask Golly that day, when she saw him, whether she could go on deck. There was plenty of fresh air in the cabin, but she wanted to scent the sea breezes and to see the light of day.

Captain Aikness called just before lunch. He did not wear his seagoing uniform, but was plainly dressed in flannels and carried a soft felt hat. He was so tall that he had to stoop as he came into the cabin, and for the first time she regarded him with dispassionate interest. Fifty-eight was nearer his age than fifty-two, she guessed. His face was tanned brown, the backs of his huge hands were covered with fine black hair. A rather terrifying figure, and more out of place in that dainty cabin of hers than Golly had been.

"Well, my dear, getting tired?"

He patted her on the shoulder, and for some reason she shrank under his touch.

"We'll have you ashore in a day or two. I've got a car waiting to whisk you off to the West of England. But for a little while I think you'd better keep out of sight."

He asked her if Oaks had been to see her that morning, and when she said "No" he seemed relieved.

"Is Lord Siniford on board?" she asked, putting the question she had meant to ask Golly.

His face puckered up a little at this, as though it was a distasteful subject.

"No, he's not," he said shortly. "You can put that fellow out of your mind, Lila: he's not worthy of you or any other woman."

Here was relief for her, and a great relief. Ever since she had been on board she had expected at any moment the door to open and the fatuous face of his lordship to appear.

The attitude of Captain Aikness was strangely different from that she remembered on their occasional meetings. He had been, as it were, in command, and she had treated him with a certain awe-stricken veneration. He was almost a mythical figure to her. But now he was strangely nervous; he made several attempts to speak, cleared his throat, stammered out a meaningless sentence and relapsed again into silence. Suddenly he asked:

"How old would you think I am, Lila?"

"Fifty-eight," she said promptly, and evidently the reply did not please him.

"I'm fifty-two," he said sharply. "Oaks has been talking. He insists on that fifty-eight nonsense. I'm fifty-two on the third of July; a comparatively young man, with twenty years of vigorous life before me."

He said this loudly and defiantly. She wondered what was coming next and half guessed.

"If you ever get married, my dear, you choose a man much older than yourself, a man of the world who can look after you."

He walked to the door, opened it and looked out, then closed it again and came back to her.

"A man who could lift you out of danger and place you safe, as quick as that!" He snapped his fingers loudly.

He surveyed her for a long time without speaking, but with such a look of gloom on his face that she was almost terrified.

"There are quite a lot of people who want to pick up an easy million. Don't lose your head if somebody comes to you with a good proposition, but remember that I'm around, and if you wanted to get

162

off this packet I could do it like that!" He snapped his fingers again.

Then he went off at a tangent.

"When I came back on this last trip for you, I knew you weren't a child any more, and you sort of got me." He thumped his chest. "You understand? You meant something to me, and you mean more and more every day. I'd take a big risk for you, million or no million——"

"What do you mean by 'million,' Captain Aikness?"

He coughed, and was palpably embarrassed.

"I thought Golly had seen you and had had a chat with you. He didn't, eh?"

She smiled. He was so obviously ill at ease, and she felt so pleasantly the mistress of the situation. It was a novel sensation and amused her, even though behind the new deference of the man she saw unhinted dangers.

"You needn't tell Golly what I said. He's a good fellow, generous and all that sort of thing, but he's touchy about certain things."

Golly generous? The little man was becoming more and more unreal. What had he to be generous with? He was poor, would often wait for half an hour till Mum Oaks came back from her shopping to borrow a little money to take him to the "Rose and Crown."

"Have you known him long—Uncle Golly?"

The big man surveyed her with smouldering eyes.

"Yes, I've known him long—too long," he said slowly.

He picked up his hat from the settee where he had dropped it, and went to the door; he stood there for a long time as though debating something with himself, and then, apropos nothing:

"To-day or to-morrow it'll easy. After that I'm not sure—just tell me when you want to go, and not a word to Golly."

Before she could answer the door had closed behind him.

He climbed steeply up the companion-way and reached the deck, not of any seagoing ship but of a great barge, its red sails furled, its spurious house flag floating busily. She bore the unromantic name of *Betsy and Jane* and was moored to the side of a meadow which stretched away to a wooded ridge. Behind her was another barge, on which two men were laboriously lowering the mast. There was nobody in sight except aft, where a little man in a coloured striped jersey and a pair of stained dungaree trousers was sitting, reading a strip of paper. He wore a huge peaked cap on his head, and even an acquaintance might have failed to recognise, in this soiled bargee, Mr. Golly Oaks of the "Mecca." He looked up over his glasses as the captain approached.

"You look pretty, I must say." There was a sneer in his voice. "If anybody come along and see you they'd think this was a houseboat or a garden party. Been down to see Lila, I'll bet."

"I've been down to see Lila," said Aikness, who sat down on the top of a hatchway and slowly filled a pipe.

Golly shook his head slowly.

"A regular houseboat party, and a couple of busies likely to come along at any minute! It took you a week to grow whiskers, and you've shaved them off because you didn't want a nice young lady to think you were fifty-eight."

"I'm fifty-two," growled the other.

Golly's lips curled so that his ginger moustache tilted ludicrously.

"You're ten," he said. And then, in a different tone: "Get out, and slip into your old duds, will you? And then I'll tell you what's happened to the *Seal of Troy*: it's in the morning papers."

The man sprang up, his face a paler shade.

"Did they hold it up?"

Golly nodded.

"And found everything," he said cheerfully. "Gold and platinum and diamonds and God knows what! And they'll find you too, Bill Aikness. Go down and change."

The man turned and swung himself through a square hatchway.

"Anything else you want?" he growled.

"Yes," said Mr. Oaks. "Bring me up a bit of black crêpe: I want to tie it round me neck."

Captain Aikness stared at him in horrified amazement.

"You don't mean——" he asked hoarsely.

Golly nodded.

"Yes, I do. All things have got to come to an end, and this one ought to have ended a long time ago."

CHAPTER XXI

John Wade had asked for a three-days' remand, to give him an opportunity of communicating with the Treasury, and in that three days the Treasury had reached no decision; was, if anything, inclined to let the prosecution of Mum Oaks drop.

"The evidence is very sketchy," said an official of the Public Prosecutor's Department, "and I doubt if you'd get a committal. Take another four days' remand if you think you can get evidence. There's no proof that Mrs. Oaks gave a drug to the police-sergeant's wife; the only charge we could make would take the form of an accessory before the act."

"Give her another four days: I think she'll talk," pleaded John, and had his way in the end.

Mrs. Oaks had been brought up early in the morning from Holloway and was lodged in a police cell. It is customary on such occasions for the friends of an imprisoned person to contribute their meals, and that morning at half-past eight a waitress from a nearby coffee-house had arrived with a substantial breakfast for the woman, and it had been taken into her cell by the wardress. John Wade arrived a few minutes after this and was in the passage of the cells leading to the woman's division when the matron came flying past him. He heard her ask the desk sergeant for a doctor, and caught the woman's arm as she ran back past him.

"Anybody ill?"

"That woman in Number Nine—your case, Mr. Wade. I think she's fainted. I wouldn't have known, but she turned over the tea tray."

He hurried back after her. The cell door was open and the jailer was inside. He had just lifted the woman on to the hard wooden bench that served as a bed. Her face was grey, her lips colourless. Bending over, John could detect neither sound nor movement of breath. He felt her hands: they were deadly cold, and, try as he did, he could feel no pulse. While he was with her, the divisional surgeon, who had been at the station, came hurrying in. His examination was brief and his verdict definite.

"She's dead."

He sniffed, then, stooping over the dead woman, smelt again.

"If that's not hydrocyanic acid I'm a Dutchman! She has committed suicide!"

But a search of her dress and the cell floor did not bring to light anything in the shape of phial or bottle. Fortunately, while the tea tray had been overturned, the teapot and milk, the only liquids, had been put on the wooden bed.

"Keep those for analysis," said John.

He was shocked, could hardly believe the evidence of his eyes. Mrs. Oaks was a healthy woman, the last person in the world to commit suicide, and she had died because—for the same reason Siniford had died a few days earlier.

It was not difficult to trace the waitress. He went in search of her with the jailer and found her serving in the drab little eating-house that had supplied the breakfast. She had no information to give. In accordance with her instructions she had taken the tray to the police court cells, which were only fifty yards from the eating-house, and she had taken the tea haphazard from several filled pots, and the milk in the same way.

"Whom did you meet on the way?" asked John.

She could not remember meeting anybody at first, but after a while she recollected that she had met two men—"Foreigners" she thought—and one had asked her to direct him to the High Street. She had turned round and indicated, with a jerk of her head, the direction he should follow.

"It was pretty simple," reported John. "One man held her attention, the other dropped the stuff in the teapot or the milk. I should think it was the milk."

"Have you got a good description of the men?" asked Elk.

"The most she could tell me was that they were foreign-looking. This damned town seems to be filled with foreign-looking people! I'm getting one of the local constables to make a sketch of the two faces from the woman's description. There's no doubt whatever Mrs. Oaks was poisoned. They thought she was ready to squeal and they were right."

He was half dead from want of sleep and anxiety but threw himself into the task of discovering the two strangers who had been seen in the vicinity of the police court that morning. His luck was in: a milkman had seen the two and noticed that one of them wore a rubber heel which had come unfastened and projected beyond the edge of the boot heel. It was a slender clue, but within a quarter of an hour after the information came to John, twelve thousand policemen were

166

examining the boot heels that passed them, and at three o'clock that afternoon two men, strolling casually along the Brixton Road, suddenly found themselves surrounded by uniformed and plain-clothes policemen. They were hustled to the station and searched. Both were aliens. Wade drove down to Brixton to interview them.

"This is where half an hour of third degree would do me a lot of good, but they shall talk," he said between his teeth.

Elk made a noise in disparagement.

"You'll get your name in the papers, my boy, though personally I'm all for a little torture. It would give variety to the business and would be a wonderful cure for policemen's sore throat."

The two men gave French names, but were undoubtedly American, though they might have been French originally. When John addressed them in their native language they could answer but with difficulty.

"We been living in France since last fall," said one.

"Why did you leave the United States?" asked John.

They were very vague about this.

Of the poisoning they knew nothing; they were just innocent people in London for a week; they explained their possession of loaded pistols by their ignorance of the law. They had never been north of the river; they did not know Mrs. Oaks, nor had they heard of the India-Rubber Men. They had come to London for the purpose of buying old French furniture cheaply, but they could not tell John where there was to be a sale of old French furniture.

Two imperturbable, leather-faced, thin-lipped men; they showed no signs of perturbation until they were handcuffed together and taken into a taxicab en route to Scotland Yard. Then, and only then, the terror of the unknown descended upon them, and one of them protested volubly, but not in French.

In the meantime a squad of detectives had descended upon the address they gave, only to learn that they were unknown. But again fortune favoured the police. They had given as their address the lodging house where they intended staying when they reached London. The place, however, was full, and they had been directed elsewhere. Fortunately, the janitor of the lodging house remembered the three lodgings he had recommended and to one of these they were traced.

Between the bed and the mattress John found three little crystal flasks, one of which was empty, the other two being filled by a nearly colourless liquid with a slightly bluish tinge. In the false bottom of the trunk John unearthed a curiosity: a curious-shaped rifle with a short barrel and a peculiarly long grip—more like a pistol grip. It was an automatic rifle that had never been fired. The cartridges were still wrapped up in damp-proof paper.

"Now what do you say about the third degree?" he demanded savagely. "These fellers would spill everything."

Elk shook his head.

"It isn't done. But—suppose the chief lets you take these fellows down to Woolwich Police Station—by river. Don't let them know where they're going. Dig 'em out at two in the morning, tie 'em up hand and foot—and take 'em to Woolwich."

"What good would that do?" snarled John.

"Suggestion's everything," said Elk calmly. "I know everything about psychology except the way to spell it."

The closest questioning at Scotland Yard by the most adept cross-examiners brought no result. They maintained an expressionless silence, understood when it was policy to do so, misunderstood when they wished to gain time. They knew nothing of the pistols, nothing of the phials; they suggested, nay, stated positively, that this evidence had been manufactured and planted in the room. They both had, they said, excellent characters, a claim which was not endorsed over the telephone by the chief of the Paris Sûreté.

John interviewed the Chief Constable and put his plan before him. That excellent man demurred. It was he who got the kicks for all that had the appearance of an irregularity. Eventually he agreed—that the prisoners should be removed by boat to Woolwich.

At two o'clock in the morning, when the prisoners were sleeping, ignorant of what was going to happen, they were awakened by two men, whose collars were turned up, and had their soft hats pulled over their eyes so that they were unrecognisable. The prisoners dressed quickly, were handcuffed, and hurried through an empty charge-room into the blackness of the courtyard. The Embankment was a wilderness; they were rushed across the road to a floating pier, where a big police launch was waiting.

There were two men on board, but these also took some trouble to hide their faces, a fact which struck terror to the prisoners' souls. A minute later the large launch cast off and went rapidly downstream on a falling tide.

They were clear of London Bridge when Elk securely strapped together the legs of the two men.

"Say, what's the big idea?" asked one with chattering teeth. "You fellers takin' us a ride?"

"Shut up!" hissed Elk.

A quarter of an hour passed; the launch sped eastwards through the darkness. Not a word was spoken. No violence was offered to either men. Their very immunity drove them crazy with fear. Opposite Greenwich Hospital one broke forth into a torrent of information. They arrived at Woolwich in the early hours of the morning, and John Wade and his companion sat over a trembling man who made a statement that was eventually to send his partner and himself to a life sentence.

At the time when the earliest citizens of London were taking their morning breakfast, two haggard-faced detectives sat with the Chief Constable and went over the points of the confession.

"This doesn't tell us who is the man who employed them," said the Chief.

He shook his head.

"He was invited to come to this country, paid a large sum, with a generous weekly wage, which came to them by post, and he knew nothing more than that on a certain date he would receive a telegram giving him a rendezvous and a time when he was to come armed."

"He practically admits the murder of Mrs. Oaks," said John.

Again the police chief shook his head.

"He admits putting in the drug, but he swears that he thought it was a dope she was using to help her escape. They had nothing to do but to carry out instructions; if the flasks were supplied to them, it will be difficult to prove they knew the drug they were administering. One of them says that he had previously doped the police-sergeant's wife and he thought it was no worse than that. The only thing he knows about his employer is that he was tall and dark——"

"And handsome," murmured Elk, and was silenced by a glance from the cold blue eyes of the Chief Constable.

"They're starting something—something big. No news of that girl?"

"None, sir."

"Funny—you thought she was on a barge, being towed up river. The police have searched every barge and found nothing. That idea seems a little far-fetched, doesn't it."

John heaved a sigh.

"All ideas seem far-fetched," he said wearily. "How far has the search extended?"

"As far as Maidenhead. The Buckinghamshire and Berkshire police are looking after the river higher up. Why don't you have a try yourself, if you think you can recognise the two barges that were lying off the 'Mecca'? Have a sleep, leave the Mrs. Oaks case to the divisional inspector and take a launch down from Henley, or from Oxford, if you like, and see if you can recognise that old tub. You don't think that this girl has got an affair and has dodged off on her own?"

169

"No, sir," said John quietly. "I believe, now that Mrs. Oaks is dead, her danger has increased to a terrible extent."

The Chief looked at him oddly.

"All right," he said.

John was outside in the corridor on his way to the street when the superintendent came to his door and called him back.

"We've traced Raggit Lane—he's been seen in London, and if there's any organisation of gunmen being built up here, he's running it."

"You've found him, sir?" asked John quickly.

"When I said we'd traced him, I meant we'd traced his dirty past," replied the superintendent. "Seven convictions in various parts of the world—ask Records to let you have a look at it."

For the moment John was not interested in Raggit Lane, although there was more reason why he should be apprehensive of that exotic man than any member of the confederacy, for Lane and his men were trailing him day and night.

CHAPTER XXII

In the afternoon a report came through that Golly had been seen in the Notting Hill district. Scotland Yard might have pursued a perfunctory inquiry but for the fact that three times in one week a report had been received that a man answering to the description of Golly Oaks had been seen in a particular area. This time, however, it was supplemented by a note to the effect that a number of "foreigners" had also been seen.

Now it so happened that in Notting Hill lived one man who, though reputedly honest himself, was an authority upon the foreign underworld. Mr. Ricordini was a naturalised Italian, who derived a large income from loaning piano organs and ice-cream barrows to his less fortunate compatriots. To say that the breath of suspicion had never tarnished the brightness of his reputation would be untrue; but it was true that the police had never associated him with even a minor crime, unless it be a crime, major or minor, to charge usuriously for the apparatus he hired.

A fat little Italian, he enjoyed the confidence not only of the police but of lawbreakers, for it was known that he had never "squealed" on an Englishman and had confined his revelations to the misdeeds of the foreign colony; and although on one occasion an attempt had been made to knife him, the assailant was a Neapolitan who had a private grievance against him.

John Wade and Elk, drove down to interview him, and he received the detectives openly in his rather ornate parlour.

"Golly Oaks I know nothing about," he began, as they expected. Even if he had known it was against his code to have spoken. "But I can tell you there are quite a lot of queer-looking fellows been around here lately, usually after dark. They go about in pairs and look as if they're getting acquainted with the neighbourhood."

"Why this neighbourhood?" asked John.

"God knows," was the cheerful reply. "They're Americans mostly, but there's been a couple of Poles. I happen to know this because a friend of mine who peddles dope—not exactly a friend of mine, but, alas! a fellow-countryman—had a talk with them. He says they're typical gunners. My friend was in Chicago till they run him out. He says there's been half a dozen of 'em walking about this last night or two."

"Are they living here?"

Ricordini shook his head.

"No, sir, that's the funny thing. If they were living here, it wouldn't be curious they should be running around the neighbourhood."

Whilst they were interviewing the Italian, local detectives were scouring the neighbourhood to find two men who had seen Oaks on the previous night. They were waiting for John outside Ricordini's house, and the story they told was most explicit. They were both ex-criminals, if such things as an ex-criminal can be, and one at least had furnished information to the police before.

"There's no doubt it was Mr. Oaks, sir," he said positively. "I saw him walking along the pavement, outside the Arbroath Building."

"Where's the Arbroath Building?"

Elk, who knew the neighbourhood backwards, explained that it was a block of shops and flats, chiefly remarkable for its ugliness and the fact that the landlords held an extravagant view as to the value of its accommodation, and in consequence of this the flats had not been occupied, and the property was something of a derelict.

"I recognised him and turned back. I said: 'Hallo, Mr. Oaks!'"

"What did he say?" asked John.

"He didn't say anything; he pulled up his coat collar and walked on. I thought I'd made a mistake, but now I'm sure I didn't, because Jimmy here saw him about ten minutes later."

"I did too, mister," said the second man huskily. "It must have been him. He was turning the corner of the block when I lamped him—saw his glasses and everything. I know him very well; I used to work in Wapping when Oaks used to buy ships' timbers and sell 'em to the hawkers."

"Did you speak to him?"

"No, sir, I didn't speak to him. But it was Oaks all right. And a few nights ago old Sorbey saw him and told a cop—a policeman—and he saw him round by Arbroath Building too."

The C.I.D. of Notting Hill had nothing to add in the shape of information. They had combed the neighbourhood pretty thoroughly without tracing Golly.

"Perhaps he's staying at Arbroath Building."

"That's unlikely," said the divisional inspector, who had arrived during the interrogation. "The place is shut up, and I'm told it's in the hands of the court, though I'm not certain about this. If you like we'll go round and see the caretaker."

Arbroath Building proved to be almost as bad as its description; a squat mass of stucco-faced concrete, the ugliness of which the shadows of evening could not wholly hide, it stood a mournful monument to the rapacity of landlords. After much knocking on a wide gate which led to the garage forming part of the building, the caretaker came to the wicket.

He was an army pensioner, well known to the police of the neighbourhood as of the highest integrity.

"Nobody's been here," he said. "I wish somebody would! I've seen the lawyers this morning. They think they've got a purchaser. I'll be glad to get away to the seaside; I've got a holiday due."

John Wade gave a short but vivid description of Golly Oaks.

"That's funny," said the man when he had finished. "I've seen a fellow like that—saw him last night when I was standing at the wicket having a smoke. He had a long brown ulster and a cap. It looked too big for him. I said 'Good night' to him and he said 'Bon soir' sort of absent-mindedly, but he wasn't French, I'll swear."

"Did he wear glasses?"

The man nodded.

"Yes, and he was smoking a cigarette and sort of singing to himself—horrible voice it was, too."

"That sounds like Golly," frowned John. "What the devil is he doing in this neighbourhood?"

The two men went back to the Yard not much wiser than they had been before they left. Elk was very thoughtful during the journey.

"I don't like this inflow of foreign labour," he said. "Our own people we can deal with—ever heard of master criminals, Johnny?"

"In books, yes."

"That's where I've read about 'em," said Elk. "And yet I smell one here."

"Aikness or Golly?"

"Golly?" There was astonishment in Elk's voice.

"Golly," repeated John. "No, I'm not mad. I'm getting a wholesome respect for that fellow. He's thorough. I shan't forget the pansies he was planting over my tomb. And he's got a sense of humour. A criminal who has a sense of humour is the most dangerous of criminals."

As they took their evening meal together Elk was reading a newspaper.

"There's an idea, Johnny; the Admiralty are sending a destroyer up to Greenwich to take part in some naval cent—what's the word?"

"Centenary?" suggested John.

"That's the kind of word they put in police examination papers to floor you," grumbled Elk.

"What is the idea?" asked Wade.

Elk folded the paper and put it down.

"Why not keep a destroyer permanently on duty in the mouth of the river? Sooner or later that's the way these fellows are going to get away. They've lost the *Seal of Troy*, but how do we know they haven't got another boat? They've been making millions. Golly or Aikness or whoever's the man has got money to burn and can pick up ships at three a penny."

That night, by the light of an electric reading lamp, Golly Oaks read the same item of intelligence, and the same thought struck him; but it was the second thought that followed upon the first which set this little man purringly aglow. So elated was he that he forgot he was at the moment waiting for news from Raggit Lane, to whom he had given a very definite commission.

That the commissioner did not carry out his orders to the letter was due to a brick which had fallen from the cart of a builder's lorry. It lay in the roadway of the Strand, and the wheel of a certain taxicab bumped over it at a critical and psychological moment.

John Wade was in the Strand at that instant. He had stopped to look at the brightly lit window of a novelty store. Scarcely were his eyes concentrated upon the goods within, when the plate-glass window scattered into a thousand fragments. He did not hear the explosion of the pistol nor the bullet as it struck the glass.

"That man's born lucky," said Raggit Lane, sinking back into the shadows of the taxicab in which he had for three hours been following or waiting for the detective.

He unscrewed the silencer of the muzzle of the long-barrelled revolver and settled himself down to the composition of a good excuse for his bad marksmanship. He had had a scribbled pencil note that afternoon, telling him to remove Wade "at all corst." Golly always put an "r" in "corst," though he wrote the Greek equivalent without an error.

A police whistle sounded loudly and was repeated. The officer on duty in the Trafalgar Square end of the Strand held up his hand and stopped the traffic. Luckily there was a jam here. Mr. Raggit Lane stepped from the offside and closed the door carefully.

"Sorry, boss—the tyre hit a brick or somep'n," said the driver.

"That's all right, Harry—I've put the gun in the locker under the seat," said Lane, and in another second was threading his way between stationary buses and cabs.

A narrow squeak that, he thought, when he reached the safety of the Square and Pall Mall beyond. This new traffic-stopping method might have unpleasant consequences—he was glad he had seen it in operation.

Lane was glad that the little adventure was over. He had accepted it with some misgiving; he had never before gone gunning in the open street, and it was not a pleasant experience.

It was getting a little too dangerous—he mistrusted the congregation of gunmen which had been drawn to London from all quarters of the world, although he had done much to organise them.

Raggit Lane's part in the game was to make clear the lines of communication. He had only once been in an actual "job"; bank-robbing and safe-blowing were more for experts. His own labours began and ended when he had made secure three lines of escape.

Lane was growing more than tired of his master, and was rich enough, if he felt a personal inclination, to quit the game; but there was a big share to come from the central fund, and that was worth waiting for. In South America was a pleasant house with a deep veranda, a jolly little yacht that would carry him over blue, sunlit seas; and a wife perhaps—the right kind.

He liked Lila Smith, before the hint had come to him that she was an heiress. There was a girl full of possibilities. There was nothing thick-witted about her.

He slackened his pace as his thoughts grew more possessive. The old man wanted her, he supposed—it was curious how nonchalantly he had taken the news that the *Seal of Troy* had given up its mystery. That meant the loss of hundreds of thousands of pounds, and if he could afford to treat this with indifference, the share that was coming must be a pretty big one. The old man was keen on her, or he wouldn't have outed Siniford. That was a dangerous trick if you like! Raggit Lane sweated at the thought. The risk—a member of the House of Lords, a prominent man of affairs, heir to a large fortune—phew! The old man took risks. He had held up the Westshire Bank in broad daylight, but that was nothing to this, because two of the clerks were in the swindle. "It is time to quit," said a still, small voice in Lane's soul. And then he thought of the big share, and the possibilities attached to that grey-eyed Lila Smith, who had become a woman under his eyes. For the old man *was* old, and who knew what impression a good-looking man of thirty-five had made upon the susceptible mind of youth . . .

A hand took his right arm almost affectionately. As he turned, another caught his left. He stared aghast into the face of John Wade.

CHAPTER XXIII

"I want you, Lane. We don't want a discussion in public, do we?"

A taxicab crawling along the edge of the kerb moved up. John opened the door and went in ahead of his prisoner, gripping his cuff. The second detective followed.

"I don't suppose you've got a gun," said John. "By the way, we've taken your taxi friend and found your artillery parked under the seat."

"I don't know what you're talking about," began Lane.

"So few people do," said Wade. "I've never arrested a man yet who wasn't as innocent as a babe. You were seen getting out of the cab by a Special Branch man and trailed up the Haymarket. I did a little search of the Strand myself and picked you up across the square. Your little soldiers will cry for their colonel to-night."

"You're talking Greek to me."

"I've been taking lessons from Golly," said John cheerfully.

He was exhilarated at the extraordinary luck that had placed in his hands one of the most dangerous of his enemies. For once fortune was on his side.

At Cannon Row police station the man was searched. Nothing was found on him, not so much as a spent cartridge.

"You'll have a little difficulty in proving your case, won't you?" said Raggit Lane triumphantly.

For answer John caught him by the sleeve and jerked up his arm.

"Look at his hand, sergeant—powder-blackened at the base of the thumb. These old guns throw back. Where are your rubber gloves, Lane—gone to the wash?"

Lane smiled.

"I suppose you're going to frame me. I got that from a backfiring fountain pen. What do you want me for?"

"Accessory to murder—which is murder," said John. "One of your little friends from Montmartre has told the whole truth and nothing but the truth."

The man did not flinch.

"You got them, did you? I saw that the police were looking for two men——"

"You saw nothing of the sort; it was not published in the newspapers, because the newspapers did not even guess we were looking for two or twenty-two men."

He administered the customary caution, and the unperturbed Mr. Lane was taken to the cells. Ten minutes later the cell door opened and John Wade appeared.

"I'm suggesting to you for your own good, Lane, that you don't take your meals from outside."

The man looked up with a smile.

"Am I a fool?" he asked.

Elk had come into the station whilst the man was being charged.

"Took it very well, that fellow—a little bit too well to please me."

"What do you mean?" asked John in surprise.

Elk rubbed his chin thoughtfully.

"You'd think, by the way he went on, that he never expected to be charged with murder, and certainly wasn't looking forward to taking the nine o'clock walk. There are too many of those India-Rubber gunmen in London to please me."

John Wade laughed.

"You can laugh!"

"This isn't Chicago," said John with a smile.

"Exactly. The policemen don't carry guns in London. A well organised squad of thugs could hold up the town—you haven't forgotten Sidney Street? Two men, or was it three, with a couple of automatics, brought out the Guards and artillery, and then they had to burn 'em out."

John waited until the formal charge was made in the morning, and when the inevitable remand was granted he drove down to Oxford. Somewhere on that river was Lila Smith, and he had a feeling that he was destined to find her. He found a motor-launch, a local detective and an official of the Thames Conservancy waiting for him, and without delay the down-river trip began.

It was a laborious business. They stopped four "tows" of barges between Henley and Hurley, and each barge had to be searched separately. John realised that the bargee had not earned his reputation for profanity without justification. It made the business all the more tedious because he was certain in every case that the craft he searched was not the one for which he was looking, and the irritation of certain of the bargemen was accentuated by the fact that one or two of them had already received two police visitations in the past few days.

One of the bargees, more polite than the others, gave him a little information.

"There's a couple of big boats lying up near Marlow," said the man. "They've been I don't know how long coming up the river. I passed 'em twice. *The Betsy and Jane* and *Bertha Brown*."

"Are they tied to the towing-path?" asked John, interested.

The man shook his head.

"No, to some private land on the right bank. I think they're all right—they've been in the river some time. I saw them in the Pool a fortnight ago."

It was late in the evening by the time they had worked through the town, but John determined to push down the river. As they cleared Hurley lock he saw the two craft lying stern to prow. They were close to the bank, overshadowed by the trees which stood at the water's edge. He saw lights burning on both and decided to wait till the morning before he made a closer inspection.

He motored up to town that night, and early in the morning was picked up at Marlow and went slowly up against the stream. A thin mist lay on the river and on the meadows on both banks. He made his approach under the stern of the rearmost barge and landed despite the printed warning that he would be prosecuted for trespassing on private land.

The approach to the barges was difficult; there was a belt of thick underbrush between the meadow and the water's edge, but presently he found a narrow track which led him to where a gangway plank spanned the space between barge and bank. On the poop of the barge a man had been performing his morning ablutions from a tin pail. He was drying his face when John crossed the gangway, and greeted his visitor with apparent unconcern.

"Captain James," he reported, when John showed his credentials. "Police, are you? You're the third lot of police who've searched this barge."

He spoke with great deliberation.

"Are you the master?" asked John. Something in the man's attitude was familiar.

"That's me, mister."

"Been promoted, haven't you? The last time you and I met you were watchman."

For a moment the man was taken aback, then he chuckled.

"Bless my life! It's the gentleman who came aboard the barge! Yes, sir, I'm the watchman, but I always like to swank a little bit. The skipper's gone ashore to get some food for breakfast."

He had slipped on his coat as John approached and had dropped his hand in his pocket. It was this little trick which had betrayed him.

"What have you got in your pocket?" asked John pleasantly. "A gun?"

The man laughed hoarsely.

"Not me, mister. What do I want a gun for?"

John saw a piece of white bandage at the man's wrist.

"Hurt your hand, have you?"

The watchman withdrew it from his pocket. It was heavily bandaged.

"Dropped a hatch on it the other day," he said. "What can I do for you, mister? Do you want to look at the hold?"

"I thought I might," said John.

The "watchman" walked slowly to the open hatchway and called down. A slovenly-looking man appeared.

"Give me a hand to take off these hatches. Good job we haven't got bad weather."

They pulled two hatches loose and John looked down on to innumerable packing-cases. On the tops of these were stencilled the name of an engineering firm in Austria.

"Take off the hatches aft," said John, and they obeyed. "She's riding rather light."

"We're on the bottom," said the man easily. "We're going to be lucky to get off, unless they let more flood water down."

Wade waited whilst the hatches were replaced, and then he drew the automatic from his pocket and regarded it carelessly.

"That's a nice gun," he said.

The watchman was eyeing him closely but said nothing.

"Come a little trip to Marlow, will you?"

"Why?" asked the other.

"You might meet your skipper," smiled John.

He backed to the gangway plank, then sidled along to the bank, never turning his face from the watchman. The other man had disappeared.

"I can't leave this barge——"

He saw the police whistle go up to Wade's lips.

"All right," he growled. "Some of you damned policemen are mighty mysterious."

He followed John to the bank, passed him and walked ahead. They made a wide detour, and all the time Wade's eyes were on the underbrush which partially hid the second barge. There was no sign of life, no sound of any kind, and the watchman was pushed aboard offering no resistance. Whilst the county detective kept his eye upon the prisoner, John sat squarely with his face towards the barge, well aware that many unfriendly eyes were watching him.

They were contented with that: the fusillade he expected did not come, and he reached the shelter of Marlow town and hurried his prisoner into the police station.

"I want you for bank robbery," said John, when the man had been searched and the contents of his pockets laid on the inspector's desk. "It seems hardly worth while mentioning the minor charge of impersonating a sergeant of the City police."

"Good night," said the man sarcastically. "You're getting a regular Sherlock Holmes, Wade."

"Quite a lot of people have told me that," said John.

"Cardlin"—he was charged in that name—made no statement, no excuse, offered no defence, did not even protest his innocence. When he had been removed from the charge-room, John Wade offered a few words of advice to the inspector.

"Bring out your reserves for station duty. I'll have this fellow shifted in a couple of hours. Don't allow anybody in the station premises unless he can prove he has good business."

He called up his superintendent at Scotland Yard.

"I think I've located the barge. It's full of dummy packing-cases that form a false roof for an inside cabin. Camouflaged Austrian packing-cases. I shall want fifty men, sir, and they had better be armed. The second barge is certainly full of Chinks."

He sent the detective along the towpath to watch the barges; a difficult task, for the mist, which had cleared, was thickening up again. A road ran through the meadow approaching where the barges were moored. With the forces available this road could not for the moment be watched, and the detective on the bank needed reinforcements. He was a long way from the nearest telephone, and his position, as John knew, was extremely hazardous.

The mist was an outlier of a deeper fog which descended on the suburbs of London: one of those unexpected and yet always to be expected phenomena to which London is accustomed. It delayed the arrival of the police tenders, and they came crawling through Great Marlow an hour late.

By this time the Berkshire police had been notified, but county police reserves are not easy to reach and concentrate, and they were only in their places when the London reinforcements went through their thin line, crossed the meadow and literally stormed the first of the two barges.

They were rushing the brushwood when John detected a smell of burning. It came from the second barge. Dense smoke was pouring from the forecastle and through the interstices of the hatches. Apparently no living soul was on board. So fierce were the flames that met a search party that they were driven back on to the deck.

The first barge was also burning when John leapt on board, but they were able to extinguish the flames. From the forecastle a small door led to comfortable sleeping quarters, apparently for half a dozen men. The party had departed in such a hurry that they had left most of their belongings behind, but John had no time to examine these. He passed into a second room and halted, amazed at the luxury of it. This had been Lila's prison: he would have guessed that even if he had not seen her one red slipper near her bed. The room was empty, and it had no other exit.

He went back the way he had come to the "general room," and, climbing up to the deck, joined Elk on the bank.

"They had half a dozen cars parked in a shed on this farm," said Elk quickly. "They must have scattered in all directions before the Berkshire police arrived. I'm sending a message to head-quarters suggesting that all the ports should be watched."

John smiled grimly.

"Don't watch the ports, watch London," he said, and he spoke prophetically.

CHAPTER XXIV

Lila had been up since seven o'clock that morning and was trying to interest herself in "Barchester Towers" when she heard a curious sound overhead. Though she did not know this, it was the noise of the hatch being opened for John Wade's inspection. She listened intently, but though she heard the sound of voices they were unrecognisable. She heard the hatch being put on again, and immediately after the door of the cabin opened and Golly came in. He put his finger to his lips and closed the door softly.

"What is wrong?" she asked in a low voice.

"Nothing, my dear," he whispered. "It's somebody who doesn't like you very much, and I don't want him to know you're here—bless my life, he'd give thousands of pounds to do you a bad turn!"

Golly in his diplomatic moments was crude but effective. Yet she had such faith in him that she believed him to be the only friend she had on board the ship.

He went out again and was gone ten minutes. When he returned he was wearing a hat and an overcoat and beckoned her urgently.

"I'm going to get you away from here; there is danger," he said in a low voice. "Come on!"

She reached for her coat but he stopped her.

"Don't touch that," he said impatiently.

He reached out into the outer cabin, and somebody handed him what appeared to be a man's dark mackintosh.

"Put that on."

It was too long in the sleeves, but in his agony of impatience he helped her turn them up.

"Will this cap fit you?"

It was a man's golf cap.

"No, I can't wear that——" she began.

"Try it, my dear, try it!"

The cap fitted rather well. Before she could look at herself in the mirror he had seized her by the arm and hurried her into the outer room. Here she saw Aikness and two other men whom she did not

182

recognise. In a corner of this room was a smaller room, the size of a cupboard. Golly beckoned Captain Aikness.

"What about 'er?" he asked in a low voice, and jerked his thumb towards the cupboard. "I don't want the girl to see her. Bring her along in the second car."

Golly had left the girl at the foot of the companion ladder, and, going back, took her hand and guided her up to the deck. She stared around in astonishment. The mist had thickened, but she could see the trees and a hint of green meadows. The scent of the morning air was glorious; she stood for a moment breathing it in ecstatically.

"The air is lovely——" she began.

"There's plenty of it," said Golly, and half pushed, half led her across the gangway plank.

It was glorious to feel the wet grasses under her feet. She did not trouble to think why Golly had lied to her or why and how the *Riki-tiki* had turned out to be a very commonplace barge.

The mist was so thick that the man walking ahead was barely distinguishable though he was no more than half a dozen yards away. Presently her feet struck a hard road and they turned to the left, and after a minute's walk there loomed out of the fog the gable of a large shed. A car was already waiting on the road. The man who had preceded her opened the door, took out a chauffeur's coat, slipped into it and buttoned it quickly, and pulled on his peaked cap. From somewhere in the mist came a companion. She saw him fixing a white dickey round his throat and wondered why, until he too slipped on a coat, and then she saw that he was a fairly good imitation of a footman.

The car was a handsome limousine. On the panel was a coat of arms—it would be a bold policeman who dared hold up this imposing equipage.

She was barely in the car before it was moving along the bumpy road. It passed through a gateway, turned sharply to the right, and, moving cautiously through the fog, came at the end of ten minutes to what was evidently a main road. Here it turned left again, and Golly, who was her solitary companion in the machine, took up a small microphonic attachment by his side and she heard a distant buzz.

"Windsor, Staines, Hampton, Esher and the bypass," he said rapidly.

He leaned back in the padded seat and chuckled, rubbing his hands.

"You've got to think of everything, Lila—can't trust nobody!" Then, suddenly: "Heard about poor Mum, Lila?"

"Mrs. Oaks?"

183

He shook his head. His curious little face had an expression of the deepest sadness.

"Dead," he said simply.

She looked at him, horrified, hardly believing her ears.

"Mrs. Oaks is dead—surely you don't mean that? How dreadful!"

"She's passed," said Golly. "As the well-known Shakespeare said——"

"Was it an accident?"

"Suicide," said Golly with surprising briefness. "She was a wonderful woman—in a way. She knew nothing about art and she had a bit of a temper."

"But I don't understand. Mrs. Oaks committed suicide—why?"

"Persecution," said Golly.

He took from his pocket a carton of cheap cigarettes, selected one with the care of a connoisseur and lit it.

"She was driven, as it were, into the grave by the police—especially Inspector Wade."

Lila was stunned at the news. She wanted to be more sorry than she was; tried to recall some momentary tenderness between them, but failed.

"She took poison," said Golly, puffing a smoke ring to the roof and watching it break against the top of the car. "Good job I wasn't there, or they'd have said I gave it to her."

"When did this happen?"

"Yesterday," said Golly. "Look!"

He pointed with pride to his tie. It was brand-new and jet black.

"I thought you might have noticed I was in mourning," he said. "Look!"

He fell into the contortions of a man taking off his overcoat in a confined space, and showed her an irregular band of crêpe around his left arm.

"Mourning," he said unnecessarily, and added: "That shows."

"Shows what?" she was curious enough to ask.

He was taken aback by the question.

"It shows I'm doing the right thing by her. I'm thinking of putting up a monument—an angel pointing up to the sky. It's not art as I understand it, but it's the best you can get in England. What a country!"

They were following a secondary road and met no obstruction or challenge. The butt of Mr. Oaks's pistol had grown unpleasantly damp from holding. He withdrew his hand to wipe it dry.

"Naturally I shan't remain single, Lila," he said. "I'm what you might term in the prime of life. I'd like to settle down, say in South

America—flowers, blue lakes, white marble buildings, roses every-where—you know."

She was too staggered to reply.

"I'm forty-three—or forty-four! I'm not sure which," said Golly carelessly. "A girl might go farther than me and miss something."

"But how terrible!" She was jerked back to realities. "Auntie Oaks dead! Weren't you awfully upset about it?"

"Awfully," said Golly, and began to whistle softly to himself.

He whistled better than he sang.

"Between her and me there was no what you might call silly love-making. It was a business arrangement, and it worked. She for-got herself sometimes—what woman doesn't? Was I a good husband or wasn't I?"

She could only reply that he was the most meek and obedient of husbands.

"I don't like that word 'meek,' " he said, bridling. "I was gentle. But that's my nature: I've always been kind to women—treated 'em as pets. That's the only way," he added.

She wanted to change the subject.

"Where are we going?"

"To London somewhere," he said. "I've got some flats there—Arbroath Building—ever heard of it? Quite a nice place, baths h. and c. I might have gone there first, but who'd have thought they'd have tumbled to the barges? I've been twelve months getting them ready. They were fitted up in Holland and came across under their own sail. Twenty-six hundred pounds each—that's a lot of mon-ey for a barge. But what foresight! That's always been my strong point, foresight. *I* knew they'd tumble to the *Seal of Troy* sooner or later; *I* knew we'd have to get the 'ole crew off at a minute's notice."

"Were there men in the other barge?" she asked.

She remembered now seeing a squat little figure moving through the mist and keeping at a respectful distance when they had stopped to enter the car.

"Twenty good fellows."

"But what is the *Seal of Troy*? Why are we running away? Have you done anything wrong?"

Mr. Oaks relit his cigarette: it was the kind that extinguishes itself at regular intervals.

"Secret Service," he said, and glanced sideways at her. "We're doing certain things for a certain Government. Naturally, the English Government doesn't want any trouble with—Italy."

She could have sworn he had searched Europe for a likely coun-try that was liable to have trouble with anybody, and picked on Italy

185

by accident.

Again they struck a main road, turned off, and, skirting Windsor, came along the Thames bank by Runnymede, and presently had left Staines behind and had entered the long section of the Great West Road. The mist had cleared now, and by the time they reached Shepherd's Bush it had precipitated into a steady drizzle of rain.

Golly had one shock: he saw two cars held up on the West Road and a cordon of police formed round them. His own was unchallenged. The stiff footman sitting by the side of the chauffeur, and possibly the coat of arms, saved him from an experience which might have been either humiliating or fatal.

Arbroath Building proved to be an island block, originally erected as a munitions factory in the latter days of the war. Such an ugly, four-square little building would never have passed a discriminating district council in peace time. The lower portion had been redesigned to hold a big garage and a number of lock-up shops. The garage had failed; the shops lost their tenants; the property had been in the market three times when an unknown syndicate had acquired it. The two upper floors had been occupied by tenants, seventy-five per cent. of whom had steadfastly refused to pay any rent, but of these the syndicate had rid itself. The garage was reconverted, though it never seemed to be used, and the flats had never been let. Probably the reason was that the rent asked was about twice the amount that any conscientious landlord could ask for such accommodation. The syndicate did not mind. They furnished one or two of the apartments, put curtains in the windows of the others, and seemed content to lose money.

It was not easy to obtain car room in the garage. There were scores of taxi owners who would have been glad to utilise the spacious yard and lock-ups, but they had no encouragement. One or two private cars were kept there, but Notting Hill regarded the building as hoodoo, and it was generally believed that the new proprietors were also booked for a visit to the Bankruptcy Court. Which was far from the truth.

The unfortunate speculator who had reconstructed this war factory had designed a series of service flats, and to this end put in a kitchen and considerable store room in the basement.

"Foresight again, my dear."

They had passed through the gates into the garage, and he had taken her in a small electric lift to the top floor. She was ushered into a small flat which was, if not handsomely, at least well furnished, though it smelt a little musty from disuse.

"I got this property for eight thousand pounds. If I'd planned it myself it couldn't have been better for me."

"But you hadn't eight thousand pounds, Mr. Oaks?"

"A friend of mine put up the money," said Golly glibly. "This is my idea of quiet: you can come and go and nobody cares who you are or what you are, and you could stay here ten years and nobody would be any the wiser."

Lila had given up wondering. She was tired, though the journey had been a short one, anxious to be alone and to reconstruct from the chaos of her recent experience a consecutive narrative which bore some resemblance to reality.

"You can have all the life you want here, but you'd better keep the curtains closed," he said.

The flat which was reserved for him looked out upon a small well, the base of which was the courtyard. She had no view of the street, and for the moment was not anxious to examine her surroundings. After she had gone he pulled up the window and looked down into the yard. Car after car arrived and disappeared down an inclined drive which seemed to burrow into the earth, but which, she supposed, led to an underground garage.

The door was locked on her, and in half an hour came the little Chinese servant with his inevitable grin, carrying a hot meal on a tray. He was setting the table when Golly returned. He looked troubled, and when the servant had gone:

"Did you hear anybody screaming?" he asked.

"No," she answered.

His face seemed a shade paler. He was for the moment at a loss for a plausible explanation.

"We've got a lady here who isn't quite right in her head—not exactly a lady, but a woman. Dippy." He tapped his forehead. "If I wasn't so gentle with women——" He shook his head, inwardly regretting his humanity.

"Does she live here?"

He looked at her oddly.

"No, she doesn't live here. She was on the barge, but she didn't give any trouble there."

"Who is she?" she asked.

"A woman," said Golly vaguely. "She's been a servant. She was quiet until she saw Aikness."

"Is he here too?"

"They're all here." He almost snapped the words, but recovered his equanimity instantly.

"It was the first time she'd seen Aikness for twenty years—she used to be sweet on Aikness. The things she called him—murderer, everything. I told him to keep out of her way; these mad people have got funny memories."

"Captain Aikness used to know her?"

"They've met," said Golly, "nearly twenty years ago. He made up to her, it appears. He's that kind of man. Anybody's good enough for him—servants, anybody. Her name's Anna."

He watched her closely as he said this, but the word had no significance for Lila.

"Can I do anything?" she asked again.

He rubbed his nose irritably, took off his glasses, wiped them violently, and put them on again.

"That's what I've been thinking. I don't see why she shouldn't see you—she's got an idea she knew you when you was a kid. Anna—you don't remember the name by any chance?"

She shook her head.

"Suppose I brought her in to-night?" he suggested tentatively. "Would you mind? You might be able to calm her down. I could bring her in now; she's got over her tantrums. She won't hurt anybody."

"I'm not afraid of that," smiled Lila. "I'm glad there is a woman here."

"Naturally," murmured Mr. Oaks, suddenly acquiring a sense of delicacy. "You're sure you don't mind? Eat your dinner first—she might take your appetite away."

She laughed at his anxiety, nevertheless ate a good meal, Mr. Oaks refusing to join her, though he sat watching her. Towards the close of the meal he brought up another subject.

"It was a great mistake putting Siniford on the board," he said, apropos nothing. "The board of this little company. It was a silly idea, but Aikness thought it was a good way of keeping him sweet. They might search the register to see what he was connected with."

"Isn't he connected now?" she asked.

Mr. Oaks coughed.

"He's gone abroad," he said, and brought the conversation back to Anna. "I'll go and fetch her."

He rose, but seemed loath to depart until he had prepared her for the worst.

"She's nothing to look at, and maybe she'll go off into one of her fits, but if she do—does—then, as old Euripides said——"

Here came a string of unintelligible words, and she repressed her smile, never dreaming of his strange accomplishments.

He was gone nearly half an hour; when he returned she thought he was looking more agitated than he had been when he had left her.

"Come in, my dear."

He stepped aside to let pass the woman behind him.

"I told you you should see her, and here she is."

She came into the room, a thin, gaunt woman, white-faced, with dark, smouldering eyes. For a minute she stood staring at Lila till the girl grew uncomfortable under her gaze.

"Is that Delia?"

Her voice was deep, rather sweet.

Mr. Oaks winked at the girl.

"That's her," he said.

She came slowly towards Lila, put out her two thin hands and took the girl's.

"Delia, darling"—her voice was little above a whisper—"you are Delia—you know me, my sweet?"

Lila shook her head.

"My name is Lila."

The effect on the woman was instantaneous. Her eyes lit, the pale, lined face became animated.

"Lila—of course you're Lila, darling! You always called yourself Lila."

In another moment the frightened girl was in her arms. Lila was bewildered, dared not struggle free, grew fearful under the torrent of wild words.

"Lila, you know me—Anna!"

CHAPTER XXV

For a moment something stirred in Lila's memory. She did remember—something. A vivid recollection that came and went instantly, leaving her more bewildered. She gently disengaged herself from the trembling woman's arms.

"Sit down, won't you?"

But the woman clung to her tearfully.

"Don't you remember the house, and that dreadful night of the fire, and her ladyship—her ladyship's dead, Lila."

The girl strove hard to think, but memory would not function. She looked appealingly at Mr. Oaks, and he nodded.

"It's quite right, my dear: she did know you; she was your nurse."

"That's true. God bless you for telling her that! I was her nurse, and they said she was dead—burnt in that awful fire. They showed me the dreadful little pieces of burnt clothing. I said you were alive, and I told her ladyship you were alive. She believed me. But I knew I should see you. I knew it—was sure of it! It was dreadful waiting. Sometimes I got tired, and then they put me away in that big house, and they wouldn't let me go out. And the men—the Chinamen—horrible little people!"

She fell into a fit of shuddering that was painful to witness. It did not pain Mr. Oaks.

"Crool to be kind," he murmured. "That's me, Lila. Nobody can ever say I wasn't gentle with a female. If I had to hurt 'em it was over in a second, and it was all for the best."

That cell of memory was multiplying. Anna was already a familiar figure to her, could almost be disengaged from the half-real, half-dreamt figures of recollection.

"You'll let me stay with you? I *must* stay with you. I'll look after you—get your clothes for you, darling. . . . I suppose I mustn't call you darling now, because you aren't a baby. And I must tell her ladyship."

"Dead," murmured Mr. Oaks.

"Yes, she's dead. Of course, she'll know——"

"I'll leave you two ladies together," said Mr. Oaks, and went out and turned the key in the door. He lifted his hat politely. It was his boast that he knew how to behave.

He passed down the uncarpeted passage and turned into a room. Aikness was sitting in a rather cheaply furnished dining-room, a glass of whisky at his elbow, the half of a cigar between his teeth.

"She's all right," said Oaks.

Captain Aikness rose and looked into the mirror, dabbed a scratch on his right cheek with his handkerchief.

"Took me by surprise."

"You took her by surprise," said Oaks sharply. "I told you these balmy people had got long memories."

"She's changed," said the captain. "She used to be a fairly pretty girl."

Oaks grunted something, poured whisky into a glass and filled it up from the siphon.

"You used to be a pretty good-looking fellow, too, didn't you, Aikness? If you hadn't been, you wouldn't have been told off to make love to nursemaids. We haven't got a good-looker left."

"She *was* good looking," mused the captain. "I got quite soft with her. She was the only intelligent servant I've ever met. What are you going to do about Lane?"

Golly lit a cigarette and smoked for a long time in silence.

"Get him out," he said.

"Do you think he'll squeal?" asked Aikness; but the other did not reply for a long time, and thinking he had not heard, Aikness repeated the question.

"He won't squeal," said Golly, staring out of the window, "but I know others who might."

Captain Aikness forced a smile.

"Not me, Golly. I'm too deeply in this business."

"So was Mum," said Oaks briefly, "yet she was ready to squeak."

Another long and painful interregnum of silence, which the captain broke.

"Lila's a bit of a problem," he said.

"Is she?" asked Golly coolly. "There's no problem about Lila: she'll marry and settle down. But she won't marry a seafaring man."

He leaned on his folded arms across the table.

"I've humoured you, Captain What's-your-name—I'm always willing to humour anybody. I've let you play papa to that kid, give her little outings, dress her up in nice clothes and what-not, and you're going to stay papa. Mum thought this idea of the girl going out to dinner with you when you came back from a long sea voyage was silly, but Mum never had foresight—that's why she's dead.

I *have* got foresight." He tapped his chest gently many times. "I never knew there was any money coming to her, but I knew she was a lady born and bred, and I thought that sooner or later she was going to be useful, and we can't let her start learning swell ways too soon. But she's not going to marry any papa, and that million six hundred thousand ain't going to build *pallaccios* for you at Rio."

For a second the two men looked at one another, a glare of hatred in the eyes of Captain Aikness which he did not attempt to disguise. Golly's eyes were cold, emotionless, deadly.

"I don't know how this thing is going to finish up," Golly went on, "but I'm aiming to teach these police birds a lesson they'll never forget. I could slip out of London easy enough, so could you; but that's not my idea of being great, Aikness." He slapped his chest again. "I'm big! I always have been big. I fenced little things for ten years to get the money to start this. I opened up at the Bank of Lyons single-handed to buy your ship. I've organised London like a general would organise it. I know every way out and every way in. I know close on three thousand coppers by sight—I'm going out with a bang, and when this is over, you and me will settle the question of Lila, and if you think that it can be settled before, or settled any way that I don't like, I'll give you a word of advice—pull your gun and get me, before I get you!"

Aikness shrank back into his chair, his mouth twitching painfully. There was a streak of yellow in this big man. Nobody knew this better than Golly Oaks, who had lived on his knowledge of men.

"That's that, Captain," he said, with a laugh. "We're all set. I can tell you what my organisation is like—I could tell you the ship me and Lila are leaving by, and the cabin number, and the name of the person who is going to marry us——"

Aikness came to his feet with an oath.

"Marry you! You!"

Golly nodded.

"I'm nearly ten years younger than you, and me and Lila understand one another. And I've got every document to prove she's Delia Pattison. Siniford gave me most of 'em and I got a few from the bank."

With a forced laugh the captain mastered his rage and sat down.

"You're a funny devil. The thing I can't understand about you, Golly, is how you allowed that old lady to bully you."

"Speak well of the dead," said Golly evenly. "That was her privilege—I gave her four hours every day when she could roast hell out of me, but the other twenty she walked on tiptoe. I'll tell you something, Aikness: she slept behind a locked door for twelve years, and she always had a loaded gun under her pillow—did you know that? And do you know why she had a loaded gun? It was in case she said something that hurt my feelings. She cast reflections on my voice once—and had a servant sleeping in her room for a month after. Mum knew me," he smiled as though, he was recalling a pleasant memory. "People who get to know me don't make any mistakes. I hope you know me, Captain."

"Sure I do, Golly," said the other, but the geniality in the voice of Captain Aikness was patently spurious.

There was a great deal of staff work to be done that night. Every other flat had its telephone, for which the owner of the block had paid for months when no call came through. Towards ten o'clock men began to drift in and were shown to their rooms: furtive, suspicious-looking men, who spoke in monosyllables and studied transcontinental time-tables and the shipping lists of those companies which have their port of departure in Italy and the South of France.

There was one man called Ambrose who, Aikness knew, was a notorious gang-leader, and it was through him that Golly communicated with his queer crew. Aikness was taken round and introduced, and reported his impressions late that night to Golly Oaks.

"Of course they dope!" said Golly contemptuously. "Ordinary men couldn't do what these men do."

In the underground garage, behind the steel doors of what had been designed as a petrol store, was a very complete armoury. Golly took the captain down and showed him its treasures. Most of them were still wrapped in oiled paper, and a man sitting on a stool in one corner was engaged in unwrapping.

"Once you decide on doing a thing," said Golly, "do it big." That was his guiding principle in life.

He had paid several visits to Lila, and was satisfied in his mind that the understanding between the girl and her old nurse was growing.

This was entirely to his satisfaction. The girl ought to have a woman companion—especially with the trip in front of her. Funny he hadn't thought of that before.

But then he had so many things to think about—planning, planning, planning.

The trouble was getting fixed ideas and refusing to budge: being bound by first intentions. For example, he had thought it an excellent idea to marry Lila to Siniford—well, he'd changed his mind. Lord Siniford was dead. And a good idea to humour Aikness all the time he had a ship. He hadn't a ship any more—but was distinctly useful.

CHAPTER XXVI

Golly's room at Arbroath Building was large and would have been airy if the windows had been opened and the heavy stuff curtains drawn. It had a bed, a chair and a table. To those you might add a strip of carpet, ludicrously inadequate, in the centre of the room. The table was of the type that can be found in architects' offices, a plain, deal, unpainted board, supported on two trestles; and neatly stacked hereon were scores of plans, survey maps, books of reference, time-tables, private tables compiled in Golly's terrible handwriting.

He was studying one of the three bank-books which he invariably carried about with him by day and took to bed with him at night. This book dealt with an account in the greatest of the Brazilian banks, and it showed so satisfactory a balance that he might say with truth that, even if Lila Smith's fortune was too dangerous to claim, he could yet live in luxury all the rest of his life.

The other two books offered him as great a comfort. He closed the little blue-covered volume with a sigh, and put it and its companions in an inside pocket.

Raggit Lane was in Brixton Prison, daily expecting a miracle, for he was full of faith in this little schemer; and in Brixton Prison, decided Golly, he would remain until the law took its usual course. Lane was happily ignorant of the fading interest of his chief. And yet Golly had planned and had intended a spectacular rescue, should any of his lieutenants by ill luck fall within the reach of the law. There was a pigeon-holed operation plan, as detailed and as exact as any drawn by a staff officer on the eve of battle. But Golly had another scheme, more grandiose, more spectacular. He was never bound by first intentions.

Even his late wife had never suspected Golly of keeping a most elaborate press-cutting book in which every detail of every successful robbery was pasted and indexed. Yet he had spent days in gloating over these cuttings. He had grown livid with rage when some extraordinarily clever move of his had gone unrecorded, and would have written to the Press supplying the omitted detail if his historical sense had not prevented him; for he knew by heart the details of every great crime that had been committed for fifty years, and he, more than any, knew just how vanity had brought the cleverest criminals to punishment. There was once a murderer, a wholesale poisoner, who wrote to the coroner inquiring into his victim's death, and those letters brought him to the scaffold. Golly never forgot this.

He had hardly put the books in his pocket when there came a knock at the door, and, getting up, he pulled back the bolt and admitted Aikness. The captain had shown unusual signs of nervousness all that afternoon. Perhaps it was the little exchange they had had earlier in the day which had upset him, but twice he had asked Golly for some details of his immediate plans, and that was not like the apathetic Captain Aikness, who hitherto had been content to accept whatsoever instructions Golly had given.

Golly bolted the door behind him and nodded to the bed. He never kept more than one chair in his working-room.

"I'm going to tell you something, Golly——"

"You're rattled: I know all about that," said Golly, searching his waistcoat pocket for his cigarettes. "All the afternoon you've been making a noise like a tin can full of peas."

"I'm no use on shore," growled the other. "I'm a sailor, and I feel like a fish out of water. Can't you let me go over to Holland and buy that boat? They want sixty thousand for her, but they'd take less. She's on the Dutch register—I could sail her under their flag, with a Dutch crew. She does nine knots."

"And destroyers do thirty-five," said Golly calmly. "I'm not going to pay sixty thousand pounds to give you the pleasure of making me seasick."

"Where have you put the Chinks?" asked Aikness irritably. "I know nothing nowadays."

"They're well hidden up," said Golly. "I've barged 'em down by Blackwall. Nobody's going to search any more barges."

"I didn't know you'd bought one," said the other in surprise.

"You don't know what I'm doing," said Golly smugly. "My mind works better when I'm asleep than yours does when it's awake. Foresight—that's my long suit."

He waited for the captain to speak. Evidently Aikness was waiting for a lead.

"Well, what are we going to do? We can't stick here until the police find us. Couldn't I go down to Genoa——"

"The trouble with you is wanderlust," said Golly.

There was a certain deadliness in his pleasantry which made the man shiver.

"You stay here, Captain What's-your-name. I've got the biggest idea that ever came out of the brain of Napoleon." He tapped his forehead. "Suppose you had a ship, what chance have you got against a thirty-five-knot destroyer? She'd be able to give you a week's start and catch you up. But I plan to get away with the biggest haul that's ever been lifted!"

He had grown suddenly excited; walked up and down the room, gesticulating as he spoke. There was a pallor in his face which betrayed the intensity of this newly awakened emotion.

"Suppose they catch us—the whole crowd of us? What's going to happen?"

He jerked an invisible rope around his neck and drew it tight with a suggestive "click."

"That's what! Can we buy our way out? We can't. Is there any way of getting a free pardon? Yes, by putting the black on 'em."

"The black on them?" repeated Aikness. "On whom?"

"The Government!" He tapped the table to emphasise his point. "We'll give 'em something at a price, and we'll show 'em what we're capable of doing before we start in on the real thing. There's two real big jewellers' stores in Bond Street where you could lift a hundred an' fifty thousand. We'll take that to start with. They owe us something for the stuff they took out of the *Seal of Troy*. Then we'll give 'em a second wallop, and then a third that'll knock 'em out, and there isn't anyone in my gang that they'll so much as lay their fingers on—they'll show us the way to Brazil or the Argentine or any old place we want to go, and they'll settle us there and be glad to settle."

Aikness thought he was mad, and the little man must have read his thoughts, for suddenly he slapped the captain on the back and burst into a fit of immoderate laughter.

"Think I'm touched, do you? But you don't know me, Aikness. You thought I was touched when I put up that bank job in St. James's Street; you thought I was touched when I said we could get the manager to open the bank in Lothbury without any fuss."

Suddenly his exuberance left him and he looked at the other glumly.

"I'd like to get Mr. Wade, though—get him fair and square, in a room like this—only me and him—pegged out on the floor, and hundreds and hundreds of big sheets of blotting-paper to catch the blood."

He laughed shrilly, and, frozen with horror, Aikness for the first time really understood this odd little man, who quoted Greek and Latin and occasionally scraps of Arabic.

"What's your scheme for blackmailing the Government?" he

196

asked.

He was anxious to turn the conversation into more comfortable channels. Well enough he knew that the fate designed for John Wade would be his if Golly Oaks suspected for one moment the half-formed scheme at the back of the captain's mind.

It was more than half formed: it was complete, except for one important particular—he had yet to decide the psychological moment when he should throw his companion to the police wolves. The hands of Aikness were clean, in the sense that he had never shed blood, though he might have been privy to the worst excesses of his master. What was the right moment to strike?

"Perfect timing, eh?" chuckled Golly, and Aikness nearly jumped from the bed at what he thought was a piece of miraculous mind-reading. "That's the secret of our success—timing! You keep your eye on me!"

He jerked a little metal watch from his pocket.

"I wonder what them girls are doing?"

"Are they sleeping in the same flat to-night?" asked Aikness, glad to escape from the nerve-racking subject.

"I had a bed taken in for this Anna. She's no more dippy than I am. She talks as rationally as a Christian. Now let me see. . . ."

He sat down at his table, took a sheet of paper and began to write rapidly. Golly had an extraordinary knowledge of London; it had been one of his studies, and he frequently mentioned places which were foreign territory to Aikness, but it happened that the sailor was well acquainted with the district about which Golly eventually spoke.

"Here's a pretty good place—lonely, and you can see the river. Practically in Greenwich and nobody will notice you've parked a car there. Anyway, you'll see a lamp signal."

He looked thoughtfully at Aikness.

"The question is, when will there be a dance?"

"A what?" asked the astounded man.

"A dance or a do of some kind I'll bet there will be, but I'll find that out."

He scribbled something on the paper, and from a little book on the table he carefully scrutinised the printed pages near-sightedly.

"If it's Friday, we'll make a wonderful job of it. It will be Friday." He slapped his knee excitedly. "I've got a feeling it'll be Friday—what was you doing in the War, Captain?"

The question took the man's breath away.

"You know what I was doing in the War," he growled. "I served two years with the Navy. You made me do it——"

"You was getting too conspicuous, keeping out," said Golly. "Jennett and Mortimer served with you, didn't they?"

Aikness nodded.

"Jennett and Mortimer are looking after the Chinks now, ain't they? Good sailors . . . They know how to load a gun, don't they?"

"What are you driving at?" asked Aikness impatiently. "What's all this talk of dances, and Jennett and Mortimer, and guns?"

Golly smiled blandly.

"I must go and have a chat with that girl," he said. Unbolting the door, he opened it, jerking his head significantly.

Golly followed Aikness out, locked the door behind him, and went, singing under his breath, along the corridor. Lila heard him, and made a gesture to the woman who was talking.

He came in boisterously, obviously in the best of good humour.

"You girls enjoying yourselves?" He looked at the scattered playing cards on the table. "I must come along and learn you a few games," he said. "You're sleeping here to-night, miss"—he addressed Anna.

"Yes, I'm sleeping here to-night." Her voice was steady and calm; there was a serenity in her face that had so entirely changed her appearance, that he would not have recognised in her the woman he had brought to Arbroath Building.

Golly strolled carelessly to the door, opened it and looked at the newly fixed bolts outside.

"You don't mind me locking you in? There's lots of burglars round this neighbourhood. It's disgraceful the way crime is spreading. The police! Fat lot of good they are! *Quis custodiat ipsos custodes!*"

"How long are we staying here, Mr. Oaks?" asked Lila, a little dazed.

Golly shrugged his shoulders.

"A couple of days, then off we go into the country. Nothing like the country to make you feel fine!"

"Mr. Oaks, what has happened to Lord Siniford?"

It was Anna who asked the question.

She was talking rationally, and this was a little disconcerting. She may know things he thought she did not know, or have seen sights which he thought she hadn't had the intelligence to grasp. Golly regarded the woman with a new interest. How much did she remember? How much had she heard? There had been some rather careless talk in front of her, for he and Aikness had regarded her as something of a lunatic. But for John Wade's warning, Anna might not have lived to hear anything. Anna was becoming an embarrassment.

"Lord Siniford, I regret to say," there was a note of pomposity in his voice—"has passed away."

"He's dead, too?"

Golly inclined his head, and gave to the gesture a suggestion of sadness.

"We've all got to come to it," he said sententiously. "He was killed by lightning"—Golly was inclined to picturesque invention—"or the act of Gawd. *De mortuis nil nisi bonum.*"

There was a silence.

"I'm terribly sorry," said the girl.

She was very grave. He guessed that she was connecting the passing of Mum Oaks with this new tragedy and reading into the coincidence something that was sinister and alarming.

"He was murdered," said Anna in her deep voice. "It was in the newspapers."

Golly shook his head.

"You can't believe the newspapers—not 'alf of 'em, anyway. Anything for a sensation, my dear—that's their motto. Anyway, he's popped off—*honesta mors turpi vita potior.*"

Again he surveyed Anna. She might be very troublesome. Mentally he cancelled the beautiful apartments he had planned for her in his South American palazzio. Her attitude was an offence, her memory deplorable. She must have heard things. . . .

"Sleep well, my dear. I'll be seeing you in the morning. Good night, miss."

His cold eyes struck terror into the woman's heart.

"Be sensible," he said mysteriously, and went out into the little lobby and Lila heard the door close and a bolt shot to its socket.

CHAPTER XXVII

Lila turned the handle afterwards; the door had been so fitted that it could not be opened from the inside. She could make sure, however, that it should not be opened from the outside and pushed home a small bolt before she came through the little lobby where Anna was waiting.

They stood looking at one another for a time.

"I don't know what to think," said Lila at last. "It seems almost impossible that he should be such a terrible man. I can't even feel frightened of him. Surely he's as helpless as we are."

Anna shook her head.

"No, he isn't. All I've told you is true. There are so many things I remember only dimly, but every word I have heard since they took me from that house by the river is here"—she laid her white hand on her forehead. "And I'm not stupid now, Lila. I was looking at my face in the glass just now, and it made me feel sick to see what I had become. It is as if I have been turned from a girl into an old woman. All the years between losing and finding you are like a moment gone—there's a hymn with a line like that—it used to be my lady's favourite—'A thousand ages in Thy sight——' I suppose I went off my head."

"Don't talk about that, please." Lila took the woman's arm in hers and squeezed it. "What are we going to do, Anna?"

"You still think I'm a little mad, don't you, darling—all this story about your being rich and Lady Pattison and the fire and everything?"

Lila shook her head.

"I don't think you're mad at all. I believe every word you say. It is difficult to realise it, but I believe it. The hardest thing is about Mr. Oaks—that he's the India-Rubber Man——"

"He is, he is!" said the woman vehemently. "You only think of him as a silly little fool who believes he can sing, but I've seen big men cringe away from him. That captain is so humble in his presence that even I was ashamed. One night I heard them talking about marriage, and I didn't realise that it was you they were discussing."

"Me?" gasped Lila.

Anna nodded.

"They never mentioned your name. They were sitting together in the cabin of the barge, and they let me out of my room to have my food. Because I was mad they took no notice of me. The captain jeered at me. But Golly never jeered. He was looking at me that night like a butcher looking over a flock of sheep and deciding which he should kill."

"Oh, don't, don't!" shuddered Lila. "Anna you make my blood run cold."

The woman's arm went round her.

"I think I must still be a little crazy to frighten you so, my pet. I'll be sensible: he told me to be! Now let us see if we can get the rest of that wallpaper off."

"There's no chance of his coming back—I've bolted the door," said Lila.

It was Lila who had discovered, behind a strip of torn wallpaper, a small section of a printed notice over which the paper had been hung. At some early period there had been pasted into each floor of the building notices which complied with the County Council regulations for the safeguarding of workmen. She did not know then that this building had been used as a munitions factory, and when she drew Anna's attention to the little scrap of printing, which she had no idea was that hidden notice, it was Anna who saw its possibilities.

The fear of interruption had made her defer the uncovering of the notice as too dangerous. With a handkerchief they dabbed the wallpaper until it was soaked, and then, with the greatest care, they stripped the paper until the notice was revealed:

In case of fire, fire party will stand by hydrants, and all employees other than those detailed for fire drill will pass in an orderly manner to the lower floor. In case of fire on the lower floor or in the basement, pull down escape ladder above and trap will open automatically. Move to the end of the roof from which wind is blowing, and throw out rope ladders which are placed in lockers at regular intervals along the parapet. Keep calm. The greatest danger in a fire is panic.

"Trap above the roof." Lila frowned up at the unbroken expanse of the ceiling.

Anna went out into the dining-room and brought in a chair, mounted it and felt gingerly at the ceiling. She pressed and the ceiling bulged upwards; cracks appeared in the surface of the plaster.

"It's behind there!"

She almost whispered the words.

And then she heard a gentle rapping on the outer door of the flat. The floor of the bath-room was covered with white specks of dust. Golly had only to take one look at the ceiling and the printed notice on the wall to know what was in their minds.

"Lock the door, and don't come out," said Anna.

She waited until Lila had fastened the door, then she went to admit Golly.

"What are you up to?" He looked at her suspiciously. "Where's Lila?"

"She's having a bath. I had to find the towels," said Anna, and the reply seemed to satisfy him.

"Having a bath, is she? Well, that's as well, because I want to have a chat with you, my girl."

He glanced towards the room whence the bath-room opened.

"She won't be coming out yet?"

"Not yet?"

Golly nodded.

"I suppose, miss, you've never been to South America?"

"No," said Anna.

"Fine country—I made a trip there once. Flowers—warm in the winter—nothing to do but just *live*! Plenty of money—or you will have; books, motor-cars, best of food—how does that strike you?"

"It sounds wonderful," she said quietly.

"That's what's coming to you." He pointed his finger at her. "If you're a good girl. Don't give me any trouble, help me with her"—he jerked his thumb in the direction of the bath-room—"don't make any more scenes, and that's what you'll have. Do you get me? But suppose you're not sensible; suppose you start kicking up a fuss, telling her this, that and the other about me—what do you think's going to happen to you?"

She did not answer.

"You know—I'll bet you know! They'll be picking you out of the river, and people will be saying: 'Who's she?—Oh, she's nobody.' That's all the notice the newspapers will take of you. You'll be 'an unknown woman,' and that'll be your finish."

"That will be my finish," she repeated slowly.

"I don't want to say any more to an intelligent lady," said Golly. He patted her shoulder paternally. "We understand each other. Give my love to Lila, and when you've got nothing better to do you can say a few words about me. I'd make a good husband—sowed me wild oats. Do you want any money?" He put his hand to his breast pocket.

She shook her head.

"I can't spend it now," she said, and Golly smiled.

"Your brain's working," he said, and with a wink he left her.

She waited some time before she bolted the door, and then she went back to the girl. Lila saw something of the old strained look in her face.

"No, no, it's nothing, my dear," said Anna.

She opened a drawer in the table and took out a knife, and without hesitation thrust at the ceiling. The plaster now came down in a shower, covering her with white powder. Thin laths were exposed; she reached up and pulled these down, and, taking the lamp which hung on a flex, she turned the bulb upwards to the opening.

"There's the trap," she said.

More plaster and lath had to come away before she could reach the square trap, and then it defied her efforts to move until she found a broom in the pantry and, both women grasping the handle and thrusting up, the trap was moved, and the handle, slipping past its edge, wedged it open.

It was a precarious business. The roof door was heavy. Perched on a chair which was placed on the table, Anna could apply no leverage. Showers of dust and debris fell upon her as she wedged the trap open wider with such articles as Lily could pass to her. Wider and wider grew the slit of night sky visible in the roof, till, at three o'clock in the morning, almost exhausted by her efforts, she dragged herself through an incredibly small space and stumbled into the open air. When she recovered her breath, she exerted all her strength and, pulling the creaking trap wide open and lying flat, she extended her hand to the girl below and drew her into the open.

Immediately they began their search for the rope ladders and the lockers, but if there were such appliances they had been removed. The two women were in despair. In less than an hour the first streaks of dawn would be in the sky. To return the way they came was to risk discovery in the morning; but that risk they must take. Had they seen a policeman and could have attracted his attention, they might have risked discovery; but there was nobody in sight.

It was Anna who lowered herself into the room below, Anna who steadied the chair and guided the feet of the girl to safety. To close the trap again was an impossibility; they must take the risk of somebody going on the roof during the day.

Though she was weary beyond belief, Lila slept fitfully, and she was awake and dressed before breakfast came, and, with it, Golly Oaks. He was not as genial as usual. Evidently something had happened that morning to disturb his equanimity.

"I shall be taking you young ladies away to-night," he said, "round about nine o'clock. I shan't be able to go with you myself, but a couple of friends of mine will travel with you. You'll give no trouble—you understand, Lila? I won't be responsible if you do."

"Where are you taking us?" she asked.

He did not reply.

"The clothes you've been wearing will do. And tell that woman it'll pay her to keep quiet—is she all right now? Not crazy or anything?"

Lila shook her head. She was nerving herself to make the request that Anna had asked her to make.

"Do you think you can manage her?"

In spite of her worries she smiled.

"I'm perfectly sure I can," she said.

"I suppose she's told you all about your grandmother and all that? Well, you had to know sooner or later."

He turned back as he was going, as though a thought had struck him.

"By the way, some of the boys got Johnny Wade last night—shot him clean through the heart."

He was watching her intently; saw her eyes open in horror and the colour leave her face.

"Bad luck, eh? Good fellow, Johnny; not much of a policeman but a good fellow."

There was something in his tone, in his intense analytical look, that told her he was lying, and that the death of John Wade had been an invention made to test her. She had to hold tight to this belief, or she would have collapsed.

"Friend of yours, Lila—dear, dear, what a loss to the Force! An active and intelligent officer, cut off as it were in his prime." He made a clicking noise with his tongue, but his eyes did not leave her face.

Now she was certain that he lied, and she felt a sense of unspeakable relief.

For his part, he saw the colour come back to her face, and misjudged the reason.

"Bit of a shock to you, Lila? Well, we all have to bear it—think of what it must have meant to me when I heard about your poor auntie. Where is Anna?"

"In her room, I think. Do you want her?"

He thought for a moment.

"No, I don't think so. I shan't be seeing much of you to-day. You girls behave."

At last she spoke the words that she had been trying to speak throughout the interview.

"Could I have some benzine?"

"What's that?" he asked suspiciously.

"There are some stains on my dress I wish to get out."

Was she acting well enough to deceive him? Apparently so.

"That's right, my girl; you keep yourself tidy. I know what you mean, but I don't know whether we've got any. Would petrol do?"

She nodded, not trusting herself to speak. He went out and was gone some minutes, and returned with a pint bottle full of the spirit.

"Tried to get you benzine," he said. "The old caretaker could have bought it; he knows the neighbourhood. But I sent him off on his holiday the morning we arrived, and the new man doesn't know where the chemist's is—or anything else."

He wiped his hands on a handkerchief and wrinkled up his nose.

"Nasty smelling stuff," he said. "I didn't know you could wash things in it—curious, I know so many things, but I didn't know that!"

He was almost good-humoured again.

"Let me put it in the bath-room for you."

She was stiff with fear at the suggestion.

"No, I want to use it here."

It had been Anna's suggestion that she should have a basin on the table and the coat she wore. He put the bottle down and left her. Anna heard the door close and the bolt shot home, and came out of her room.

"Why do you want the petrol? I don't understand. I nearly died with fright when he said he'd put it in the bath-room."

But Anna would not satisfy her curiosity. She poured a portion of the contents into the basin. The smell was overpowering; and since there was some cleaning to do, Lila had not been wholly deceiving the little man.

But he might come back to discover how the petrol was being used. He trusted nobody, but apparently he saw nothing odd in her request, for he did not return until late in the evening.

There was great activity at Arbroath building that day; meetings and telephone conversations; one of the more innocent-looking "tenants" went into the City, dispatching telegrams at every post office on his way. Aikness was called in for a consultation. He was shaking with fear, could hardly control his lips, for Golly had confided his plan to him, and its very daring was sufficient to shatter stronger nerves than the sailor's.

"I've promised the boys a clean-up and a getaway, and they're going to have it," said Golly, "but you needn't be in it. You'll take the girls to Greenwich and join me when you get back." He pushed a paper across the table. "The car will get you there"—he made a mark on the plan before him—"in exactly two minutes. I'm allowing you three. There'll be a launch to pick up you and the girls——"

"Do you think it will go as smoothly as that?"

"Don't interrupt me," snarled Golly. "Listen! At nine-eleven we open Kinshner's"—he mentioned the greatest jeweller's in Bond Street—"at one end, and the West End Diamond Syndicate at the other. We'll have to blow the safe at Kinshner's, but that'll be dead easy; it's old-fashioned, anyway. They're getting a new one in next year. I'm not asking you to stand in on this—there'll be shooting and you won't like it. We ought to get a hundred and fifty thousand pounds to-night from the two places, and that'll be all we want." He rubbed his hands gleefully. "I'd like to be here to see the papers in the morning."

"You said 'Friday'—why to-night?" almost wailed Aikness.

"I thought there was a dance on Friday; it's to-night. If I said Monday week and started to do it this morning, does that make a hell of a difference to you?"

It was a new Golly who spoke, dramatically, menacingly. Captain Aikness wilted under the glare of his eyes.

"Don't think you're going to try anything with me, Aikness." Golly thrust his face into the other's. "There are two men going with you—one on the box and one inside with the young ladies. They'll gun you the first time you show the sign of a white liver—that's clear, ain't it?"

"Clear enough for me," said Aikness, steadying his voice with an effort.

His own private plan was crumbling to dust.

CHAPTER XXVIII

A pencilled note, hurriedly scrawled, came from Ricordini to Elk.

There's something doing to-night—in the West End, I think. I've had a tip not to go anywhere near Piccadilly.

Such a warning from Ricordini was not to be ignored. He very seldom went out of his way to communicate with the police. Elk got his superintendent on the phone.

"Warn the divisional inspector," said that gentleman. "I'll be up right away—where's Wade?"

"He's at Brixton interviewing Lane. I'm expecting him any moment."

John was, as a matter of fact, hanging on to the wire at the other end, trying to get Elk, and soon after the inspector had hung up, he came through.

"Lane wants to give King's evidence. He's told me a lot already. Do you remember Arbroath Building?"

For a moment Elk did not recall the place.

"This building may be their head-quarters if they start big trouble. Lane isn't sure—Golly never takes people into his confidence—but he's pretty certain it is somewhere in Notting Dale, and his description tallies, although he only saw the place once and does not know the neighbourhood. He says the gang is making a clean-up on Friday night."

"Make it to-night," said Elk, "and rush up here."

By the time John Wade arrived, the West End was filled with plain-clothes men; but it seemed that their vigil was to be unrewarded until, at about ten past nine, a dull explosion shook Bond Street and was followed, as by an echo from the other end, by another. A police whistle blew and then another. A flying squad car, racing to the scene, was completely wrecked and two of its inmates injured by a motor-lorry which drew across its path. The driver of the lorry escaped.

While this was happening and detectives were flying down Bond Street, a high-powered motor-car drew up by the kerb, the door of

Kinshner's was thrown open and four men came out. A policeman turned to grab them, and the first shot was fired in that amazing battle which will remain an unpleasant memory for many years.

The policeman went down with a broken shoulder, but as the car moved forward, two plain-clothes men sprang on the running-board, and paid for their temerity with their lives. Suddenly the West End was startled to hear the rattle of machine guns. The car flew across Piccadilly, dodged between two swerving vehicles into Jermyn Street, turned into St. James's Street, travelling against the traffic, and was in the park and lost before the first of the police motor patrols swung out of Pall Mall.

The second party of raiders did not escape so easily. They came from the back door of the West End Diamond Syndicate into a knot of armed detectives; there was a quick exchange of fire, which brought one of the burglars to his knees. The other three shot their way clear, spraying their pursuers from an automatic rifle projecting over the back of the car.

As they turned into Oxford Street, a motor-bus driver, realising what was happening, brought his vehicle across the road to bar their path. They dodged behind him, fired at the conductor, without hitting him, and sped along Oxford Street. But their pursuers were on their heels. Oblivious of the bullets which jerked every few seconds from a machine gun, a flying squad car flew after them, until a lucky shot smashed the front wheel and brought the machine into collision with a lamp-post.

Instantly every outlying station was notified. Reserves were swarming to divisional head-quarters, and additional cars had been seized or borrowed to take up the chase.

John Wade heard the first staccato rattle of the automatic as he was walking along Piccadilly with Elk. He saw the car dash across the thoroughfare and disappear. . . .

"It's the most daring thing they've done," said a breathless divisional officer whom they met in Bond Street. "Smashed the jewellers', and didn't even attempt to hide themselves. In fact, one of our men saw them at work on the safe and phoned for help—if he'd blown his whistle we might have got them."

John did not even trouble to examine the burgled premises: he hurried back to Scotland Yard, Elk with him, and passed on to the hastily gathered chiefs who were within call the statement made by Raggit Lane.

"He may have gone back there," said the superintendent who had arrived in the meantime. "There will be no harm in cleaning up this place. Pick your men; you'd better take rifles with you."

It was twenty minutes to ten when the first of the police cars ran into the street leading to Arbroath Building. As they did so, there was a clang of gongs and a motor fire-engine came out of a cross-road, swerved, missing them by inches, and went before them. They picked up a running policeman.

"What's the trouble?"

"Arbroath Building is on fire. It's a block of old——"

John did not wish to hear any more about Arbroath Building. He saw a bright light in the sky, and wondered if history was going to be repeated.

"Two women in there—a young girl and another one," said the policeman. "I saw 'em waving their hands, and went to ring the fire alarm."

"What?" John Wade went cold at a thought. Something told him that one of those two was Lila.

CHAPTER XXIX

Golly had made his appearance and taken a ceremonial but admonitory farewell. He was by turns fatherly and majestic.

"Don't forget, I'll be seeing you in an hour's time. No monkey tricks, you"—he pointed at Anna. "I'm relying on you to keep her sensible, Lila."

The girl nodded.

Mr. Oaks sniffed fastidiously.

"Don't like the smell of your petrol, and you can't have the windows open. You've brought it on yourself. You'll go with Aikness, Lila—you understand?"

She nodded again.

"Aikness an' a couple of friends. You can trust the friends."

He was scarcely out of the room and the door locked before she was in the bath-room and Anna was pushing her through the trap.

"I'll turn out the light now, but if he comes back again I'll switch it on again. You'll be able to see the light shining through the trap."

The girl crept along the concrete roof and peered cautiously over the parapet. She had to wait ten minutes (with many backward glances for the signal) before she saw the first of the cars emerge from the garage; it was followed by a second, and then she heard the gates close. She came back and whispered the news through the trap-door. In the meantime Anna had collected light chairs, a towel rail, and a blanket from her bed, and, turning on the lights, she handed them up to the girl at the end of a broom.

"Now take the bottle, and be careful," she warned her.

Lila reached down and grasped the bottle, which was three parts full of petrol; her hand was trembling so much that she thought she would drop it. When she had deposited these and came back, Anna was on the table.

"There's somebody knocking at the door," she said in a low voice. "It must be Aikness."

The knocks were repeated, louder, more peremptory. Anna, with extraordinary and unsuspected strength, drew herself up to the edge of the trap, her last act being to kick away the chair beneath her. Lifting the trap together, they let it fall with a crash into its place.

"Aikness and his friends won't try to push that up. If they do we'll stand on it," she said.

She gathered the blankets and furniture into one corner of the parapet and looked over. There were several people walking about in the street below. Not far away she thought she saw the figure of a policeman, and, stooping, uncorked the bottle and poured its contents on the heap. She struck two matches and then a third, but the wind blew them out. The fourth light held, and she dropped it on the petrol-soaked blanket. Instantly a tongue of flame leapt up, illuminating the roof and the houses around. She heard a police whistle blow and saw men running towards the building.

She was visible now in the light of the flames and waved her arms. Lila heard a sound behind her, and, turning, saw the trap slowly moving up. With a scream she flew towards it and sprang upon the top. It fell into its place, and she heard a crash and a roar below. Just then Anna heard the sound for which she had been waiting—the distant jangle of fire bells, and, regardless of danger, she stood up on the parapet and extended her arms.

She was seen by the crowd that had gathered below. A roar of warning, encouragement and fear for her, came up from the packed street. She stepped down again on to the roof, and as she did so she saw a third car run out from the garage below, scattering the crowd left and right; it disappeared round a corner.

"They've gone," she called hoarsely. "Thank God, they've gone!"

Fire engines were coming from other directions—two, three—then suddenly a red ladder-head came over the parapet, and a brass-helmeted man, followed by another, leapt upon the roof. Then Lila saw a man in civilian clothes jump from the parapet, and as his foot touched the roof, she ran into John Wade's arms.

CHAPTER XXX

There was a ball at Greenwich Hospital, and every officer except the officer of the watch on His Majesty's torpedo-destroyer *Meridian* was ashore. Shore leave had been granted to one of the watches, and the crew of *Meridian*, which, though not very large, was the fastest of her type, was a small one.

The sentry on the gangway challenged the boat approaching, and when somebody in the boat said there was an urgent letter for the commander, the sailor called the officer of the watch. As the sentry leaned down to take the letter there were two muffled reports, and officer and man died at their posts. Instantly the craft was boarded by twenty yellow-faced little men and, taken by surprise, many of them sleeping, the crew were summarily disposed of.

It was afterwards described as an impossible happening, yet it was easily achieved. An officer of a tramp steamer lying near by heard noises which sounded like shots coming from the ship, and thought it was rather remarkable that naval men should indulge in rifle practice at that time of night.

One sailor alone escaped, slipping into the water and swimming ashore. And then a black launch approached the side of the destroyer noiselessly, and Golly and the remnants of his gunmen climbed on board. Already his signal lamp had summoned Aikness; but ten minutes passed, and fifteen minutes before the launch which had been sent to fetch him arrived. He had with him the two guards whom Golly had appointed to accompany him, but the women were not there. He was so frightened that he could hardly articulate. Golly heard the word "fire."

"We'll talk about that later," he said, livid with fury. "Get on to the bridge!"

The mooring was already slipped. *Meridian* was due to leave that night and had steam up. The possibility that she might not have a full head of steam had not occurred to Golly, though Aikness had drawn his attention to this chance.

Already the Chinese firemen were below; a quartermaster took the wheel, and the destroyer went downstream, gathering speed. In the officers' cabin Golly interviewed his captain.

"Now let's hear you!" he said ferociously, and Aikness told his story.

"Got through a trap?" He bit his lip. "I never thought there was a trap."

"I saw a notice on the wall—a fire notice. They must have found it; it mentioned 'trap' there——"

"Started the fire—that's what they wanted the petrol for. I'll come back for her."

He showed his teeth in a grin, but he was not amused.

"They'll be after us——" began Aikness.

"Be after us, will they?" said Golly. "Haven't I told you they can't come after us? I'm picking up the first P. & O. boat and lying alongside of her. There's one out of London this afternoon. And if they send cruisers to catch me, I'm sinking that P. & O. boat and the passengers! D'ye hear? I'm blowing 'em to hell out of the water! They don't carry guns in peace days."

So that was the plan! It was the part that he had not told before. That was the blackmail he had threatened.

The destroyer went at full pelt, ran risks which would have turned the hair of its skipper white, and came at last, in the dark of the morning, to the smell of the open sea.

"There she goes!" Golly stood by the captain behind the chin-high bridge, focusing a pair of night glasses. "I can pick her up! I've got a man on her. Give her a signal."

The signal lamp flickered, and a light winked from the liner's stern.

"Now let them——" began Golly.

At that moment a great white beam of light swept out from the land, moved slowly along the water until it held the destroyer.

"Whack her up," snarled Golly. "Every ounce of steam and then some! We've got to overtake that packet ahead."

Flames flew from the destroyer's three funnels; she shivered and shook under their feet; but the light held. And then Golly, staring landwards, saw a red pencil of light, and a little later heard the roar of an explosion. He did not see the shell strike the water; it fell outside the focus of the light.

Again came the red pencil and something screamed overhead.

"They're straddling us," whispered Aikness. "My God! They'll get us!"

He gazed, fascinated, at the hidden battery, saw the red flicker of light again.

"If we could only——" he began.

He said no more. A great shell struck the vessel amidships and there was a terrific explosion.

* * * *

The searching boats found one survivor, a little man, his spectacles fastened securely to his ears, a ludicrous figure within a large lifebuoy.

"My name's Oaks," he said when they hauled him on board. "I'm giving no trouble—I'm not that kind of man. I'm all for peace and quietness and humanity. I saved a little baby once; the other fellows wanted to leave her, but I couldn't bear the thought of it. Name of Lila Smith."

He was slightly hysterical, but calmed down later and gave nobody any trouble.

When, after he had been sentenced to death, he took to singing, the other prisoners, and the warders who watched him, made bitter complaints. But nearly dead men have their privileges. He sang on the morning of his execution in his reedy falsetto, and when the trap dropped with a clang, the warders were not as sorry for him as they had been for quite a number of men who had passed out of life by the same route.

www.ingramcontent.com/pod-product-compliance
Lightning Source LLC
Chambersburg PA
CBHW031415250626
47155CB00004B/1496